HALLOWED FALLS

JESSICA YUEN

Chapter 1

Leah slowly opened her eyes, becoming increasingly aware of the incessant knocking on her bedroom door. She let out a groan, then flung the comforter off her body and sat up. She ran her fingers through her straight, dark red hair and tucked her side-swept bangs behind her ear. The sunlight was beaming into her bedroom and she waited for her eyes to adjust before she walked over and opened the door.

"Morning, sis. Did I wake you?" asked Hazel as she stared at Leah with her roundish-almond shaped eyes.

"Yea, but it's okay. What's up?" asked Leah as she rubbed her eyes.

"Just checking to see if you wanted to head down to the garden together before breakfast," said Hazel. Her wavy, unbound shoulder-length blonde hair swayed as she spoke.

Leah scratched her forehead and yawned.

"Yea, I'll be ready in a bit." said Leah as she turned and walked into her bathroom. She stared at herself in the mirror as she began to

brush her teeth and noticed the dark circles underneath her green eyes. She'd been working quite a few overnight shifts the past week at the Luna Valley Medical Center. When she was done brushing her teeth, she patted some concealer over the dark circles, then went into her closet. Hazel waited for Leah to get dressed and they headed downstairs together.

It was a cool and sunny spring morning in Luna Valley, Euphorya. A peaceful and prosperous state in the mid-western region of Charmesa. The April rain from the previous night drenched the garden at the Plumeria estate. Flame robins sung their sweet song as Leah and Hazel walked down the dirt path on the side of the house. The scent of wet grass and fragrant jasmines greeted them as they entered the garden.

Hazel headed for the camellias that seemed to have wilted a bit and examined them for a second before raising her left hand over the flowers. Her fairy wings shimmered as they slowly spread open under the sunlight and a bright golden glow formed under her palm. She had cast the Blossom charm. When the golden glow faded, the camellias looked fresh again. Hazel smiled and fluttered her wings with delight.

Hazel's forewings were slender ovals and her hindwings were wide triangles with rounded corners. The tips began with iridescent shades of purple fading into aquamarine-blue. Tiny golden specks dance gracefully along the edges. When her wings were not spread, they were folded flat against her back.

The Plumerias come from a long line of fae. Leah was born a fairy, however, a couple years ago, she decided to give up her fairy powers and alchemize into a witch by taking the Enchantress elixir. Some of their ancestors had chosen the path of other snupes, just as Leah did. Snupes was short for preternatural beings, a term that everyone began using when they were in high school. There were only two fairies known in the Plumeria lineage that chose to take the Enchantress Elixir, Gregoro Plumeria and his wife, Henrietta. A decision made over a century ago, that changed the reputation of the Plumerias and the lives of many.

Leah took her witch's stylus out from the pocket of her maroon cotton dress and waved it in a figure eight motion, then aimed it at a sunflower in front of her. A purple, shimmery mist floated out of her stylus and swirled around the sunflower. When the mist subsided, the sunflower had turned into a corn stalk.

"Damn, I was trying to turn it into a peony." said Leah. She sat down at a bench in the center of the garden and examined her stylus. A witch's stylus is made of stainless steel and tempered glass. Inside the glass is a mixture of gemstones, precious metals, and flowers. Every witch's stylus has a different combination of these materials inside. It usually contains two types of gemstones, one flower, and one type of precious metal. Leah's stylus had crushed amethyst, blue lace agate pebbles, a 14-carat gold wire, and a plumeria flower.

"There's actually something I've been meaning to ask you," said Leah as she looked up at Hazel. "I've been thinking about moving to Hallowed Falls for a while now and I wanted to ask if you'd consider moving there with me?"

"Hallowed Falls, the town mother said our ancestors inhabited a long time ago? What made you consider moving there?" Hazel wrinkled her brow as she started to water the wolfbanes.

"Well...before I even decided to take the Enchantress Elixir, I've always wanted more...to discover more....and to *do* more with my powers. Don't you want to learn more fairy charms and auras? My intuition tells me, Hallowed Falls is where we can do that," said Leah as she stuck her stylus back into her dress pocket.

Three years ago, when Leah was twenty-six years old, she started her hematology residency. This past Fall, she received the hematology license that she worked so hard for. Hazel had great admiration for Leah's passion and ambition. She had always known that life in Luna Valley was never enough for her older sister. Even Hazel began to feel the same way recently, but she had to continue to push those thoughts away, to focus on tending their garden. But ever since she turned twenty-four last month, the feeling only grew stronger.

Leah could see that her sister was close to considering it. "I *need* to go there. With or without you. I'll be okay you know. We can always keep in touch," said Leah sarcastically.

Hazel's eyes shot up at her sister.

"You know I would never let you do that. Just...let me sleep on it," said Hazel, her wings lifting her one foot off the grass as she drifted towards the manor.

Their parents moved from Hallowed Falls to Luna Valley when they were pregnant with Leah. It was known throughout the history books that all magical beings originated from Hallowed Falls. Their mother, Fleur had always told them stories about the Plumerias, her family the Beauroses, and all the different snupes that thrived there.

The following day, Hazel woke up incredibly tired. After staying up late agonizing over her decision, she was firm in her resolve to consider moving to Hallowed Falls overnight. She had made a decision and was going to talk it over with Leah over breakfast.

"Good morning, dear," Fleur was at the breakfast table sipping tea and reading the morning paper. "It's unlike you to wake up so late. Are you feeling alright?"

"Morning, mother. Yea…I just stayed up a little later than usual. That's all." Hazel took a seat at the breakfast table and poured herself some hot tea.

"Of course, dear. Moving to Hallowed Falls isn't a quick and easy decision." Fleur responded, peeking over her newspaper now. Hazel nearly choked and spit up her tea.

"You know?! How?!" Hazel exclaimed.

"I told her about it last night," Leah interjected as she pulled out a chair, joining them at the table. She seemed to have appeared out of nowhere.

"Your sister tells me everything. You know that," Fleur winked and smiled at Leah.

Leah had her witch's stylus in her hand waving it in a figure eight motion before pointing it to the pot of coffee. Hazel watched as the pot of coffee floated six inches above the table. It hovered over Leah's mug and slowly poured coffee into it.

Leah has always had a special bond with their mother. Not that Hazel didn't but Fleur and Leah even looked similar. They were often mistaken for sisters when they were together in public. Fleur had green eyes, high cheek bones, and light blonde hair. Her iridescent wings were spread out and shaped like a cicada's. The tips of her wings started off with a rosy pink and faded into a deep purple. Although Leah had been born with blonde hair, she dyed it dark red in medical school. She inherited her mother's green eyes and high cheek bones, but her wings disappeared after she took the Enchantress Elixir.

Hazel inherited her mother's blonde hair but has her father's hazel eyes, which is how she got her name. Back when Leah was still a fairy, she even told their mother before telling Hazel that she had decided to become a witch. She knew that the decision would break Hazel's heart, but Hazel had taken it well. She would always stand by her older sister, no matter what. Between the three of them, they've always felt the most powerful when they were together.

"And you're…okay with this?" Hazel asked suspiciously.

Fleur let out a heavy sigh.

"As a parent, a fairy one nonetheless, is never *okay* with anything." said Fleur. "But I recall a time when I, too, had to make a similar decision like this one." Fleur's thoughts flashed to her past.

Hazel could tell their mother was deep in thought. She didn't know what it could be, but she sensed that it was a traumatic event. Fairies are the most intuitive magical beings and can sense what others may be feeling. Fleur quickly snapped back from her thoughts.

"Anywho, you girls are adults now. It's time you created your own stories." said Fleur as she resumed to reading the newspaper.

"Well that settles it. You in?" Leah asked Hazel.

"Yea...yea, let's do it," Hazel replied as she took another sip of tea.

Two weeks later, the sisters were all packed up and ready to go. They stood in front of the manor's gates and bid their parents goodbye.

"You can always call us if you need anything, love," Gregorio said as he gave them hugs and kisses. Gregorio was partly named after his great-great grandfather, *Gregoro* Plumeria. Gregorio had always been a supportive father to Hazel and Leah, just as he continued to be at this moment.

"Let us know when you get settled in. And a word of advice, girls...don't be afraid of dark corners. Sometimes, it's the best place to be," Fleur whispered in a conspiratorial tone as she gave them a wink.

The girls got into Leah's car and drove south towards Hallowed Falls, Mystland.

Dusk had fallen when they arrived at 160 West Gardenia Road. It was the address of the old Plumeria estate in Hallowed Falls. Their father's great-great-great grandfather, Brodrick Plumeria purchased the land and built the estate to what it is now. Their father, Gregorio kept a staff to help maintain the property all these decades.

They drove past the gates and up the dirt filled road towards the front door. The road to the house seemed long and lined by trees with branches that seemed to be making an archway over their heads. As they pulled up to the old Plumeria manor, Hazel felt unusually at ease. Almost as if she was *home*.

"This place *feels* familiar. Have we been here before?" Hazel asked as she gazed out in awe, both at her surroundings and the sense of familiarity.

"I'm not sure. Perhaps when we were younger. It's amazing, isn't it?" Leah asked.

Hazel nodded as she continued to stare out the window in amazement. At the front of the manor was a round-about yard with a two-tier stone water fountain at the center. The Georgian-style manor was made with peach-colored bricks and every window had a set of bright white shutters. The porch lights and what seemed like every light in the house, were all on, shining brightly in the approaching dark. It was a beautiful property and all the glowing lights made Hazel feel welcomed.

They stopped right in front of the porch and as they got out of the car, a young woman stepped out of the house. She seemed to be about the same age as Leah. Her reddish-orange hair was up in a bun and her curtain bangs framed the sides of her diamond-shaped face. The woman waited for the sisters to get out of the car before approaching them.

"Hello…Miss Plumeria. Welcome to the old Plumeria manor. My name is Lucinda and I'm the new head housekeeper. May I take your luggage?" She asked politely.

"Hello, Lucinda. I'm Leah and this is my sister, Hazel. That's okay, we can take our luggage up ourselves. Do you…live here as well?" Leah asked.

"Yes, ma'am. I live on the property. In the east building, just over there." Lucinda pointed over the trees behind Hazel. There was a four-story building and the first two floors had lights on.

"Are you the only staff on the estate?" asked Hazel.

"No…ma'am. There is another housekeeper, Amber Greene and a groundskeeper, Oliver Gates. They were given the night off today," Lucinda answered.

"Oh, okay. Will you kindly show us to our rooms? It's been a long drive. And you can just call me Leah."

"Of course, Leah."

They grabbed what they could from the car and followed Lucinda through the front doors. The foyer seemed enormous. It had a high ceiling and polished white marble floor. In the middle of the foyer, a large glossy black grand piano stood proudly, just behind it they could see a glass shelf stocked with different colored liquor bottles. A staircase to the left of the foyer curved grandly upwards, its banister gleaming like the hood of a polished car and to the right was a set of dark mahogany doors.

"Those doors lead to a study room, there's also a bathroom back there to the left, the dining room is straight ahead, and the kitchen is in the back, to the right. The main manor has two floors. There are ten full bathrooms, three kitchens, one dining hall, four studies, and twelve mini-suites on the estate. The east building has four floors. It is where the housekeepers and groundskeeper reside. The west building has one mini-suite, one full bathroom, and a study on the second floor. The ground floor of the west building has an indoor gym and is fully equipped. The southeast building is fully furnished and is normally used as a guest house. Brodrick Plumeria's dream was to be able to house multiple generations of Plumerias on the estate." Lucinda explained as she started to climb the staircase.

Hazel and Leah continued to follow her silently, both a bit overwhelmed but excited.

The second floor was more impressive than the first. Across from the stairs was a beautiful aquarium tank and to the right was the great hall. There was a large statue sitting in the middle of the open floor. Made of white marble, the statue depicted a fairy woman looking up and holding a lavender flower. Curious, and a little more comfortable with her surroundings, Leah opened the first door to the left.

"Wow, check this out! This room is huge. I am *so* claiming this room!" Leah shouted. There were two large French-style windows that were almost floor to ceiling across from the door. The wallpaper was maroon with a fleur de lis pattern throughout the entire room. A medium sized crystal chandelier hung above a queen size bed between the two French-style windows. On the far right of the room was an archway that led into a walk-in closet and bathroom.

Hazel opened the door across the hall from Leah's room.

"Whoa," whispered Hazel as she stepped through the door. The suite had the same layout as Leah's. The wallpaper had a floral pattern against a light blue background and there were hummingbirds printed randomly throughout the entire room. A beautiful light gray wooden canopy bed stood in the middle of the suite.

Lucinda knocked on Hazel's door.

"Dinner will be served down in the dining hall, shortly. I'll see you downstairs." said Lucinda as she closed the door behind her.

Hazel went downstairs after unpacking some of her clothes. She pressed a few keys on the grand piano as she walked by. Playing the piano was something she'd always loved, and she couldn't wait to get her hands on this one. Next to the stairs, she noticed a black marble bar table.

"The old Plumeria household must've loved entertaining and held many grand parties here." Hazel thought to herself.

Leah was already in the dining hall when she walked in. She took a seat at the table as Lucinda came through the kitchen door with a covered tray. The aroma smelled delicious and Hazel's stomach growled.

"Lobster Fra Diavolo. It's my specialty!" Said Lucinda as she uncovered the tray on the table and headed towards the kitchen.

"Won't you join us?" Leah asked.

"Well...sure, if you don't mind," said Lucinda. She set the metal lid down and sat across from Leah.

"So, you mentioned earlier that you were newly hired?" Leah asked as she cracked open a lobster claw.

"Yes, I saw an ad at the library a week ago. I moved in three days before you guys arrived," said Lucinda as she twirled the pasta with a fork.

"Oh. I'd like to check that out some time. Where is the library?" asked Hazel.

"The library is in the middle of town. I can write down the address for you after dinner," said Lucinda.

"That would be great, thank you. Have you always lived in Hallowed Falls?" asked Hazel as she wiped her mouth with a napkin.

"I've also lived in Crystal Brooks for a bit. It's a town not too far from here. So, what do you ladies plan on doing after you settle in?" Lucinda asked as she took a sip of water.

"I actually applied for a hematology position at the Hallowed Falls hospital last week. I'm still waiting to be called for an interview." said Leah.

"That's wonderful, good luck!" said Lucinda.

Leah and Hazel explored the manor together after dinner. They went into the study next to the foyer. There was a grand fireplace built into the wall across from the door with a sitting area in front of it. On the far left of the room was a huge bookshelf.

"Oh boy, we need to get some updated furniture around here." Leah said as she looked around the room.

"Well perhaps at least a tv and a computer? Everything else is fine, it keeps with the whole Georgian-style theme in the manor," said Hazel.

"I agree" said Leah.

The sisters explored the rest of the suites on the second floor and then called it a night.

A couple of days after settling in, Hazel decided to visit the library. She threw on a light blue, off-the-shoulder cotton dress and went downstairs. She walked into the study and found Leah reading a book in front of the fireplace.

"Hey, I'm planning on checking out the library today. Do you want to come with me?" Hazel asked Leah.

"Actually, I think I'm going to explore the property some more, maybe another time?" Leah replied.

"Alright, I'll see you later!" Hazel turned on her heel and walked out the front door to her car. Her mother insisted on getting it for her and it had arrived just yesterday from Luna Valley. It was a pale blue Chevrolet Spark, perfect for running errands in a small town.

The library was only ten minutes away from the manor. It was a five-story, red brick building that took up about one-third of the street. She parked across the road and once she was inside, she began to browse the aisles. Before she knew it, she was on the top floor. No one else seemed to be around and it was dimly lit by sconces on the walls. As she walked down the aisles, she noticed that each one had a name, unlike the numbered aisles downstairs. "Powell, LaMeur, Alexander, Griffin, Summerland, and..." Hazel gasped. *"Plumeria."* She whispered to herself.

"You're a fairy, aren't you?" A voice from behind startled her. She turned around to find a young woman about her age staring curiously at her.

"Wait...you can see my...?" Hazel began to say.

"Wings? Yep, I can see your wings," said the girl with a friendly smile.

Hazel was surprised to hear that. A fairy's wings were invisible to the human eye and only magical beings had the ability to see them.

"I'm a witch, you see," said the girl. She took her stylus out and pointed to a book on a nearby shelf. It began to slide out and float in mid-air.

"Put that away! There are humans around!" Hazel whispered loudly and pushed the girl's hand back down.

The book plummeted to the floor with a loud thud.

"Relax, you're in Hallowed Falls. We're safe here." The girl explained. "My name's Olivia LaMeur, of the LaMeurs." she continued, pointing to one of the signs above the aisles.

"I'm Hazel Plumeria… of the… Plumerias." said Hazel, still confused.

Olivia's eyes widened. "You're a…Plumeria? That's wonderful!" Olivia grabbed Hazel and hugged her. "We've always wondered when the Plumerias would be back!" said Olivia with excitement.

"Wait…what do you mean *we're safe here*?" Hazel asked as she took a step back from Olivia.   "There isn't a big population of humans in Hallowed Falls like most folks think. The handful that are left know about us magical beings. They have voluntarily sworn in under a spell, to protect us. They are bound by *magic* to keep our secret," Olivia explained.

"Okay…What are these aisles and why does it have our family names?" Hazel asked suspiciously.

"These aisles are named after the founding families of Hallowed Falls. The most prominent members of each family were Brianna Powell, Phillip LaMeur, Adrian Griffin, Honora Summerland, Gregoro Plumeria, and Leo Alexander. They were the founders of the Aster Elites. Each aisle holds books on their family history and their magical findings," said Olivia as she glanced down on her phone.

"Oh, crap! I've got to go. It was great meeting you, Hazel." She said as she began to walk down the stairs then turned her head back to Hazel.

"By the way, you should check out Delphina's Emporium on the other side of town on Stone Street. They've got some *really* interesting stuff there. See you around!" Olivia said as she waved and hurried down the stairs.

"Wait, what's the address?" Hazel asked as she walked towards the stairs, but Olivia had already disappeared.

Hazel picked up the book that was laying on the floor and stuck it back onto the shelf. She looked through the aisles for a while longer and checked out a book from the Plumeria section. When she exited the library, she decided to search for Delphina's Emporium. She got into her car and typed the store name into her GPS but nothing came up.

"That's strange. Maybe I'll just drive around for a bit. It's a small town, how hard could it be to find?" she thought to herself.

It had been over half an hour and Hazel felt as if she had been driving in circles. She was close to calling it a day and head back to the manor when she stopped at a red light. Her eyes landed on a street sign up ahead, perpendicular to the road she was on.

"Stone Street," she read out loud.

When the light turned green, she drove up the next block and made a right turn on Stone Street. She immediately noticed how different this road was from the rest of town, it seemed darker and secluded. At the end of the dead end road, Hazel could see a dark green awning over a storefront window that read 'Delphina's Emporium'. She parked her car in front of the store and got out.

A bell chimed as she pushed the door open.

"Welcome to Delphina's, I'll be right with you!" a voice yelled out from the back of the store.

She stood at the door and looked around for a second. It reminded her of the antique shop she frequented back in Luna Valley. There were shelves filled with books, candles, and soaps. She passed a table of jars filled with oddities in some kind of yellowish green liquid.

"Does that one have a two-headed lizard in it? Probably just a prank display." she thought to herself.

"Hi!" a voice came from directly behind her and made her turn around instantly. She looked up at the man and his gray eyes met hers. He wore a fitted white button-down shirt with the sleeves rolled up and a dark olive-green apron with 'Delphina's' embroidered in gold across the bottom.

"Uh...Hi." said Hazel, she immediately noticed a witch's stylus sticking halfway out of his apron pocket.

"Do you…always stare at strangers like that?" he asked as he walked behind the counter.

"Uh…I apologize. It's just that where I'm from, we don't really meet too many snupes. Let alone witches." She said as she continued to browse the store.

"Snupes?" he asked with a raised eyebrow.

"It's short for preternatural beings back where I'm from." she replied.

She stopped at a golden vitrine with rounded glass windows in a nook to the far right of the store. Inside the glass case were three egg-shaped objects sitting on top of a black satin pillow. They were a shimmery sky-blue and faded into silver halfway down. For a second, she could've sworn she saw one move.

"What in the *world* are these?" Hazel asked.

"They're authentic dragon eggs. We get different ones every six months." The man said from behind the counter.

"Where do they come from?" asked Hazel as she stared at the eggs in wonderment.

"There's a couple of places where dwarf dragons dwell. Those three are from the Misty Briars Forest," said the man.

"Oh…I've never heard of that forest before." said Hazel.

"Only a few have. It's up in the northeast somewhere and it's *extremely* hard to find." said the man.

"How hard could it be if one had a map?" asked Hazel.

"Like I said, *extremely*. The Misty Briars Forest can only be found on the night of a full moon." said the man.

"Wow," she said. "I'd like to buy one,"

The man came around the counter with a set of keys and unlocked the glass case. He gently lifted an egg off the satin pillow and walked back to the counter.

"That'll be $450." The man said as he typed away on the register.

Hazel paid for her dragon egg and the shopkeeper gently placed it in a small blue wooden box with a gold satin interior. She tucked it into her bag and exited the shop through a side door. Once she stepped out, she noticed a beautiful garden surrounded by bright colored flowers and against the garden fence was a beekeeping house. She suddenly felt homesick and missed tending to the garden back at her parents' manor. Her thoughts were suddenly interrupted by an excruciating pain on her right calf.

"OW!! WHAT THE HELL?!" she yelled as she bent over in pain.

The shopkeeper rushed out the side door.

"What?! What?!" he shouted as he looked around frantically. He saw her leaning against the wall on the side of the building with her hand over her calf. He walked over to her and examined her leg.

"Oh geez, you got stung. Hold on, I've got something that will help." He said as he walked back into the shop. He came back rather quickly with a clear glass vial in hand. He opened the bottle and she caught a whiff of it when he poured the amber liquid onto his fingers. It smelled of lavender, honey, and a hint of mint. As he gently patted the substance on her calf, she immediately felt relief from the bee sting. The swelling had gone down as quickly as it had appeared, almost as if it never happened.

"Wow, what is that? A magic potion or something?" she jokingly said as she twisted and turned her leg to double check it.

"Yea...actually. It's the Salixantho Elixir, made for bee stings....and other ailments alike." he explained. She noticed a flash of sadness as he closed the bottle. He stood up again and tucked it into the pocket of his apron.

"Thank you, uh," said Hazel, realizing that she hadn't gotten his name.

"Victor, Victor LaMeur," he said as he gazed down at her.

She looked into his eyes and it felt like her stomach did a flip.

"Whoa! What was that?" she thought to herself and she suddenly became very aware of her heart rate.

"Thank you, Victor, for tending to me." She turned to walk out through a gate and back to her car.

The sun had begun to set as Hazel drove down West Gardenia Road. She couldn't wait to tell Leah all about her day.

"Leah?! Lucinda?! You would not *believe* what I found today!" she called out as she walked into the dining hall.

"Hi, Hazel. I heard you yelling in the foyer, what'd you find?" Lucinda asked as she continued to set the table for dinner.

"What's up?" Leah asked, walking in from the foyer.

"I was looking through the library today and I ended up on the preternatural archives floor. Each aisle was named after a founding family of this town. One of them was Plumeria." said Hazel. She happened to glance over at Lucinda who was scooping salmon onto a plate. Hazel's eyes widened.

"There was another familiar name that I saw. It was... *Griffin*." said Hazel.

Leah looked at Lucinda.

Lucinda stopped what she was doing. She took in a deep breath, then slid a chair out and sat down.

"Yes, I am a descendant of Adrian Griffin...I come from a long line of witches," Lucinda explained. Then, she pulled her left pant leg up and took her stylus out of her boot.

"Garnet, black diamonds, gold, and the protea flower make up my stylus," said Lucinda.

"Mine has blue lace agate, amethyst, gold, and the plumeria flower...I chose to drink the Enchantress Elixir a couple of years ago." said Leah as she took her stylus out.

"I know. Fleur told me," said Lucinda.

"What?…Why would our mother mention that to you?" Leah pulled her brows together.

"Because…I am actually your cousin. Our mothers were sisters," Lucinda said with a doleful look on her face and stared down at the table.

"You're Aunt Lucia's daughter? How come our mother has never mentioned you? I mean…don't get me wrong, I'm ecstatic that you are our cousin. I just didn't *expect* to find any relatives here." said Leah, still in shock.

"Mother rarely ever talked about Aunt Lucia. How did she get in contact with you?" Hazel questioned.

"Aunt Fleur has always been there for me. Ever since…ever since my mother died trying to save another fairy," Lucinda said. She paused to keep her voice from cracking. "I was only fifteen when she died. A fairy was trapped in quicksand in the Sunset Forest. My mother was there for research when she heard someone yelling for help. She tried to calm the fairy down so that she could slow the sinking. But the fairy was in such panic that when my mother reached in, the fairy pulled her in as well. By the time her team found her, it was already too late." Lucinda explained.

"Lucinda…I'm so sorry." Hazel said as reached over to touch Lucinda's hand.

"Thanks. That was almost fifteen years ago and I miss her dearly. That's why I joined the Aster Elites. I want to help protect human and magical beings just like she did." said Lucinda.

"That's incredible, Luce. Would you be willing to teach me what you know and help me hone my craft?" Leah asked.

"Of course. That is the reason Aunt Fleur requested that I move into the estate. When you told her that you were going to come live in Hallowed Falls, she asked if I could help watch over you guys. She didn't want you girls to think she was being overprotective, so she asked me to come up with a cover. But I'll just give her a call and explain it to her tomorrow," said Lucinda.

"What's the Aster Elites? This girl I met at the library mentioned it earlier as well." Hazel asked.

"The Aster Elites is an agency dedicated to safeguarding the preternatural world and was founded by the household names you saw at the library. An accord was created when they formed the agency where all the founding families had agreed to live and work together in amity. Where once werewolves and vampires were on opposite sides, they had come together to keep the peace. Where once fairies looked down on witches, they began to trade certain secrets of their magic. To stray from the accord was to be shunned and possibly *executed*. But a little over a century ago, one of Leo Alexander's sons, Marco discovered that drinking the blood of other magical beings increased his powers. His ability to hypnotize were heightened. Most vampires could only hypnotize humans but by consuming the blood of magical beings, he was able to hypnotize the preternatural when we were in a vulnerable state of mind. Many fairies began to mysteriously disappear and their corpses would turn up days later all over town. Eventually, a couple of the towns' lycanthropes and witches started turning up dead as well. It was later discovered by Honora Summerland that it was Marco Alexander who had been responsible for the killings. By the time the A.E. got to the Alexanders' estate, Marco was already gone and was never seen in Hallowed Falls since. Until about 30 years ago, the killings started up again. Many fairy, witch, lycanthrope, and even vampire families began to move far away in fear that Marco Alexander had been back," Lucinda explained.

"That must have been why our parents moved to Luna Valley." said Hazel.

"My mother urged your parents to move there when they were pregnant with Leah. She suspected that Marco was back and targeting fairies. Fairy blood made vampires more powerful than the other snupes' blood did. He was able to move quicker, heal faster, and gave him five times the strength of a normal vampire. Your father was the last Plumeria descendant to have lived in Hallowed Falls. The A.E. opened an investigation on the murders but they were not able to link it to Marco and before they knew it, the murders stopped abruptly. Only recently did fairy families start moving back again. There still aren't too many of them though. They don't really socialize with the other snupes around here." Lucinda said.

"What happened to the rest of the Alexander family?" asked Leah.

"They were pretty much shunned by all the founding families. The descendants still live in Hallowed Falls and are rarely spotted in town because they aren't really welcomed when they do come around. The Alexanders live on a property at the west end of Dragon's Breath Trail. Rumor has it that they keep their elders in coffins down in their basement. That's what I heard back in college." said Lucinda.

"That's *really* creepy." Hazel said.

"Welcome to Hallowed Falls." Lucinda said with a smirk.

The next day, Leah got up bright and early to get a workout done. She was in her suite on the second floor of the main manor and walked to the end of the great hall where there was an enclosed bridge connecting the main building to the west building. Once she crossed the bridge, she entered a mini-suite with a balcony overlooking the maze garden. The suite had mauve colored walls and white furniture.

To the left of the door was a set of stairs that led down to where the workout equipment was. After running on the treadmill for an hour, she went back upstairs. She unlocked the French-style double doors and went out onto the balcony. The sunlight hit her eyes, making her squint. She used her hand to block the sun as she looked out into the distance. It was difficult to see what was at the end of the maze garden, but she was able to see large ponds surrounded by multi-colored flowers and shrubs. Behind the large ponds were small hills. It was such a beautiful property and Leah felt reassured of her decision to move here.

She turned around and walked back across the enclosed bridge to the manor. Once she was back in the great hall, she noticed something gold and glimmering in the corner of her eye. It was coming from the bookshelf to the right of the bridge. There was a book with gold binding, shimmering in a particular way. Almost as if it was calling out to her. Leah walked over to the bookshelf for a closer look and reached for the book. As soon as she pulled it out, she heard a loud mechanical sound. The bookshelf started to move to the left, revealing a small dark nook with a spiral staircase.

"Whoa" she whispered to herself.

She began to slowly ascend the stairs. Her footsteps echoed in the dark space around her. When she reached the top, she could tell that it was a large room but it was still pretty dark. Leah put her hands parallel to each other in front of her body. A bright golden orb started to form between her palms and grew to the size of a baseball. She gently tossed the glowball into the air and it hovered just above her right shoulder.

She carefully walked around the room and could see shapes of furniture covered by large purple sheets. The walls were made of dark red brick and there were a few paintings of dragons hung around the room. A crystal chandelier hung from the center of the ceiling. It looked like large pieces of shattered glass just floating in the air. Underneath the chandelier, stood a wooden table with vials and bowls.

"*That must be an alchemy station.*" Leah thought to her herself.

"Whoa!" Lucinda exclaimed.

Leah jumped and turned around. "Geez, you scared me!" Leah shouted with her hand clutching her chest.

"Sorry…wow, look at this place! I've only read about it in the Plumeria archives. I didn't think we'd find it this quickly." said Lucinda.

"Well, I was doing a quick workout in the west building and there was this book on the shelf…it was practically calling out to me. What is this place, Luce?" Leah asked.

"It was said that back when Gregoro Plumeria inherited the manor, he built a lair to practice his craft. Gregoro was one of the greatest master alchemists of his time. Many of the potions and elixirs that are in the A.E. archives are because of his extensive researches." said Lucinda as looked around the room.

"He actually enchanted this room. Any spell, good or bad will only last twenty-four hours within these walls. This is where we can work on your enchantment skills. But first, I'll have to clean up a little in here." said Lucinda.

"You know, you don't have to pretend to be housekeeping anymore. We have Amber to help us out," said Leah.

"I know, but I enjoy taking care of family since I've never really had any," said Lucinda.

"What happened to your father...if you don't mind me asking?" asked Leah.

"He also works for the A.E. and helps locate precious materials. For years, he's worked under the Department of Assets to help find precious resources needed to create potions and elixirs at headquarters. He was eventually promoted to senior director. He is constantly moving around the globe but he still oversees the department," Lucinda explained.

"Wow, so being an A.E. agent is practically in your blood," Leah mused.

Lucinda nodded with a half-smile.

"C'mon, let's see what Amber made for us in the dining hall." said Lucinda as she walked towards the stairs.

Leah followed behind her.

Chapter 2

Hazel woke up the next morning feeling fully rested. It was the first night she had slept well since the move. She looked over at her egg and gently petted the shimmery blue shell. It was still in the wooden box on her nightstand.

After breakfast, Hazel decided to visit the Fabled Tale bookstore. She remembered driving past it when she was looking for Delphina's. When she got there, she purchased two books. 'Horticulture & Beyond' for herself and 'Alchemy Level Three' for Leah. Right as she approached the door, it swung inwards and knocked the books right out of her arms.

"I'm sorry ma'am… I didn't-" Victor said as he looked up at her apologetically.

"Hazel?… Hi," said Victor as he bent down to pick up the books. He was wearing a black three-quarter sleeve baseball shirt. She almost didn't recognize him without the apron.

"Victor… right? Good to see you again," she said with a polite smile and felt a flutter in her stomach.

"*Ugh, what the heck is that?*" She thought to herself and blushed as if he were able to hear her thoughts.

"Are you in a hurry to get anywhere? I'd like to get a cup of coffee with you if you're up for it," said Victor.

"Sure," Hazel answered with a nod.

They got a couple of coffees and sat on a bench outside the bookstore. Victor tilted his head and glanced at the books on her lap.

"Alchemy Level Three, eh?" he asked and took a sip of his coffee.

"It's for my sister, actually. Leah's a witch, too." She told him.

"Really?" said Victor.

"Yea, Leah took the Enchantress Elixir a couple of years ago." Hazel explained.

"That's a tough decision for someone to make. She must be really brave," said Victor with a smile.

"Yea, she even started talking about wanting to join the Aster Elites," said Hazel.

His smile slowly started to fade and he knitted his eyebrows.

"My cousin, Liam and I were agents for the Aster Elites....he was killed during a mission about three years ago," said Victor.

"Oh...I'm sorry to hear that. You don't have to talk about it if you don't want to," said Hazel.

"No, it's alright. We were on a mission to retrieve a lightning opal that headquarters found on their satellite radar. It was located up in the Acacia Mountains. The mountains are guarded by trolls who are known to be very possessive. They did not like the fact that we were there, let alone retrieving a lightening opal." Victor paused and looked into the distance, a faraway expression in his eyes. He sighed heavily and continued, "we were attacked on the way down the mountain. Liam was slashed on the side of his torso and one of the trolls had spiked his sword with poison. I was fighting a horde of trolls and was not able to get to him in time. I had an antidote in my pocket, the Salixantho, but by the time I got the trolls to retreat, it was too late." As Victor finished, his head was parallel to the ground and his hands were crossed.

"No wonder he was sad the day he used the Salixantho on my calf. It reminded him of his cousin and he still blames himself." Hazel thought to herself.

"I'm so sorry that happened to you, Victor. That is absolutely horrible. But you can't blame yourself for what happened." Hazel tried to console him.

He nodded. "That is why I left the agency. I needed time away." Victor slowly got up and tossed his cup into a nearby trash can. He stood there for a few seconds and turned back to Hazel.

"Want to check something out with me?" he asked as he reached his hand out to her. Hazel gladly took it with a grin.

Hazel followed Victor to his car and he held the passenger side door open for her. She was hesitant to get in.

"I promise, I don't bite," said Victor with a smirk.

"Fine, I just better not end up in the newspaper tomorrow," she said jokingly, as she got into the car.

Victor shook his head and chuckled. He drove a few blocks and parked in front of a public park. Hazel looked out the window and noticed a mirrored glass building in the middle of the park. They got out of the car and walked in. There were oak trees and rose bushes all throughout the small park.

"What is this place?" Hazel asked.

"It's the Hallowed Falls arboretum. It is rumored that the souls of ancient fae live in the fairy houses inside," Victor said as he looked up at the arboretum.

The arboretum was a rectangular shaped building with mirrored glass all around and a dome shaped roof. Once they were inside, Hazel could hear the sound of musical chimes and she wondered where it came from. She looked around the ceiling for speakers but there were none.

"Where is that sound coming from?" she asked.

"What sound?" asked Victor.

"The musical chimes. You don't hear that?" asked Hazel.

"I don't hear anything," said Victor.

Hazel frowned but the chimes quickly left her mind when the sight of the most beautiful fairy house at the center of the arboretum caught her eyes. It sat on top of a gold tree stump and stood about four feet tall. The exterior was adorned with gemstones and bright colored flowers wrapped around the house. She noticed a few more fairy houses as they walked closer to the center, one on each corner of the building.

"This place is heavenly," Hazel said with amazement.

"Yea, I used to love coming here. I haven't been here for years. Many *snupes* as you call them, believe that one day the heir of Honora Summerland would return and would be able to access the center of the arboretum. The heir would inherit the most powerful fairy magic known to the preternatural world. Powers that could even bring back the dead," said Victor.

"Is that really true?" asked Hazel.

"Well, there's nothing in the archives about it. So, who knows?" Victor shrugged and turned to face her.

"That is so fascinating," said Hazel as she turned to face him. She almost gasped when she realized how close he was standing. They were only inches apart and she couldn't help but notice his chiseled jawline as she looked up at him. The warmth from his body made hers feel even hotter. Her eyes slowly moved down to his full mauve colored lips. She suddenly became very aware of her breathing and took a step back.

"I should…probably head back to the manor now. Thank you for showing me the arboretum. This place is breathtaking," said Hazel.

He chuckled. "Sure, let me drive you back to your car," said Victor as they walked back to his car.

After he dropped her off, he waited for her to drive away and replayed the moment they just had in the arboretum. He was sure that he felt a spark between them, and he began to regret not asking for her number. Then, he remembered telling her about Liam earlier.

"I wonder if that scared her away. Maybe I shouldn't have told her I was a former A.E. agent. Not that it matters now, anyway," he thought to himself.

He shook his head as if it would shake the negativity out of his mind as he pulled out onto the road and headed home.

Hazel walked in through the front door as Leah came out of the study and grabbed her wrist.

"Geez! Are you trying to break my wrist?" Hazel shouted.

"Come, quick! You *need* to see this!" Leah said as she pulled her across the foyer. They ran up the stairs, through the great hall, and towards the bookshelf next to bridge. Hazel noticed a book that started shimmering. She watched as Leah pulled the book out. The bookshelf started to move, and Hazel took a step back.

"Whoa!" said Hazel.

"Don't be afraid of dark corners, mom said that before we left, remember?" Leah said as she grabbed Hazel's hand and led her up the spiral stairs.

"Wow! This is incredible! What a great place for you to practice your magic." Hazel said as she continued to explore the room.

"You can use it as well to practice your charms and auras. Lucinda said this room was enchanted by Gregoro. Any magic, good or bad will only last twenty-four hours in here." Leah explained as she turned back to face Hazel.

"What'd you do in town today?" asked Leah as she picked up a flask from the table.

Hazel's thoughts flashed back to the moment she had with Victor just before they left. The thought made her blush and Leah caught it.

"Um…why are you turning as pink as a tulip right now? What's going on with you?" asked Leah with a suspicious smile.

"I was at Delphina's Emporium earlier this week and I purchased a dragon egg there. When I went out to the garden, I got stung by a bee and the shopkeeper, Victor graciously tended to my wound. He was…really nice. We bumped into each other again today and went out for coffee today and…I felt something. Every time we talk, I feel a flutter in my stomach. I don't know what it is. I've never felt anything like that before," said Hazel.

"It's looovve." Leah teased.

"No way. We've only seen each other twice," said Hazel.

Leah laughed. "Well, where's the dragon egg now?" Leah asked.

"It's on my nightstand. I should probably go check on it," Hazel said as she started towards the stairs. Leah followed. When Hazel opened the door to her suite, she suddenly heard something that sounded like a small hiccup and a small flame flew up into the air.

"The egg hatched!" Leah exclaimed.

"It's a baby green dragon! She's beautiful. I'm going to name her Sage," said Hazel as she looked down at the six inch green dragon on her nightstand. She slowly reached her hand out and tried to pet the top of Sage's head. Sage sniffed Hazel's hand.

"I've read about dwarf dragons back in college. They can grow up to about two feet long with a wing span of five feet. Back in the days, they were common household pets but eventually people began to feel like they were a nuisance. The dragons began setting houses and the woods on fire because they were not trained correctly when they were young," said Leah.

"Oh, I'll see about getting those training books. Wouldn't want to set our old family estate on fire now, would we?" asked Hazel as she continued to pet Sage.

Leah shook her head and chuckled. "I've got to prepare for my interview tomorrow. I'll see you downstairs," Leah spoke over her shoulder as she walked out of the suite.

The following day, Leah left early to go to the Hallowed Falls Hospital for her interview and waved goodbye to her sister before walking out of the dining hall. Hazel finished her breakfast and stood in front of the white French-style doors, gazing out at the maze garden. She opened the doors and after deliberating, decided to explore the garden. The worst that could happen is that if she did get lost, she could just fly out of it. She walked down the steps of the deck and towards the entrance of the maze.

It didn't take long for her to reach a small clearing. There was a wooden bench with iron rails against the tall shrub wall. In the corner of the enclosed clearing, was a small fairy house with different colored rose bushes behind it. The house was made of stone and was covered with morning glory and trumpet creeper flowers.

"My own fairy house!" she thought to herself with excitement.

Then, she remembered something she read in the book she recently got. It was said that if a fairy takes good care of the flowers growing *inside* the fairy house, it can produce magic nectar. The nectar can help fairies nurture their powers. Some have said that it could even be used to make powerful elixirs, like the Fertility Elixir. That was how the fairy, Honora was said to have brought her daughter to life. In a section of the book, it was said that Honora never fell in love and so she never had a mate. She used the Fertility Elixir and a strand of her hair to create her child, Lavender Summerland.

Hazel spent the rest of the day fixing up the fairy house. First, she trimmed down the wilting flowers and used the Blossom charm to grow fresh ones. Then, she weeded the plants and cleared up the small greenhouse she found behind the east building. She didn't realize it was already dark until Lucinda called out to her for dinner. Hazel got cleaned up then met Leah and Lucinda down in the dining hall.

"Hey Luce, have you ever met Victor LaMeur? He was a former agent at the Aster Elites." Hazel said as she stuffed a piece of ravioli in her mouth.

"Victor LaMeur? I didn't know him personally, only in passing. He was a director at A.E. up until a couple of years ago. I'm not sure what his reason was for leaving the A.E. though," said Lucinda.

"He left because his cousin, Liam was killed by a troll while they were on a mission in the Acacia Mountains. He needed time away after that incident," Hazel explained.

"Oh wait, I do remember that mission. I knew Liam. He was one of the top agents in the Department of Assets." said Lucinda.

"Victor? The guy who helped you the other day when you got stung by a bee? And Liam LaMeur? Of *the* LaMeurs?" Leah asked.

"Yes, they are the descendants of Phillip LaMeur, one of the co-founders of the Aster Elites. He was a geology professor back in the day and headed the Department of Assets when they formed the agency. Phillip LaMeur also founded the emporium. He named it after his wife, Delphina," said Lucinda.

"I just remembered, the girl who approached me at the library the other day said her name is Olivia LaMeur. They must be related," Hazel pondered.

"Olivia LaMeur is Liam's younger sister. Her father, Andrè owns the emporium now. It's been passed down in their family for generations," Lucinda offered.

"Oh, what an interesting family," said Hazel with fascination.

"By the way, how'd your interview go, sis?" asked Hazel as she turned to face Leah.

"It went very well, actually. Turns out that one of the doctors who interviewed me is also an alumni of Luna Valley University," said Leah as she cut a piece of ravioli in half. Choosing to eat her dinner a bit more delicately than her sister who continued to shove ravioli in to her mouth whole as though she'd been starved for a year.

"That's fantastic, I'm so proud of you!" Hazel exclaimed.

"Leah, we can practice in Gregoro's lair tomorrow, since I don't have to report to headquarters," said Lucinda.

"Sure, that sounds like a plan. Actually, I wanted to suggest this earlier. Why don't you move into the main manor with us? It'd be nice to have all three of us under the same roof. After all, we're family," said Leah.

"That sounds great. I'd love to!" Lucinda beamed.

Amber, the housekeeper walked out of the kitchen with a basket of chocolate chip muffins. "Those smell delicious, Amber." Leah closed her eyes and took in the delectable aroma. "Have you seen the groundskeeper today? I wanted to know if he was able to get the security system set up," asked Leah.

"Yes, ma'am. Oliver is in the study setting up the system right now," said Amber.

"Great, thank you. And please, just call me Leah," said Leah with a smile.

"Of course, Miss Leah," said Amber as she went back into the kitchen.

A few days later, Hazel decided to make another visit to Delphina's. She wanted to pick up some tea leaves and also had hoped to bump into Victor there. She hadn't heard from him since that day at the arboretum. As soon as she walked in, she saw Olivia wave at her from the other end of the store.

"Hey! Hazel, over here!" Olivia called to her. She was standing in front of the dragon egg case. Hazel walked over to her and noticed there was only one egg left in the vitrine. Then, Olivia turned to face Hazel.

"Isn't he beautiful? I named him Garwyn," said Olivia. She held out her arm to show Hazel the baby purple dragon. He was stunning, with scales that were a deep purple and it even had a shimmer to it.

"I also purchased one of the eggs recently and named her Sage, she's a baby green dragon. I've never owned one before. My mother always told us that her family owned a few when she was younger," said Hazel, admiring Garwyn.

"They are such majestic animals and loyal, too." said Olivia.

"I've noticed the eggs are all blue and silver colored. How do you get different colored dragons to hatch?" Hazel tilted her head slightly to the side.

"It really depends on whoever owns the dragon egg. Unless you're human of course. Only magical beings would be able to get the dragon eggs to hatch. As you already know, everyone has a natural aura around them, and only fairies have certain visible auras. That aura is absorbed by the egg when they are near it. It is also how the dragons familiarize themselves with their owners before they hatch.

Green dragons are born to owners who are always honest, natural healers, and those who are protective of their family and friends. Purple dragons are born to owners whose loyalty knows no bounds, natural leaders, and social butterflies. So, depending on what kind of person you are and how often you are near that egg determines the color of the dragon," said Olivia.

Just then, they heard the bell chime at the front of the store.

"Oh, it's my cousin. Hey, Vick!" said Olivia.

Hazel turned around and blushed instantly when she saw Victor. He had on a police officer's uniform.

"*That's odd. I thought he worked here at the emporium, why is he in a police uniform?*" She thought to herself.

She had to admit, he looked really good in the uniform and the thought made Hazel blush even harder.

"Hey, Liv…Hi, Hazel, you got a second to take a walk with me?" He asked. Olivia winked and smiled at Hazel.

"Yea, of course." Hazel replied with a nod.

They walked out to the garden through the side door. Hazel was reminded of the horrible bee sting she got on her first visit there.

"You're a police officer?" Hazel asked with a raised brow.

"Uh…yea actually, I was only working here for my uncle while I was in the academy and I just got sworn in not long ago. That's why I've been MIA. I was just patrolling in the area when I saw you in here with Liv," said Victor.

"Oh, I see." Hazel nodded her head slowly.

There was an awkward pause between them, and she couldn't help but sense that he was a bit nervous. She racked her brain for something to say but as usual, her mind went blank as soon as her eyes met his.

"I'm glad to have bumped into you again, I wanted to know…if you would like to go out to dinner with me tomorrow night?" He asked with a smile.

"Um…I'd be happy to!" Hazel replied with a smile. On the inside, she was doing a happy dance.

"I'll pick you up around six o'clock. I've gotta go. See you tomorrow," said Victor as he flashed her a smile.

Hazel hadn't felt this excited in a long time. She said goodbye to Olivia and headed back to the manor.

The following evening, Hazel was getting ready in her suite for her date.

"You're going on a date with Victor?" Lucinda asked with excitement.

"Yea, tonight at six and I have no idea on what to wear!" Hazel said as she rummaged through her walk-in closet.

Lucinda was petting Sage who was napping snuggly on her lap.

"I've asked people at work about him. Turns out, that the agency has been trying pretty hard to get him to come back in the past year. But since he joined Hallowed Falls PD, they're just keeping an eye on him for now," said Lucinda.

"I'm sure he has his reasons for not returning to the Aster Elites," Hazel said from inside her closet.

"I guess." Lucinda shrugged. "Hey, maybe we could host a barbecue next weekend? You can invite Victor and Olivia and I'm sure Leah would like to invite a couple of her new coworkers as well. Bring some warmth back into the old Plumeria manor." Lucinda suggested.

"That's actually a great idea!" Said Hazel as she walked out of the closet with a black dress in hand.

"What do you think?" asked Hazel as she held the dress up against her body.

"It's perfect!"

An hour later, the doorbell rang and Lucinda opened the door.

"Oh, hi..." said Victor. "Lucinda Griffin, right? Pleasure to finally meet you."

"Y-you know who I am?" she asked.

"A few years ago, when I was still with the A.E. I heard that Aaron Griffin's daughter joined the agency. I've also seen your file back when I was recruiting for the department of assets and heard great things about your work. Also, Hazel mentioned that you were her cousin on the phone earlier." said Victor.

"Oh," She replied with a nod and a smile.

"Hey, stranger," Hazel said from behind Lucinda. She wore a black, off the shoulder dress that ended just above her knees along with a pair of nude peep-toe heels.

"Well, it was great to finally meet you as well, Victor. Have a great night, guys!" Lucinda said and went back upstairs.

"Good night!" Hazel waved back at her.

"Wow, you look…stunning," said Victor, in awe.

Hazel felt the familiar warmth creep up from her neck to her face.

"Thank you. You don't look too bad yourself." she said trying her best not to seem nervous.

She wasn't the best at flirting and on top of that, she hadn't been on a date in a long time. He opened the passenger side door for her, then walked around the front of the car and got in.

"So, where are we going?" asked Hazel.

"The Fabled Tale Bookstore," said Victor.

Hazel cocked her head. "We're going to…the bookstore?" She drew her brows together.

Victor couldn't help but chuckle.

"Yes, but it's not what you think. You'll see when we get there," said Victor as he continued to smile.

She squinted her eyes at him in suspicion eliciting another chuckle from him.

Victor parked across the street from the bookstore and waited for her to step out before crossing the road. When they reached the storefront, a white rectangular 'We're closed' sign hung across the front door. He slowly turned the doorknob and when he heard a click, he pushed the door open with ease. He stepped in first and Hazel reluctantly followed behind him into the lightless building. She glanced around the store. There was no one else around besides the two of them.

"Um, this date is starting to feel like an episode of Unsolved Mysteries waiting to happen," said Hazel as she stood in the middle of the store.

"C'mon, this way," he said as he waved her over.

"I don't know about this. Are you sure we're allowed to be here right now?" asked Hazel as she wrapped her hands around her upper arms.

"Don't worry, I won't let anything bad happen to you," said Victor as he extended his hand out to her.

Hazel gave him a once-over glance before unfolding her arms and gently placing her hand in his. Victor's hands were twice as big as hers and they were slightly rough but warm. His touch sent a tingly sensation through her fingers and up her arm. He pulled her towards the back of the store. Then, stopped abruptly when they reached a dark hallway lined with bookshelves on both sides. The hallway was pitch black but Hazel could see something reflective from a distance.

As they approached the end of the hallway, she noticed a large wooden cheval mirror that stood at least eight feet tall against the wall. Their reflections were black silhouettes looking back at them.

Victor turned to face her, but she avoided looking directly into his eyes. She was afraid that he could see right through her and would know how vulnerable she was feeling, so she kept her eyes down at his chest. His breathing seemed to have quickened and she caught a whiff of his cologne. It was a mixture of seductive citrus and bergamot. As he stared down at her, he could tell that she was still feeling uneasy.

"Trust me?" He asked with his chin tilted towards his chest and his brows drew together.

"Well, he hasn't given me any reasons not to," Hazel thought to herself.

She let out a breath of air and looked up at him.

"Okay," she said as she let him lead her into the dark once again, her hand still in his.

Hazel watched as Victor lifted one leg and slowly walk through the mirror. She gasped and her eyes widened, then carefully reached into her reflection. The silvery surface of the mirror acted like metallic fluid. As she stepped through, it felt like she was walking into a freezer but only for a brief second. Once they were on the other side, the cold had dissipated and they were standing in a dimly lit restaurant.

There was a live band playing smooth jazz music on a small stage in the corner and every table seemed to be occupied by a couple. A bar table lined the wall on one side and right above the glass shelves behind the bar was a wooden sign with black letters that read '*The Hallowed Nook*'.

The bartender picked his head up and noticed them standing by the podium in front of the mirror. He walked out from behind the bar and walked over to them.

"Good evening, monsieur et madame. Reservations?" The waiter asked with a French accent.

"Yes, under LaMeur." Victor politely replied.

The waiter glanced down at the top of the podium.

"Ah, oui! Right this way." said the waiter.

They followed the waiter to a table near the stage and he pulled out the chair for Hazel.

"Thank you," said Hazel as she sat down.

Victor pulled out the chair across from her.

"What a cool speakeasy! How did you find out about it?" asked Hazel, excitedly.

"I'm glad you like it. I heard about it from a friend a while ago. Apparently, it's been here for ages but it's my first time here as well," said Victor.

Just then, their waitress approached the table.

"Good evening, my name is Charlotte. Can I get you guys any drinks?" she asked.

"Yes, a glass of pinot grigio for me, please," said Hazel.

"And a whiskey and coke, thanks," said Victor.

Charlotte nodded and walked towards the bar.

"You know, you really had me back there," said Hazel.

"What do you mean?" asked Victor, feigning innocence.

"I thought we would either be arrested or I'd end up on the local newspaper the tomorrow morning," said Hazel.

Victor laughed.

"Well, I wanted it to be a surprise and... I meant what I said before, I won't let anything bad happen to you," said Victor with a smile.

Hazel glanced up at him from across the table and smiled shyly.

Charlotte came back with their drinks and set them on the table.

"Are you guys ready to order?" she asked.

After ordering their food, Hazel pulled her chair closer to the table.

"So, I heard from Luce that the Aster Elites has been trying to recruit you again?" Hazel asked as she reached for the wine glass.

Victor scratched the back of head and leaned back.

"Yes, it's true. They've reached out to me several times and I've turned them down every time. Ever since I left, I hadn't thought about going back," said Victor as he leaned forward again over the table. "I don't know, maybe someday I'll return but I'm pretty content with how my life is going right now." he said as he stared down at his whiskey and coke. He turned the glass round and round with one hand, leaving wet rings on the white tablecloth.

When he snapped out of his thoughts, he looked up at her with a half-lidded gaze.

She didn't need her fairy senses to understand what he was feeling. There were dark stormy clouds behind those gorgeous gray eyes. She knew he was still grieving the loss of Liam.

He gave her a half-smile.

"Enough about me. I asked you out so I can get to know *you* better," said Victor with a grin now and crossing his hands on the table like a student in class.

Hazel opened her mouth but as usual her mind suddenly went blank as soon as his attention lands on her.

"I'm really not as interesting as you may presume," she managed to say as she shifted in her seat.

"That's not true. You and your sister chose to move from the bustling Luna Valley to little ol' Hallowed Falls when usually people can't wait to get *out* of small towns," said Victor as he brought the glass of brown liquor to his lips and tilted his head back slightly without taking his eyes off of her.

"Well, if you *really* must know. I moved here because of Leah, not that she forced me to. It's just that I know being here means a lot to her and I just couldn't bear to let her be alone here without anyone looking out for her."

"It seems that your sister's pretty lucky to have you."

"We've always had a really strong bond. In fact, I've always been the one whose felt lucky to have her as a sister. Her passion for healing others and ambition inspires me every single day."

"She certainly sounds like an incredible person."

"She is the best!" Hazel said with delight.

Just then, Charlotte approached them once again and placed their food on the table.

"Bon appètit," she said with a smile before walking away with her tray.

"Everything smells delicious!" Said Hazel, unfolding the white napkin and placing it on her lap.

"Yea, my buddy who recommended this place says he's never been disappointed and he's been coming here for years." said Victor.

They ate in silence for a few moments, enjoying each other's company.

Back at the manor, Leah was slowly pulling up to the front yard and put her car in park. It had been a long day at the hospital, and she was relieved to finally be home. She sat there as her thoughts drifted and she recalled when she first began as an intern at the Luna Valley hospital. She remembered how incredibly lucky she had been to have Dr. Rachel Guerisseuse as her mentor at the time. Not only was she also a witch, but Dr. Guerisseuse was one of the top hematologists at the hospital and had also been her professor at the Luna Valley University. Dr. Guerisseuse helped Leah tremendously through the process of researching and producing the Enchantress Elixir. It was only after getting her residency at Luna Valley Hospital that Leah decided to take the elixir.

Leah researched all throughout college just to ensure she was making the right decision when it came time to take the elixir. Fairies were not able to cast spells like witches can. Witches were not able to produce auras and charms like fairies could but there were certain healing spells that could be combined with elixirs that were stronger than any fairy charm or aura.

"Hey, are you alright in there?" Lucinda knocked on Leah's car window. She didn't realize how long she'd been sitting in the car.

"Uh, yea. Long day," Leah said as she opened the car door and stepped out.

"Amber made mac and cheese tonight. Come on," Lucinda said as she walked back into the house. Leah followed.

"Got something brewing on your mind?" Lucinda questioned.

"Just thinking about the time I took the elixir. It was shortly after I had started my residency at Luna Valley Hospital." Leah reminisced.

"What made you decide to do it? If you don't mind me asking," asked Lucinda.

"I've always wanted to do more with my powers and to help all magical beings, just like Gregoro did," Leah explained. Just then, they heard a car door shut and ran to the window that looked out to the front yard.

Victor parked in front of the manor, behind Leah's car. They watched as Victor got out of the car and opened the passenger side door for Hazel before walking to the front door together.

"I had a great time tonight. Thank you," Hazel simpered.

"I did as well and I hope we can do this again soon," said Victor and smiled back.

"Actually, we're having a barbecue this Saturday. I'd really like for you and Olivia to come." said Hazel, biting her bottom lip.

"That sounds like fun. I'll let Liv know." He took a step closer towards her. "Good night, Hazel." he said as he gave her a kiss on the cheek and walked back to his car. He gave her another big smile before getting in.

Hazel turned on her heel and got her keys out. She couldn't stop smiling. Just then, she noticed someone peeking out from the window and when they realized they've been spotted, the shadows darted behind the curtain. Hazel shook her head before unlocking the door and stepping in.

She also knew Victor waited until she was inside the house before driving away and it warmed her to know that he really meant what he said earlier.

"Well isn't he a gentleman? He opened the car door and everything," Leah teased.

"He really is," Hazel as she replayed the moment his hand first touched hers.

"I'm just teasing. He seems like a nice guy," Leah smiled.

"He and Liv will be coming to the barbecue. You'll have a chance to get to know him as well," said Hazel as she kicked her shoes off her feet.

"So...how was the date? Give us the juicy details!" Lucinda squealed.

Hazel laughed and began to recount the events of the date. When she was finished, they all got up and walked towards the stairs.

"I've never felt like this on a first date before...I really think he's different from all the others." said Hazel as they climbed the stairs.

"I'm looking forward to meeting the guy my sister is head over heels for." Leah teased.

The girls giggled and went into their own rooms for the night.

The girls got up early on Saturday morning. Hazel busied herself with decorating, while Lucinda and Leah prepared the food for the grill. The first guests to arrive were Leah's coworkers; Maryann Wong, Tyler Charmont, and Heidi Hendrix. Olivia and Victor arrived shortly after with Victor's best friend, Duke Bryant.

"Welcome to the Plumeria manor!" Lucinda greeted them excitedly.

Hazel walked into the foyer to give Olivia and Victor a hug.

"Duke, this is Hazel Plumeria. She recently moved here from Luna Valley with her sister." Victor grinned and placed his hand on Hazel's waist as he introduced her.

"Pleased to meet you Hazel. You have lovely home." said Duke as he extended his hand to her with a friendly smile.

"Thank you, it's a pleasure meeting you as well." Hazel shook his hand and smiled back. She didn't know much about Duke aside for the fact that he is Victor's best friend and is currently Lucinda's boss. She also didn't expect Duke to be so polite but she appreciated it and he seemed very genuine.

"Everyone's out on the deck, you guys can follow me," Lucinda gestured for them to follow her as she began to walk towards the back.

Olivia and Duke followed her out to the deck while Victor pulled Hazel to the side.

"I made this for you. It's Salixantho, the elixir I used on you when you got the bee sting. Just in case you ever need it again," Victor said as he held out a small mason jar filled with amber liquid and a blue bow tied around the lid.

Hazel carefully caressed the mason jar with both hands, as if it were a fragile dragon egg.

"That's very sweet and thoughtful, thank you." She gave him a kiss on the cheek and grinned from ear to ear. They slowly made their way to the garden together and found Duke by the picnic table.

"I'll get you guys margaritas. I made it myself, be right back." Hazel turned and headed over to the drinks table.

"I'm going to grab a burger." Duke walked over to the grill just a few feet away.

Victor grabbed a paper plate and started to scoop fruit salad onto it.

Leah's coworkers, Heidi and Maryann were sitting on the corner of the patio when Heidi suddenly stopped talking to Maryann and froze. She noticed Victor standing at the picnic table across the deck and was surprised to see him here. The shocked look on her face worried Maryann.

"Heidi, are you okay?" asked Maryann with concern.

"Uh...yea. I just spotted an old friend. Excuse me for a second." Heidi said as she kept her gaze on him.

She got up and walked towards Victor.

"Hey... Vick, it's been a while," said Heidi, nervously with a half-smile.

Victor turned around from the picnic table.

"H-Heidi...h-hi!" Victor stuttered as he placed the paper plate down.

Heidi's shoulder length, light blonde hair seemed to glow under the sun and her deep blue eyes stared right into his. She could tell he was just as surprised to see her and she smiled.

"I am doing great actually. I recently took on a position as a trauma surgeon at the Hallowed Falls hospital. How about you?" asked Heidi, tilting her head slightly to the side.

"That's awesome, I've been helping my uncle with his store and I recently joined the Hallowed Falls PD," said Victor, tucking his hands into his pockets.

"Hallowed Falls PD? Kind of a step down from when you were at A.E. isn't it?" Heidi gave him a friendly shove with her hand.

Victor chuckled and rubbed the back of his neck.

"Uh...I guess so? But I like the way things are going for me right now," he replied with a cheery tone.

Hazel, Leah, and Lucinda were at the drinks table on the other side of the deck.

"Who's that talking to Victor?" asked Hazel.

"That's Heidi, we work together at the hospital. I didn't know they knew each other. Man, this really *is* a small town," said Leah as she continued to mix more margaritas.

"Heidi Hendrix used to be an agent at the A.E. She wasn't there for long and resigned shortly after Victor left. I think they briefly dated back then. From what Duke has told me, she's also a descendant of the Alexanders." Lucinda said.

"That's...interesting." Hazel raised her eyebrows as she poured margaritas into two separate glasses.

"I have to run now, but we should have lunch together some time. Are you free tomorrow? I'd really like to catch up," asked Heidi as she gently rested her hand on Victor's bicep and gave him a kiss on the cheek.

"Sure, it would be nice to catch up." Victor nodded with a smile.

Heidi waved goodbye to him as she looked for Leah to say goodbye.

Hazel looked over right when Heidi gave Victor a kiss on the cheek. She felt a small prick in her chest and her stomach tightened.

"*What was that? Was I...jealous?*" she thought to herself. "*No, I don't want to be that girl,*" She grabbed the two glasses of margaritas and walked towards Victor.

Duke rejoined Victor at the picnic table.

"So, this is the Plumeria manor. My folks were friends with the Plumerias before they moved. I've always wanted to see what the inside of this place looked like," said Duke as he took a bite out of his burger.

"Okay guys, let me know if this is good," said Hazel as she handed the margaritas to Victor and Duke.

Duke took a sip. "Wow, we've got to come over more often for these margaritas, Vick," Duke teased and nudged Victor's arm with his elbow.

Victor shook his head and laughed.

Leah stepped onto the deck and set a tray of cooked patties on the picnic table. Hazel grabbed her arm as she passed by.

"Duke, have you met my sister Leah?" Hazel said and gave Leah a wink.

"No, we haven't been introduced yet. Hi, Leah. Thank you for having us over," Duke said, flashing her a smile before taking another bite out of his burger. His bright white teeth and dimple made him look like a model in a toothpaste commercial.

"Uh…hi and y-you're welcome," said Leah as she started to make herself a plate of food.

Duke had dark brown hair in a quiff style. His piercing blue eyes seemed incredibly vibrant against his olive skin and as he stared at Leah from behind the burger.

While Duke and Leah were getting acquainted, Hazel grabbed Victor's hand and pulled him away.

"Looks like you saved me from another boring conversation with that one," said Victor.

Hazel giggled.

"I want to show you something," she told him as she led him towards the ten foot tall shrubs and guided him through the maze garden.

"What a beautiful garden," said Victor in awe, as he looked all around.

"I come out here sometimes to clear my mind and practice my charms," Hazel said as she crouched down over a closed up purple tulip.

She fluttered her wings and waved her left hand over the bulb. A bright glow flashed from under her palm. Victor watched as Hazel encouraged the flower to bloom, the petals slowly unfurling.

"That's incredible. Must be awesome to be able to do something like that," said Victor.

She stood back up and dusted her hands off.

"Yea, but sometimes I feel kind of...blah. Ya' know? I mean...yes, it's great that I can bloom plants but what actual good can I even do with that? I really admire Leah and Lucinda. They both worked really hard on their magical skills to be able to help others....and all I can do are minor auras and charms," said Hazel, sounding disappointed as she looked down at her hands.

"Fairies are the most special of all magical beings. You have the power to heal others in ways other preternatural beings can't. Did you know that fairies can produce Restoration auras not only for themselves, but for anyone else they choose? There are other healing auras you can cast when you start honing your magic," said Victor encouragingly.

"I didn't know that I can project my aura on to someone else. The only training I've ever had was from my mother. She's always withheld from teaching me higher level fairy magic, in fear that it would give us away to the humans. Come to think of it, I don't know why I've never questioned it. I guess because I've always been too busy tending to our garden and learning about the different species of flowers to realize it" said Hazel thoughtfully.

"I can try to help you with what I've researched during my time at the A.E," said Victor.

"Thank you," Hazel responded and gave him a half-smile.

"We should probably go check on Leah. I'm sure Duke has bored her to death by now with his work stories." Hazel laughed. They began to make their way back through the maze garden. Meanwhile, Duke and Leah were still in conversation by the picnic table.

"So, you work at Hallowed Falls hospital, huh? That's great that you want to help heal others," Duke was saying to Leah.

"Yea, I've always wanted to do more with my powers and Hallowed Falls seemed to be the place to do that," Leah responded as she took a bite of her burger.

A light breeze swept past them and blew Leah's hair away from her face. Duke couldn't help, but notice how pretty Leah was. Her light beige skin seemed silky smooth and she had the most unique shade of green eyes that Duke had ever seen.

"What do you do?" Leah asked.

"I work at the Aster Elites Headquarters. I am one of the senior directors there," he explained. He glanced back at her again and chuckled.

"What?" asked Leah with her mouth full.

"You've got something right…there." Duke said as he pointed to his own lips. "Here let me get it for you."

He grabbed a clean napkin off the table next to him and wiped the ketchup off Leah's chin. Leah froze. For a second, it felt like a spark running through her body. It went from her chin, down her arms and the rest of her body. She felt her heart begin to race and she held her breath. Duke looked down at her and noticed the golden specks that decorated her green eyes. Duke suddenly froze, too. Then, quickly snapped out of it.

"Uh, I'm sorry. I've…gotta go. Thank you for the food and drinks," said Duke. Leah sensed a bit of panic in him but she didn't understand why.

"Oh…okay…bye," Leah frowned.

Duke tried to find Victor to let him know he was taking off but he was nowhere to be found. He decided that he'll explain it to him later and walked towards the back door to the dining hall.

"What was I thinking?" Duke thought to himself.

He had just gotten out of a serious relationship. He shouldn't have flirted with Leah.

"If that even counted as flirting," he thought to himself.

That's why he had to leave. He was still trying to get over Savannah and didn't want to give anyone any ideas.

Victor and Hazel made their plates of food, before heading back to Leah.

"Where'd Duke go?" Hazel asked as they sat down next to Leah.

"He left and in a hurry, too. I must've scared him away," Leah said with a shrug.

"It's not *you* that scared him away," said Victor as he took a bite of his burger.

"What was it then?" asked Leah.

"Duke just went through a really bad breakup with a girl named Savannah Powell. They had been dating for a few years and Duke finally proposed about a month ago, but Savannah declined. Claimed that she wasn't ready or whatever. He hasn't admitted it but I could see that he's been feeling completely broken. That's why I brought him here today, to try and get his mind off of it," said Victor.

"Poor Duke," said Hazel.

"That's awful," Leah said, furrowing her brow in concern.

The rest of the barbecue went smoothly as everyone hung out and talked. As the day grew dark, the last of their guests left and Hazel, Leah, and Lucinda started to clean up.

"That was fun, wasn't it ladies?" asked Lucinda as she cleaned up the picnic table.

"You and Victor seem to be getting along well. And Leah, I saw you with Duke. Is he okay? I heard about the breakup a couple of weeks ago." asked Lucinda as she continued to clean. Leah went around with a trash bag to gather anything disposable.

"The conversation was going pretty well or at least I *thought* it was. It was nice to talk to someone new for a change, aside from you guys and my coworkers," said Leah.

"Hey! Offense taken!" Hazel joked.

"Sorry! You know what I mean…He helped me wipe ketchup off my chin and suddenly, he was taking off. I thought it was kind of strange until Victor explained the situation." Leah shrugged.

"The barbecue really was great though, Luce. I definitely had a good time," said Hazel with a smile.

As they finished cleaning they realized how exhausting the day really was, what with the prep, entertaining and the cleanup. They wandered off to bed not too long after cleaning up, and settled in for a peaceful sleep.

The following afternoon, Victor had taken on a shift at Delphina's. He was checking in the new shipments when Duke walked in.

"Hey." said Duke as he awkwardly stepped into the shop.

"Hey, what happened? You left pretty early yesterday. You alright, man?" asked Victor as he continued to pull packing peanuts out of a box.

"Yea, I just had a moment... with Leah. It reminded me of Savannah. It's stupid," Duke explained. He felt awful as soon as he had gotten home from the barbecue.

"No, I get it. It's only been what, a month since you guys broke up? It's going to take some time," said Victor.

"Yea, I guess," said Duke as he glanced down at his car keys. "Anyway, I was in the area and thought I'd stop by. I was invited to the opening of the new lounge next Friday night, Siren's Cove down on Dragon's Breath Trail. Interested?" asked Duke.

"Sure man, sounds fun," said Victor as he continued unpacking boxes.

"Alright, I'll see you later," said Duke as he walked out of the store.

Shortly after Duke left, Victor heard the shop's door open again.

"Welcome to Del-oh...hey, Heidi," said Victor, caught off guard. He forgot that they agreed to have lunch together today.

Victor couldn't help but do a double -take. Heidi was wearing a white tank top with a low neckline, revealing quite a bit of cleavage, paired with short shorts. Her hair had been curled, soft ringlets fell around her tanned shoulders.

"Hey! You about ready for lunch?" Heidi asked with curled red lips.

"Uh, yea, just one sec," said Victor. He walked over to the stockroom door.

"Daryl! I need you to cover the front for a bit!" yelled Victor.

"Alright, I'll be right out!" a voice yelled back.

"I was thinking, how about we try Pixie's Grill down Emerald Street? I heard that the Pixie Pasta there is amazing," said Heidi.

"Yea, that sounds great." said Victor, excitedly. He remembered how great of a friendship he had with Heidi before Liam died and a part of him wanted that friendship back.

He untied his apron and flung it over the counter. Heidi smiled, put her arm through Victor's, and they walked out of the store together towards Pixie's Grill. The air was dry and hot as they stepped outside. When they approached the restaurant, Victor held the restaurant door open for Heidi and they went inside to wait for a table.

Back at the Plumeria manor, Hazel was playing with Sage in the garden when her cellphone rang.

"Hello?" Hazel answered.

"Hi, Hazel! Great barbecue you guys threw yesterday. Listen, I was wondering if you'd like to grab lunch and go shopping with me later?" asked Olivia, cheerfully.

"Sure, I don't really have any plans today. Where should I meet you?" asked Hazel.

"We can meet at Tempra's Café. It's down the street from Delphina's. Let's say...in one hour?" asked Olivia.

"Great, I'll see you there," Hazel answered. Hazel picked up Sage and went upstairs to get ready.

By the time Hazel arrived, Olivia was waiting outside of the café when she pulled up to the curb. Hazel had thrown on a pale yellow, spaghetti strapped dress with a pair of white espadrilles, she looked fresh and pretty in contrast to the hot day.

"Cute dress! I'm so glad you're free today." Olivia grinned as she walked up to Hazel and gave her a hug.

"Hi! Thank you! I got it from my favorite store in Luna Valley," said Hazel as she looked down at her dress.

"What's Leah and Lucinda up to today?" asked Liv as they began to walk.

"They're actually both at work. I'm glad you called. I don't really know anyone else around here and it gets kind of boring, walking around town alone sometimes," said Hazel.

"No worries, I got you. In fact, I wanted to ask if you'd be interested in coming with me and a couple of my friends to Siren's Cove lounge this Friday? You should bring Leah and Lucinda along," said Liv.

"I've never been to a lounge before. Count us in!" said Hazel with a smile.

Olivia stopped in front of a restaurant.

"Awesome. This is Pixie's Grill, it's been here for over a century and the food is fantastic!" said Olivia.

"Sure, sounds great!" said Hazel. They walked in, feeling a little relief at the cool interior. Hazel took a quick glance around the restaurant. The restaurant had a sports bar feel to it, the walls were painted black and the furniture seemed to be made of rosewood with a glossy finish. Large windows were installed all around the restaurant, allowing the natural light to illuminate the entire place.

"Welcome to Pixie's Grill! Just two today?" asked the waitress in a friendly tone as she pressed some buttons on her monitor.

"Yes, thank you," said Olivia politely.

As they were waiting to be seated, Hazel looked around the restaurant and spotted Victor sitting at the bar alone. She was about to walk over to him but just then, she saw Heidi take the seat next to him.

"*They're together on an afternoon date? What the hell?!*" she thought to herself.

"Oh, what a coincidence. Hey, Vick!" Olivia shouted and started speed walking towards the bar.

Hazel followed behind her slowly, choosing to glance around the restaurant instead of straight ahead.

"Heidi, good to see you again," said Olivia in a surprised tone.

"Hi, Olivia." said Heidi with a forced smile.

"Hey…w-what are you guys doing here?" asked Victor, suddenly feeling and not sure why.

"We were just stopping by for lunch before doing some shopping. What a coincidence that you guys are here, too! I thought you were working today?" said Olivia.

"I was. I mean, I'm taking a lunch break." said Victor as he kept his gaze on Hazel.

"Yea…what a coincidence," mumbled Hazel.

Just then, they heard someone from the front of the restaurant announce Olivia's name.

"Oh! Looks like our booth is ready. Enjoy your lunch. See ya!" said Olivia. She grabbed Hazel's arm and started skipping towards the booth.

"See ya," said Hazel as she got dragged away.

They walked back to the waiting area where the hostess waited for them with two menus.

"This way, ladies," said the hostess.

Hazel glanced back at Victor and Heidi for a second, then followed behind Olivia to their booth. They were seated on the side of the restaurant next to a large window looking out onto a main road. Hazel looked out the window noticing the streets seemed pretty busy today. Across the street was the arboretum and it reminded her of the day Victor had taken her there.

"Is something wrong?" asked Olivia with a concerned look on her face.

"No," said Hazel with a half-smile.

Olivia smirked.

"I wouldn't worry about them too much. I mean, yes. They briefly dated a few years ago but I *know* for a fact, that Victor is really into you," Olivia winked.

"How can you tell?" she asked.

"Whenever I stop by Delphina's, he is constantly talking about you. And of all the relationships I've seen him in, I've never seen him this excited about someone." said Olivia.

"Really?" asked Hazel with a raised eyebrow. She wanted to believe Olivia but the sight of Heidi and Victor together kept her skeptical.

"Really." Olivia assured her with a nod and a smile.

Hazel felt a bit reassured by this and decided to try and just enjoy the rest of her day She waved the thought of Victor and Heidi out of her mind for now, determined not to let it bother her.

Later that evening, Hazel was sitting out on the deck with a glass of wine, the day of shopping had been fun, but the thought of seeing Victor with Heidi was harder to dismiss than she cared to admit. Leah opened the backdoor and stepped out, disrupting her silent reverie.

"Hey, you alright sis? You rarely ever drink alone. Where's Lucinda?" asked Leah and sat down next to her.

"She called and said she's working overnight. Yea…it's just that…I was out in town with Olivia today when we bumped into Victor and Heidi. They were on a lunch date at Pixie's Grill," said Hazel, blandly.

"I thought you guys were a thing?" asked Leah.

"Not exactly…we never actually said we were a *thing*. We've only been on one date, but I just can't help but replay that evening. There was something between us. Well, at least I *thought* there was. I guess I'm overthinking it. Maybe he's not that interested after all." said Hazel morosely started down at her glass of wine.

"Hey…cheer up. There's plenty of guys in Hallowed Falls. He just happened to be the first guy you met here that was nice to you," said Leah as she grabbed a beer out of the mini fridge on the deck. "You could be right but I'm tired of thinking about him. What about you? Have you been thinking about Duke? He's actually pretty hot," Hazel teased.

"Yea, but unfortunately he is emotionally unavailable. I just want to focus on my work and strengthen my craft right now, anyway," said Leah as she took a swig from her beer.

"Olivia invited me to some lounge this Friday. We should all go together!" Hazel suggested.

"I haven't been to a lounge in a long time. That might be fun," said Leah with a smile.

Hazel nodded and rocked her glass of wine.

"Did you know fairies can project certain auras onto another person?" asked Hazel.

Leah shook her head and wrinkling her nose a little, "No, I had no idea."

"Yea, Victor was the one who told me that," said Hazel as she kept her eyes down at her glass.

Leah tilted her head and narrowed her eyes.

"Wow, you really *like* the guy," she said.

Hazel lifted her head.

"It doesn't really matter now, anyways. I'm not sure what he has going on with Heidi," Hazel responded as she heaved a sigh.

Leah gave her a sympathetic look and kept her company in silence as they finished their drinks.

Friday evening came around in a blink of an eye. It had been raining all day so Hazel decided to tend to the greenhouse. She was slowly adding more herbs and flowers to their collection. Soon, they'd have almost everything needed to create any potion they wanted. She had frequented Delphina's Emporium the past couple of days and it just occurred to her that she hadn't seen or heard from Victor in a while.

"Perhaps he really has gotten back with Heidi," she thought as she repotted the white orchids.

After cleaning up the soil on the floor, she headed back into the manor to get ready for tonight. They were meeting Olivia in front of Siren's Cove in two hours and she still hadn't decided on what to wear.

Leah, Hazel, and Lucinda drove up to Siren's Cove lounge. When they got there, Olivia and two of her friends were standing by the entrance.

"Hazel! Over here!" She waved at them excitedly, bouncing on her toes.

They walked up to Olivia together.

"You guys look gorge! Come on! I got us the VIP table," said Liv as she started walking into the lounge.

Victor and Heidi were sitting at the table when the girls walked in. He smiled and waved at Hazel when he saw her.

"Did you know he was going to be here?" Leah whispered to Hazel.

"No," Hazel replied flatly. She kept her gaze on her for a minute and then looked away as she tried to fight the feeling of jealousy.

"I'm gonna go get us some drinks!" Leah shouted as she walked towards the bar.

"Let's get on the dance floor!" Olivia grabbed Hazel's arm and pulled her to the dance floor.

Victor got up and was prepared to walk over to her when Heidi grabbed his hand.

"Vick, will you get me another long island iced tea?." Heidi pouted as she held up the empty glass.

"Uh… yea, sure. I'll be back in a sec." said Victor as he gave Hazel a quick glance before heading towards the bar. He watched as Olivia dragged her away and decided he would catch up to her later.

Duke walked in shortly after they did. He scanned the room before spotting Victor by the bar and walked over to him.

"Hey, so you made it." said Duke with a smile as he continued to look around the lounge.

"I said I would. The girls are here as well." said Victor as he tried to get the bartender's attention.

Duke glanced around the room to see who Victor was referring to. His eyes landed on Leah who was on the opposite side of the bar.

"I'll be right back," said Duke as walked away.

Victor smirked as he watched his friend walk around the large bar.

"Hi, Leah." The voice came from just out of her eyeline, forcing her to turn to see who it was.

Duke was standing next to her, leaning against the ledge of the bar table with his arms crossed in front of him. He was wearing a fitted navy button-down shirt that hugged his V-shaped torso nicely, and black jeans. His biceps looked like it would tear the sleeve if he made the wrong dance move.

"*Ugh, why does he have to look so damn good in that shirt,*" Leah thought to herself.

She gave him a polite smile.

"Listen, I'm sorry for leaving so abruptly last week at your barbecue. I'm just going through some stuff right now and I didn't want to give you the wrong idea," said Duke over the loud music.

"Don't worry about it. I didn't get any ideas…I hope you have fun tonight, Duke," said Leah, trying to seem unbothered. She grabbed the drinks and was about to walk away but turned her head.

"Or at least *stay* long enough to," she said before continuing towards Lucinda.

Leah handed Lucinda drink as she approached her.

"Thanks! I saw Duke come over to you. What did he say?" Asked Lucinda as she took a sip of her drink.

"He apologized for leaving abruptly at the barbecue. He said he didn't want to give me any *ideas*. What ideas does he think I'm going to get, anyway? We literally spoke for two minutes before he freaked out and left. That was all," said Leah. She started to feel increasingly annoyed the more she thought about the brief conversation and Lucinda could see it on her face.

"Forget him, let's go dance!" said Lucinda.

The girls danced all through the night. Hazel couldn't remember the last time she had this much fun. Then, she happened to glance back at the table where Heidi and Victor were sitting. Heidi had her hands wrapped around Victor's arm. They were talking and laughing. It confirmed Hazel's suspicions that they were back together. Why did it bother her so much? She hadn't known Victor for that long. But still, as hard as she tried to not let it bother her, it was eating her up inside. She stopped dancing and leaned over to Lucinda and Leah.

"Hey, guys? I think I'm going to head home," Hazel shouted over the music.

"Okay, we'll go with you," said Lucinda as she gestured to Leah that they're leaving.

Leah nodded in agreement. They said goodbye to Olivia and her friends, then headed back home.

As soon as they got back to the manor, Hazel headed straight for the shower, trying to wash away her hurt as much as the layer of swear she worked up dancing. When she was done, she went down to the dining hall where Lucinda and Leah were having cheesecake.

"Amber left this for us in the fridge. We saved you a slice." Leah said with a smile and pushed a plate towards Hazel.

"Are you feeling any better? You looked like you were sick to your stomach before we left." Lucinda asked as she poured a hot cup of tea for Hazel.

"Not really but I'll be okay," Hazel said as she sipped the tea.

"It's cause of Victor isn't it…and Heidi?" Leah asked with concern.

"I shouldn't feel like this, we aren't even in a relationship." said Hazel as she poked at the cake with a fork.

"It's understandable…you have feelings for the guy. You should probably talk to him about it. Maybe he has an explanation?" Lucinda suggested.

"Yea…I'll think about it," said Hazel. They stayed up talking for a while longer and then went to bed.

After a couple days of laying low, Hazel decided to stop by the local florist. She wanted to see what other flowers she could plant in their garden.

"Welcome to Primrose's Flower Shop. I'm Amarie, please let me know if I can help you find anything," said the woman behind the counter as she was trimming a bouquet of roses.

Hazel greeted her in return, unable to help staring at Amarie's butterfly-shaped wings. They were a beautiful, iridescent light blue shade that faded into an ethereal light green. Amarie nodded and smiled politely at Hazel. The store smelled like fresh cut flowers and she wondered if she would be able to find gardenias. She looked up at the door when she heard it swing open and saw a familiar face.

"Hey...Hazel," said Victor.

"Victor...? What are you doing here?" asked Hazel.

"I was just across the street at the bookstore and I saw you walk in. I thought maybe we could talk," said Victor hesitantly.

"Talk about *what*?" asked Hazel tersely.

"Us," he suggested. He could tell she was annoyed.

"There's an *us*?" she asked as she continued to walk through the flower shop. She clearly knew what he meant but she wanted to hear him say it.

"You know what I mean," he said beginning to feel frustrated.

"Actually, I don't," she stopped and turned to face him.

"I thought there was something between us, that night on our date. But I was wrong because you are obviously dating Heidi. There is no *us*." said Hazel responded, unable to hide the hint of irritation in her tone.

"We're not dating. We're just...friends. We've always been good friends. She was there for me when Liam died. I will admit that the last couple of times we were together, it may have seemed like something else. But we were just catching up. We only went out a couple of times before I left the A.E. I had shut everyone out after that," said Victor.

"You guys are really *just* friends?" asked Hazel with a raised brow.

"Yes. Back then, I thought there was a spark and we had been close friends for so long. But then I realized shortly after, I didn't feel anything more for her other than friendship. I didn't feel anything for anyone after Liam died. I had gone numb and I hadn't felt anything for anyone in years. Until recently...when I met you." Victor paused and waited for her to respond.

"Oh..." said Hazel. She felt like an ass now for jumping to conclusions.

"I know we haven't really seen or spoken to each other much after our date that night. I've just been picking up a lot of shifts at the station since I'm still a rookie there, but I'd to spend more time with you if that's okay," said Victor shyly.

"I feel like a jerk now. Will you let me take treat you to out to lunch?" She asked apologetically.

"I never say no to lunch." said Victor with a relieved smile.

Chapter 3

I t was a rainy Tuesday afternoon when Leah decided to go to the library. It felt like forever since her last day off. The large wooden door creaked open as she pushed through. She immediately noticed a group of college students sitting at a round wooden table whispering and laughing to the left. A few other people who were browsing the aisles and a man, who she assume, is the librarian was putting books away in another aisle. She decided to explore the preternatural archives floor and began climbing the curved stairway to the right of the entrance. When she got to the top step, she almost turned back around. The floor was poorly lit and she thought perhaps it was a closed floor, but the names above each aisle caught her eye.

"This must be what Hazel was talking about. How fascinating!" Leah thought to herself.

And began to browse through the aisles. She picked up a book from the Plumeria archive and began to flip through it. Suddenly she heard a loud thud, startling her out of her reverie. The noise seemed to have come from one of the aisles to the left of her. She pulled out her stylus and slowly walked up the aisle. Her breathing quickened and it was so quiet that she could practically hear her heart pounding inside her chest. When she reached the end of the aisle, she carefully peeked around the corner to where she heard the noise. There was nothing there. All of a sudden, she heard something like a swooshing sound coming at her from behind. Before she knew it, she felt something forceful knocking her down to the ground and landed hard on her right elbow.

"Who's there?!" she yelled, trying not to sound afraid.

At first, she was only met with silence. Then she heard footsteps walking down the aisles. It was getting closer and closer. Whoever it was, was approaching her aisle.

"What are you doing on the floor? You okay?" asked Duke with concern.

"Duke? Y-yea...I think so. I was knocked down," said Leah shakily as Duke helped her up.

"Knocked down by what?" He asked, sounding a bit confused as he scanned the floor.

"I-I'm not even sure. I heard something fall onto the floor from the next aisle, so I walked over, and someone came up from behind me. But I didn't see them. What are you doing here?" asked Leah as she dusted her pants off.

"There was a book I wanted to see, research for the A.E.," Duke replied. As he took a closer look at Leah, he realized how shaken up she really was.

"Hey, would you want get a cup of coffee with me?" Duke asked.

Leah thought about it for a second. She didn't really want to after their awkward interaction at the lounge, but she also didn't want to be alone right now.

"Sure, I could use a cup of hot coffee," she decided.

The rain had stopped and the sun was already breaking through the clouds by the time they stepped out of the library and walked over to Tempra's Café.

"Why don't you have a seat out here. I'll be right back." said Duke, motioning to one of the outdoor tables, before walking inside.

Leah took a seat at one of the small tables by the entrance. She began regaining her nerves and steady herself but the sound of a motorcycle passing by made her jump again. Duke came back out a few minutes later with two coffee cups and an ice pack in his hands.

"Here you go. How's your elbow?"

He seemed genuinely concerned. Leah looked into his deep blue eyes. His light brown hair was still wet from the rain earlier and he had swept it back from his forehead. He looked even more attractive now than when she first met him at the barbecue.

"It...um...still hurts but I'll bandage it once I get home. Thanks for asking," said Leah as she held the icepack to her elbow.

"Leah...I want to apologize for the way I've acted. I haven't given you the best first impression."

"No...it's okay. If anything, I should apologize for not hearing you out. Victor told me about your situation. I'm sorry that happened to you" Leah responded, her sincerity apparent in her tone.

"Yea...It's been rough, but I'll be alright...eventually. Vick told me that you and your sister just moved here. What brought you guys to Hallowed Falls?" Duke changed the subject hoping to avoid any awkwardness.

"Good question. I'm still trying to figure it out. I mean, I guess it's because I've always felt out of place in Luna Valley. The cliché way of explaining it, would be that...I felt I had a calling here. Also, as you may already know, generations of Plumerias were born and raised in Hallowed Falls. I was reassured of my decision when Lucinda came into our lives. I just...feel it in my bones that this is where I needed to be. What about you? Have you always lived here?" Asked Leah. She set her ice pack down and took a sip of coffee. The warmth from the hot drink somehow made her feel less jumpy.

"Actually, I live at the A.E. headquarters. It's a forty-minute drive from here. I come into Hallowed Falls for the library and to see some friends most of the time. But before that, my parents and relatives also lived in Hallowed Falls for generations. I moved out of town when I was recruited by the A.E. years ago." said Duke.

Duke focused on his coffee and Leah took the opportunity to look closely at him again. She was surprised he was being so nice to her, especially since she hadn't been the last time they spoke. He looked up at her and she quickly looked back at her elbow.

"Um...I should probably get this bandaged up," she said with a smile. "Thank you for the company and the coffee, Duke." She got up and headed back towards the library where she'd parked her car.

"Are you sure you can drive like that?" Duke shouted after her.

"I'll be fine, really!" Leah shouted back as she continued to walk.

On her way to the car, she smiled to herself, feeling relieved that they got to chat for a bit. She really did feel bad for what she said the other night and he didn't deserve that.

Hazel was playing on the grand piano in the foyer when Leah walked in holding her elbow. She stopped playing and looked up at Leah, her smile fading as she noticed her elbow.

"Oh my God, what happened to you? Are you alright?" Asked Hazel as she got up and hurried over to Leah.

"Yea, I'll be fine. I was at the library earlier and someone knocked me down," said Leah as she walked towards the bathroom.

"Wait, who attacked you?" Asked Hazel, worried for her sister.

"I don't know…it happened too quickly and it was too dark to see," Leah replied. She grabbed the first aid box from the cabinet under the sink and went into the dining hall as Hazel followed.

Shortly after Leah sat down and began tending to her elbow, Lucinda walked in.

"That was a *long* day," she said as she peeled her jacket off and slung it over a chair.

"You have no idea," said Leah as she continued to bandage her elbow.

"What happened to you? You hurt your elbow?" Asked Lucinda.

"I was attacked at the library on the top floor. I didn't see who or what it was. But Duke found me and…actually *comforted* me." said Leah, still surprised to have seen the gentle side of him.

Hazel looked at Leah in surprise, but she seemed to be zoning out for a second. She snapped her fingers in front of Leah's face.

"Hold on. You didn't tell me that Duke found you. How'd he even know you were there?" Hazel demanded.

"He mentioned he was researching something in the archives. After he found me, he stayed with me and we got coffee. We talked for a while and got to know each other a little better. He's actually pretty sweet. I was a bit surprised," said Leah.

"Really? I've never really seen any other side of him, apart from being at work. I would never have guessed that he had a soft side." said Lucinda thoughtfully

"I was a bit thrown off as well from how gentle he was, but I really appreciated that since it really shook me up. I'm beginning to think that I was wrong for thinking he was a jerk," said Leah.

"Well, you're not alone for jumping to conclusions about someone. By the way, I took your advice, Luce. I spoke to Victor and he did have an explanation. I felt like a jerk afterwards, so I took him out to lunch…and after a long talk, we decided to become exclusive." said Hazel with a smile.

"That's great, Hazel!" said Lucinda.

"He apologized for being MIA after our first date, we had a great conversation and I really feel that we are on the same page now," said Hazel.

"I'm so happy for you!" said Leah.

Hazel giggled. "Thanks, guys."

The following afternoon, Leah and Hazel headed to town. Hazel showed Leah some of her favorite shops before deciding to take her to the arboretum. It was such a beautiful place and she knew Leah would love it. When they reached the park, Leah's eyes widened with awe.

"Wow! This place is *magnificent*. How'd you find it?" Asked Leah.

"Victor brought me here a few days after we first met." Hazel replied.

Once they stepped inside, the warmth from the sun and the sweet scent of ylang ylang welcomed them. Leah also felt lighter, as if a weight she didn't even know she had, was lifted off her shoulders and she felt more relaxed.

"It feels *right* being here, doesn't it?" Asked Hazel.

"Yea…it does. Feels really familiar but I can't quite explain it," Leah marveled.

"I know. Ever since we arrived at Hallowed Falls, I've felt a sense of belonging. The same feeling as you've just described. I can't explain it either, especially since we've never actually been here before," said Hazel.

"I've read about the Hallowed Falls arboretum in one of the books I checked out of the library. The book was from the Summerland archives, in fact the Summerland family built this place. It was said that this place has been blessed by powerful fae and is supposed to be a safe haven for all fairies," said Leah.

"That explains the fairy houses." Hazel nodded her head in the direction of the fairy house at the center of the floor.

"Legend has it that before Honora died, she stored some powerful fairy magic in the center of the arboretum in hopes that one day when the heir of Summerland returned, they would have something to protect themselves. There was nothing in her research journals about her plans to do that though and no one's ever been able to prove that she did," said Leah.

"I do recall Victor mentioning something about that as well when we were here. But why did she do that? Where was her daughter, Lavender Summerland?" Asked Hazel as she glanced over at her sister.

"According to the book when the killings first began, Summerland had ordered her daughter to move far away. This was to keep her safe. Lavender left and never came back to Hallowed Falls, not even after the death of her mother. No one heard from her and no one was able to find her," said Leah.

"That's really sad. They probably never really got to say goodbye."

"I know, that's terrible...I wonder if any of her descendants are even alive to this day. But I guess no one will ever know."

Hazel looked up and realized the sun was beginning to set.

"Come on, it's getting late and I still have to pick up lilies from the flower shop," said Hazel.

The flower shop was only a couple minutes' drive from the arboretum. Leah took in a deep breath once they stepped inside the shop.

"I love the smell of fresh flowers," she said happily.

Hazel noticed that there was a different fairy behind the counter, from the last time she had been there.

"Hello, welcome to Primrose's Flower Shop. I'm Primrose Evans. Is there anything in particular that I can help you find?" she asked in a friendly manner.

Hazel and Leah couldn't help but notice how beautiful she was. Primrose had wavy light purple hair that went down to her waist. Her wings were stunning iridescent orange, also a set of two, like Hazel's but they pointed lower than hers.

"Hi, do you have sunset lilies?" Hazel asked, hoping she hadn't noticed her gawking.

"Yes, they're actually over here in the back," said Primrose with a smile and leading the way.

Hazel followed as Leah browsed through the shop, admiring the flower variety. Primrose walked to the back of the store and into the greenhouse.

"Here they are. Are you getting them as a gift or for yourself?" Primrose asked.

"I plan on adding it to my garden. I restored my family's old greenhouse a couple of weeks ago and I'm slowly adding more flowers to it," said Hazel.

"Oh, that's sounds fun! I find that tending to the garden is really calming. I'm sure you feel that way as well since you're also a fairy. What's your name?" asked Primrose.

"Hazel Plumeria. And that's my sister, Leah," Hazel said as she nodded in Leah's direction. "Plumeria! Wow, I've read about your family's history at the library. You must be a descendant of Gregoro Plumeria. I really admire his work. I didn't realize there were any Plumeria's left in Hallowed Falls." said Primrose.

"Yes, Gregoro was our great-great-great grandfather. My sister and I just moved here about a month ago from Luna Valley. It's comforting to see another fairy here, actually," said Hazel with a smile.

"I haven't seen that many around here either and only met a couple of others as well. My parents and I moved back here from Charmsville about a year ago to be closer to some relatives. Well, it was a pleasure to meet you. Let me know if I can help you find anything else!" said Primrose cheerfully.

"Thanks!" Hazel replied.

When Leah and Hazel got home, Lucinda was on her laptop in the dining hall.

"Did you notice the wings on the flower shop owner? She's like the second fairy I've met since we moved here. The other one that I've met works for her," said Hazel as she took a seat across from Lucinda.

"There are a few that work at the hospital, but they pretty much keep to themselves," said Leah.

"I don't blame them after what happened a few months back," said Lucinda as she kept her gaze at the laptop.

"What do you mean?" Asked Leah, curiosity peaked.

"A few months ago, two of our A.E. agents from the Department of Assets were conducting research at the Bloodstone Cemetery. Red diamonds have been detected there by our radars. While they were digging for the rare gemstone, they heard a scream coming from a nearby cave. They investigated and when they found the source, they discovered a young female fairy laying lifeless on the dirt. She had been murdered... her blood had been drained," Lucinda explained in a matter-of-fact tone.

"That's horrible...do you think that the Alexanders had something to do with this?" asked Leah with concern.

"Given the history of Hallowed Falls and the two devasting events that happened, most people did raise suspicions against them. So, the Hallowed Falls PD and the A.E. opened an investigation. It is still ongoing, but they haven't found proof that the Alexanders were involved. Especially, since Heidi's parents have been so cooperative and working with the detectives. It's also due to the fact that there are also other vamp families that live in town. Everyone's a suspect at this point," said Lucinda.

"Hazel, you should probably be a bit more cautious when you go into town. We don't know if they killer is still around." said Leah.

Hazel nodded.

"I'm going to wash up before dinner." said Hazel as she walked out of the dining hall.

Hazel woke up the next day with Sage snuggled up next to her. She got dressed and went downstairs for breakfast. As she walked through the foyer, she smelled the sweet scent of waffles coming from the dining hall.

"Morning, sunshine!" Leah greeted Hazel as she walked in.

"You're...more energetic than usual. What's gotten into you? Asked Hazel suspiciously.

"The sun energizes me. I just love it when the weather is like this. Warm, bright, and sunny. Not a cloud in the sky!" Said Leah with a big smile.

"Okay...who are you and what have you done with my cousin?" Lucinda said as she walked into the dining hall with a plate of bacon and a plate of waffles.

"I *love* you, you know that?" Hazel stated.

"Yea...yea...you just love me because I cook for you" said Lucinda rolling her eyes.

Hazel smiled and winked at her. Just then, Lucinda's phone rang.

"This is Lucinda. Oh hi, good morning...wait what?" Her expression went from relaxed to concerned. "Okay, thank you for notifying me," said Lucinda as she hung up.

"Is everything okay?" Leah asked with furrowed brows.

"No...they just found another body...at the Bloodstone Cemetery. They identified her as Serena Bennett. Duke called to let me know since we live in the area," said Lucinda with a worried look on her face.

Leah gasped and raised both her hands to her mouth. Tears started to form in her eyes.

"I know her...Serena Bennett is a nurse at the hospital. She's a fairy," she said shakily.

"Oh my God! It must be starting again!" Hazel gasped. Her eyes widened with shock and horror.

"We don't know anything yet." Lucinda put her hand up slightly to calm them down. "Just...be careful if you guys are going into town the next few days. Stay home unless you absolutely need to go out. I'll let Oliver and Amber know to stay close to the manor, I'll be right back." Lucinda headed to the east building to look for Amber and Oliver.

They nodded and looked at each other.

"I'm sorry about your friend, Leah. Are you okay?" Asked Hazel, hoping to comfort her distraught sister.

"Yea...it's just that...I spoke to her last night, right before we left the hospital. I-I just can't believe it," said Leah, still in shock over this news.

Hazel gave her sister a reassuring hug.

"I'm just glad you're off today. We can keep each other safe," said Hazel as she rested her cheek against Leah's.

Just then, their front doorbell rang and Hazel got up to get the door. She was surprised to find Victor standing there in his police uniform.

"Hey, I just stopped by to make sure you're okay. I heard that they found a body early this morning," he said. She could tell he had been worrying about her by the look on his face.

She nodded and gave him a half-smile. "Yea…we're okay. Come on in."

Their footsteps echoed in the foyer as they walked into the dining hall.

"Hi Vick," Leah greeted him and quickly wiped her cheeks with both hands.

"Hey Leah, what's wrong? Were you just crying?" Asked Victor, concerned.

"The body of the fairy they found was a friend of Leah's from work," Hazel explained.

"I'm sorry to hear that. Serena Bennett, right? I heard about it this morning. When was the last time you saw her?" Victor asked shifting in to investigation mode.

"Last night, right before my shift ended. She mentioned that she was going to pick up dinner from Blue Wolf's Tavern after work," said Leah, composing herself enough to be sure she was giving accurate information.

"That information may be helpful to the investigation. I'll head back to the station and let the detectives know." He assured them and glanced at Leah. "We'll get down to the bottom of this, Leah. I'm sorry again about your friend. I'll see you later, Hazel. Call me if you guys need anything." He quickly gave Hazel a kiss on the cheek and left.

Later that night, when Lucinda went downstairs to get a glass of water, she noticed that the light in the study was on.

"Hey, you're up later than usual," said Lucinda as she leaned against the door frame with her arms crossed.

Hazel was sitting on the blue velvet Georgian sofa, reading a book next to the grand fireplace.

"I couldn't fall asleep so I started reading one of the books that Leah checked out from the library. It's one of the books from the Alexander archives. I didn't know they owned the property that the Bloodstone Cemetery sits on. Even their family's main mausoleum is located there," said Hazel.

"Yea, they actually run the cemetery and funeral home next to it. Amongst a couple of other business investments they have in town," said Lucinda.

"Have you heard anything else about the investigation?" Asked Hazel.

Lucinda sat down next to Hazel. The heat from the fireplace warmed her skin and it felt nice.

"We were told that Serena was last seen at Blue Wolf's Tavern. Our agents are in the process of reviewing the surveillance footage that they gave us," said Lucinda, tiredly.

"That's what Leah told Victor earlier. Serena had mentioned it to Leah before leaving work yesterday," said Hazel.

"Correct, I won't know anything else until they get through the footage. I'm going to get a glass of water and going back to bed. Goodnight." said Lucinda.

"Night," said Hazel.

The investigation of Serena's murder had bene ongoing for the past few days, with no major leads. Other than, she was last seen at the Blue Wolf's Tavern, before the subsequent findings of her body at the cemetery.

"How did she end up there?" Lucinda thought to herself.

Lucinda hadn't been assigned to this particular case but she needed to know, so she returned to the Bloodstone Cemetery, to look for clues that could have been missed in the initial investigation. According to the surveillance footage that the restaurant handed over, Serena walked into the tavern and headed straight to the bar area to order take out. Then, she walked towards the restrooms in the back. It appeared that she had spoken to several people on the way to the restroom, most likely just saying hello. There was one person in particular though, who walked into the restroom right after her. Due to the lack of clarity of the footage, it was hard to see what the person looked like. All they could identify was that the potential suspect was wearing all black. Then, it showed her coming back out and paying for her take out. Apparently, she had walked out alone and the figure in black never came out of the bathroom.

"Whoever it was, probably escaped through the bathroom window and waited for her to leave the tavern." she thought to herself.

She arrived at the Bloodstone Cemetery just as the sun was setting. She gazed out towards Rose Gold Beach. It was just a quarter mile down the road from the cemetery. The water seemed calm and she could see the pink sands glimmering on the beach. She turned back to face the gates of the cemetery and walked through. As she continued further into the cemetery, a large mausoleum ahead of her came into view. It sat on a small hilltop with stone steps that led up to it. There were many mausoleums on the property, but she wanted to investigate this one in particular. Mainly because she knew it was the Alexander family mausoleum.

"Can I *help* you?" A gruff, slightly annoyed voice came from behind Lucinda.

She turned around and saw an elderly man standing there.

"Uh, no. Just visiting," said Lucinda.

"You a family member?" Asked the man.

As she opened her mouth to answer him, she saw a silhouette run from one tree to another in the back of the cemetery. She took a step forward to go after it, but the elderly man stepped in front of her.

"Ma'am! Visiting hours end at dusk. You need to leave, *now*," he warned her.

Lucinda narrowed her eyes at him for a second, then turned around and left, feeling annoyed.

When Lucinda got back to the manor, she gave a heavy sigh as she walked into the dining hall. Hazel looked up at her.

"Hey, Luce. Did you just get back from work? I thought you were off today?" She asked.

"Uh, no. I was off…I just came back from the cemetery. I wanted to see if I could find anything else that would help the investigation," said Lucinda.

"You went by yourself? What are you, crazy?" Hazel asked with a raised eyebrow.

"I go on investigations alone all the time for work. I'm well practiced in my defensive spells. Don't worry." said Lucinda as she walked towards the kitchen and patted the top of Hazel's head.

"Hey, what's for dinner?" Asked Leah as she walked in.

"Lucinda went to the cemetery today…by herself!" Hazel exclaimed and threw a hand in the air.

Lucinda comes back out with a couple of plates.

"Thanks, tattletale. I went to do some investigating," said Lucinda.

"Well, were you able to find anything?" Asked Leah.

"No, I was shooed away at closing," said Lucinda, disappointedly.

"What about the surveillance footage, did you hear anything about that?" Asked Hazel.

"Yes, Serena had spoken to several people at the tavern, but she left alone and it didn't seem like she was followed. She had gone to the restroom before leaving, though. Someone went in after her, but the footage wasn't clear enough to identify who it was," said Lucinda as she gave each of them a plate. She sat down and was about to take a bite of her mashed potatoes but then paused.

"What's wrong?" asked Leah with knitted brows.

"I just remembered…when the cemetery worker was asking me to leave, I noticed a silhouette of someone running across the back of the cemetery. It was almost as if the person was watching me and ran when I looked over," said Lucinda thoughtfully.

"Maybe I should come with you next time. I've gotten a lot stronger with the defensive spells, since the last time you trained me," Leah suggested.

"Yea…I'll consider it next time," said Lucinda with a nod.

The next day, Hazel was in the garden tending to the plants when she noticed that her sunset lilies hadn't bloomed. She tried the Blossom charm again, but it had no effect.

"Perhaps, I should go see Primrose at the flower shop. Maybe there's something I'm doing wrong." Hazel thought to herself and frowned.

She cleaned herself up and got ready to head into town. When she arrived at the flower shop, Primrose was tending to the peonies in the greenhouse.

"Hello," said Hazel.

"Oh!" said Primrose with her hand over her chest.

"I'm sorry, I didn't mean to spook you." said Hazel apologetically. "I didn't see anyone up front so I figured I would check the greenhouse."

She took a second to glance around. A broad-tailed hummingbird perched on a branch of a small tree and in the corner, a small waterfall fountain burbled quietly. The sound of the water made her feel relaxed.

"This is a beautiful greenhouse, I didn't really get a chance to admire it last time. It's so…tranquil. And you have hummingbirds?" Hazel remarked.

"Oh, ha! They kind of pop in occasionally when I have the windows open. I like to think that they are checking in on me," said Primrose with a grin as she continued to water some more plants.

"What can I help you with today?" She asked.

"Remember the sunset lilies I purchased from you? It's been a while and they haven't grown at all. They also didn't react to my Blossom charm," said Hazel.

"That's because the plants I sell here don't react to magic. The secret is in the way I cultivate the seeds. It makes them the purest ingredient for potions and elixirs. The technique has been passed down to us from my ancestors. What you need to do, is to continue to give them affection….and talk to them. They react to all of that, in addition to the normal care of course," said Primrose with a smile.

"If you say that works, then I'll keep trying," Hazel shrugged. "Thanks, Primrose!"

"See you soon!" yelled Primrose as Hazel headed towards the front of the store.

Hazel passed the checkout counter and was about to approach the door to leave when suddenly, the lights shut off and she stood there in the dimly lit store. The only illumination was the sunlight coming in from the window.

"*Must be a power outage in the area,*" Hazel thought to herself as she looked up at the ceiling.

Out of nowhere she felt someone grab her from behind. She tried to scream but whoever it was, had their hand over her mouth and an arm across her chest to keep her from leaving. She could tell it was a man due to his height and strength. He dragged her back further into the store and for a second, she was paralyzed with fear, but she wasn't going to let her attacker win. She began to wiggle her body aggressively in hopes that it would loosen his grip while trying to catch a glimpse of his face at the same time but he held onto her so tight, she couldn't turn her head. He removed his hand from her face for a second and she started to scream.

"Primrose!" she yelled at the top of her lungs.

Suddenly, she felt something hit her hard on the head and before she knew it, she dropped onto the hard tiled floor and blacked out. Just then, Primrose ran into the room and gasped when she noticed a dark figure dressed in all black standing over Hazel's body. Her eyes widened with fear as she tried to see who it was, but due to the big hood over his head and lack of lighting other than the natural light behind him, she couldn't make out the features of his face.

He bent down and began to lift Hazel off the floor. Primrose was instantly struck with panic but she knew she needed to act fast. She grabbed a fire extinguisher and began spraying the contents of it at the attacker. He fell backwards and caught himself with both hands, then quickly scrambled to his feet and ran out the front door.

Primrose dropped the fire extinguisher and it landed with a loud sound of metal hitting the tile floor. She kneeled down beside Hazel and made sure she was still breathing, then dialed 911. As she waited for the ambulance, Primrose casted the Mend aura onto Hazel and was able to close up the cut on the side of her head but a huge bump remained on it.

An hour later, Primrose was in the waiting area talking to Leah when Lucinda jogged over to them.

"Hey! I rushed over here as fast as I could. How's Hazel?" Lucinda asked, trying to catch her breath.

"Hey, I spoke to her doctor earlier and she would have to stay overnight so that they can monitor her due to the blunt force trauma. I'll take you guys to her," Leah replied and began walking towards a hallway. "Luce, this is Primrose. She was the one who brought Hazel in."

"Nice to meet you, Primrose and thank you." said Lucinda gratefully.

Leah brought them to the room Hazel was in.

"I'll be right back," said Leah as she walked towards the nurse's station.

Lucinda knocked on the door and walked in. Hazel was sitting up on the bed and a man in a dark blue suit stood next to her with a notepad in hand.

"Well, I think that's all I need for now. I'll reach out to you if I have anymore questions. I'll leave you to rest, Miss Plumeria. Good day," he said with a nod.

"Thank you, detective," said Hazel politely.

He gave the girls polite nod and walked out the door.

"Hey, how are you feeling? What happened?" Lucinda asked.

"I'm okay for now. I was at the flower shop and was about to leave when I was attacked," Hazel explained, her eyebrows scrunched together and she tried to remember what happened.

"Did you see what your attacker looked like?" Asked Lucinda.

"I tried but I couldn't turn my head enough to see." Hazel rubbed her forehead as she began feeling frustrated with herself.

"Hey, I'm sorry. Is there anything you'd like me to do?" Lucinda asked with concern.

"No, but I'll let you know if anything comes up," Hazel responded with a smile.

Just then, there was a knock on the door and Leah walked in with another doctor. He seemed to be about Leah's age, with black hair and friendly hazel eyes.

"Hey, guys. This is Dr. Tyler Charmont. He was the one who examined Hazel earlier," said Leah.

"Hey, Primrose," said Tyler.

"Hey," Primrose responded.

"You guys know each other?" asked Leah.

"Yes actually, we're cousins." said Tyler.

"Oh, that's why you look so familiar. You were at our barbecue, weren't you?" asked Lucinda.

"Yes, I really enjoyed the food by the way. Especially the chicken pasta salad, it was out of this world," said Tyler with a smile.

"I made that myself. Secret ingredient," said Lucinda with a smile.

"Maybe you can share that recipe with me some day," Tyler continued to smile.

Lucinda felt herself blush a bit. Hazel grinned and stared at the two of them.

"But if you and Primrose are cousins, why don't you have fairy wings?" asked Hazel.

"My mother is a fairy and my father is a witch. When a fairy and a witch reproduce, there is a fifty percent chance of the embryo being one or the other," Tyler explained.

"Oh," said Hazel with a nod and winced at the pain caused by her quick movement.

"Hey…you've got to be gentle with your movements and get lots of rest. I've gotta run, but I'll come by before I leave for the night. Love ya'!" said Leah and gave her sister a pat on hand.

"Leah's right, you need to rest as much as you can," Tyler said firmly. "It was a nice seeing you again, Lucinda. Primrose, I'll talk to you soon." He said before walking out the door.

"I should go, too. I've got a lot of cleaning up to do. I hope you feel better soon," said Primrose.

"Thanks again, Primrose," said Hazel and waved her goodbye.

Primrose gave her a friendly smile and closed the door behind her.

"I saw that," asked Hazel with a smile.

"You saw what?" Asked Lucinda, crossing her arms and holding back a smile.

"The spark I saw between you and the doc," Hazel responded slyly.

"What spark? There's no *spark*. I mean, he's not unattractive…I guess. I'm sure he's got a girlfriend or a wife or something…" said Lucinda, rolling her eyes.

"I looked and he didn't have a ring on. Maybe we can ask Leah to invite him over again soon," Hazel smirked.

"How about you just focus on healing? I've got to get back to work. Take care, sweetie." said Lucinda blowing her a kiss as she walked out the door.

As soon as Lucinda left, Victor walked in and rushed over to her.

"Hey, are you okay? What happened?" asked Victor, concerned.

"Hey, I'm okay," said Hazel fixing the part of her hair that wasn't covered by the gauze. "I was attacked at the flower shop, but my friend Primrose was able to stop the attacker before he was able to do anything else. I also filed a report and they are investigating it."

"When I find out who did this, I'm going to kill them," said Victor angrily.

"I hope they do find out who it is. I don't know why they would've done this when I barely know anyone around here," said Hazel.

"Maybe I can get more information from the detectives. I'm just relieved that you're okay," said Victor with a calmer voice.

"Thanks for coming to check on me," Hazel smiled.

"Of course," said Victor as he leaned towards her and gave her a kiss on her forehead.

Victor stayed with Hazel until visiting hours were over.

Lucinda decided to visit the flower shop the following day. As she pulled up to the store front, she noticed a man speaking to Primrose inside. She recognized him as the detective who questioned Hazel at the hospital. She got out of her car and went in. Primrose waved to her once she was inside. Primrose finished speaking to the detective and approached Lucinda when he left.

"Lucinda, what brings you here?" Asked Primrose as she walked towards her.

"Hi, Primrose. Hazel asked me to check in on you to make sure you're okay. Maybe I can help clean up a bit?" asked Lucinda as she grabbed the broom leaning on the wall next to her.

"Thanks, I appreciate it" said Primrose as she grabbed a rag off the counter.

"So, did the detective find out anything else?" Asked Lucinda.

"No, they weren't able to find anything left behind by the attacker," said Primrose disappointedly.

"Oh..." Lucinda replied. "Do you have cameras in your store?"

"I don't have cameras in here but the craft store across the street had a security camera facing the street and my shop. They were able to see someone enter the store but because of the distance, the footage wasn't helpful in identifying the suspect," said Primrose.

"Can you think of anyone who would harm you or your store?" asked Lucinda shifting into investigation mode.

"I don't know. I can't think of anyone who would do this," Primrose responded with a frown.

Lucinda continued to help Primrose clean up the shop. When she was done, she returned to the manor.

A couple of days had gone by since the attack at the flower shop. Leah went to visit Hazel during her lunch break.

"Hey, how are you feeling today? What did Dr. Charmont say?" Asked Leah as she sat on the bed next to Hazel.

"He said I can be discharged today. Lucinda will be picking me up in a bit," said Hazel.

"Oh, okay. I just wanted to make sure you're alright before I get back to work. I'll see you tonight then, rest up," said Leah as she closed the door behind her.

Lucinda was running a little late to pick Hazel up from the hospital. She was out of breath by the time she reached Hazel's room.

"Hey! I'm sorry. I got caught up with something at work. You about ready?" Asked Lucinda.

"Yea, I just need to get changed," said Hazel.

"Alright, I'm going to use the restroom. I'll be right back," said Lucinda as she closed the door behind her.

Once Lucinda got back into the room, she noticed a nurse changing the bed sheets. Hazel wasn't in the room and her handbag was still on the chair.

"Excuse me, did you see where the patient went?" Lucinda asked.

"She was escorted out of the room in wheelchair just a few minutes ago. It looked like they were leaving," said the nurse.

"What? Did you see what the person looked like?" Asked Lucinda.

"No, all I saw was someone dressed in all black with a hood on," the nurse replied.

"Oh…thanks." said Lucinda with a frown.

She grabbed Hazel's bag and ran out of the room. Lucinda noticed Leah walking the opposite way down the hall.

"Leah!" Lucinda shouted down the hall.

Leah turned around and saw Lucinda running towards her.

"I think someone took Hazel. I stepped out to use the restroom and when I got back, she was gone. One of the nurses said she saw someone with her. It looked like they were leaving," said Lucinda.

"Let's split up. They couldn't have gotten far and I'll call Victor to make sure it wasn't him," said Leah, attempting to stay calm.

A couple of hours passed, but they still weren't able to find Hazel. Victor, Lucinda, and Leah were all sitting in the study back at the manor.

"Hazel doesn't really know anyone in town aside from Olivia and Primrose. Olivia is out of town and Primrose was confirmed to be at the flower shop. Who would have taken her?" Asked Lucinda with worry.

"I'm worried that if we don't find her soon, she might get seriously injured." said Leah as she paced the room.

"What if we tried to cast the Locator Spell for lost items? I know it usually works on objects only, but it's better than not trying anything at all," Lucinda suggested.

"We can give it a shot," said Leah sounding hopeful.

Lucinda looked into Hazel's bag and found a hairbrush. She held it tightly and closed her eyes.

"*Powers help me find, what my eyes cannot seek, before I am out of time, help me find what is lost,*" Lucinda chanted.

A white glow surrounded Lucinda's entire body and flashed for a second. She gasped and her eyes popped open.

"What? What is it?" asked Victor.

"I saw a glimpse of a location. But it was just for a split second. I saw...the gates of Bloodstone Cemetery," said Lucinda, her eyebrows mashed together.

"Then that's where we need to go. I'll drive," said Victor as he took his car keys out of his pocket and headed towards the door.

"Wait, I remember something my mother taught us when we were younger. There was an incident when Hazel and I were kids. Our babysitter took us to the mall. Somehow, I got distracted and strayed away from them. I was eventually found but when we got home that night, our mother taught us the Seekers aura. It's an aura that only fairies can use to find another fairy they've already met. You see, fairies leave pollen residue wherever they go. It comes from their wings and is only visible to another fairy. When fairies meet at a close distance, they get introduced to that fairy's unique pollen. When they turn on the Seekers aura, they can track that fairy within twelve hours." said Leah.

"Okay...so what are you suggesting?" Asked Victor.

"What if we got Primrose to help track Hazel?" Leah suggested.

"Oh my God, why didn't I think of that?! Let's go!" shouted Lucinda.

"I doubt the flower shop is open at this time. Let me call Tyler to see if he can give us her address," said Leah as she took out her phone and dialed Tyler's number.

"Hi Tyler, I'm sorry to bother you but is there any way that you can give us Primrose's address? We need her to use the Seekers aura to find Hazel," said Leah.

"Yes, why don't I go pick her up. I'm just leaving the hospital now. Where should I meet you guys?" asked Tyler over the phone.

"Bloodstone Cemetery. Thanks, Tyler," said Leah.

Leah hung up and the three of them ran out the door. It was after dark when they arrived at the cemetery. Tyler and Primrose had not arrived yet.

"'The cemetery is already closed. The front gate is locked," said Leah as she shook the gate.

Just then Tyler's car pulled up behind Victor's. Primrose and Tyler got out of the car.

"Hi Primrose, thanks for coming to help," said Leah.

"Don't thank me yet. I'm not sure how strong my Seekers aura is since I haven't really been around Hazel that long," said Primrose as she walked up to the cemetery's gates.

Lucinda kept watch of their surroundings to make sure no one was around. They watched as Primrose jumped about two feet up and off the ground. Her wings fluttered, causing a strong gust of wind around them. A bright golden glow surrounded her whole body for a few seconds. Then, she slowly floated back down onto the ground and opened her eyes.

She saw a glowing substance that almost looked like sparkling dust on the grass.

"I see it! It's leading towards the back of the property. But how do we get in?" Asked Primrose.

"Here, step back," said Tyler as he moved closer to the gate.

Tyler took his stylus out and pointed it at the lock. A light blue mist floated towards the gate and when they heard a click, the gate opened slightly. Primrose pushed the gate open wider and everyone else followed behind her. The grass crunched beneath her feet as they walked and a low lying fog hovered over the ground. The pollen led them to an incredibly old mausoleum, hidden in the back of the cemetery.

"This is where I saw the dark figure the last time I was here," said Lucinda.

"The pollen goes into that old mausoleum over there," said Primrose, pointing.

"It looks ancient and decrepit. I wonder who it belongs to?" Asked Leah.

As they got closer, they were able to see the name on the top of the mausoleum door.

"Alexander? I thought their family mausoleum was near the entrance?" asked Lucinda.

"This must be the *original* Alexander mausoleum. I'll go in first." said Victor.

Victor put his hands in front of his body and conjured a glowball. He gently tossed it up and it floated over his head. As he began to walk, it stayed just above his right shoulder. They walked in and saw an enormous sarcophagus in the middle of the room.

"What the…" said Primrose with a confused look on her face.

"What's wrong?" asked Lucinda.

"The pollen…it's going *into* the stone coffin." said Primrose.

"How can we get it open?" asked Leah.

They all tried to push the lid off but it wouldn't budge. Victor examined the sarcophagus. He looked all around it looking for any possible opening. While running his hands along the edge, he felt a piece of stone that stuck out. It looked like some kind of button so he pushed it. Immediately, he heard a click and the lid of the sarcophagus started to move.

"Look! This side is lowering….it looks like…a staircase leading down somewhere!" Leah exclaimed, bending down slightly to examine the staircase.

Victor began to walk down the stairs and the rest followed. It was a dark tunnel, but they could see a dim light visible towards the end. They discovered a room to the left of the tunnel where the light originated, and as they drew closer, they realized they could hear voices.

"Good job, I didn't think you'd actually get one," a man's voice said.

Victor waved his hand at the glowing orb and it dissipated.

"I can't say that I'm not disappointed in your lack of confidence in me," the female voice responded.

"That woman's voice sounds familiar," Leah whispered.

They stayed against the cold stone wall and crept closer to the entrance of the room. Victor peeked his head in aorund the door. He spotted Hazel, tied to a chair and unconscious. A tall figure in a hooded jacket stood on one side of the chair and a blonde-haired woman in a white lab coat on the other. The woman turned around enough for Victor to identify her. Heidi Hendrix. Victor hid behind the wall again.

"It's Heidi. She's the one that kidnapped Hazel. There's also someone else in there with them but I can't see who it is," whispered Victor.

"Dr. Heidi Hendrix? But why…?" Leah whispered, upset and confused at the same time.

"I don't know but we're going to find out. You guys stay here. I'll go get Hazel," said Victor.

"I'll go with you," said Tyler as he took his stylus out.

"I'll text Duke and let him know what's going on," said Lucinda.

Victor waited until Heidi and the other person disappeared through a door on the opposite side of the room from where they were. He slowly inched towards the chair where Hazel was tied up and took out a small knife. As he started cutting the rope around her wrists, Hazel began to stir.

"Victor?" she mumbled.

"Shh, you'll be okay. We're going to get you out of here." he whispered.

"I hear footsteps. Hurry!" Whispered Tyler urgently.

He was cutting the last piece of rope on her right ankle just as Heidi came back into the room.

"Tyler?! How the hell did you get down here?! Marco!" Heidi shouted.

Victor was able to cut through the last of the rope. Within a split second, a man about six feet tall with dark blonde hair appeared next to him. He grabbed Victor and his bright blue eyes bore into Victor's before sinking his fangs into his neck. Victor grunted as he slammed against the hard surface and dropped to the ground.

Tyler picked Hazel up with both of his arms and ran towards the door. Lucinda put her arms on her side with her palms parallel to the ground.

Bright fiery orbs started to manifest in each of her hands, then threw the fireballs at Marco and Heidi while Leah ran over to Victor. Leah threw Victor's arm over her shoulders and they started to run up the dark tunnel. Lucinda continued to launch fireballs at their assailants. Just then, Marco used his right arm to block a fireball but his sleeve caught on fire and he fell to the ground attempting to extinguish it. He yelled in panic and Heidi ran over to him to quickly put it out.

"We can't let them get away. We need her to get the blood of the Summerland heir!" Marco yelled to Heidi. Heidi got up immediately and ran after them.

Lucinda and Leah helped Victor out of the mausoleum, while Tyler and Primrose helped Hazel. They ran as fast as they could towards the front gates of the cemetery and back to their cars. Lucinda grabbed Victor's keys out of his pocket and helped him into the backseat. Then, she got behind the wheel and Leah jumped in next to her. They drove up the street towards the beach and made a U-turn, passing Tyler's car.

Tyler jumped into the driver's seat while Primrose sat in the back with Hazel.

"Go, go, go!" Primrose shouted at Tyler.

Primrose reached into her bag and took out a small vial containing some kind of light blue liquid.

"Here, drink this. It might help you." said Primrose as she brought the bottle to Hazel's lips.

Hazel drank the concoction and made a face.

"What is it?" she asked groggily.

"I call it the Blue Butterfly elixir. It's made with begonias and blue peas. If a sedative had been used on you, this would counteract the effects," said Primrose calmly.

"Thanks, Primrose." said Hazel as she closed her eyes again.

By the time Heidi reached the front gates, in pursuit, the other cars were already down the road and out of sight. She decided to run back into the mausoleum and check on Marco.

"I can't believe that Marco Alexander is back and with Heidi as his accomplice! We need to call the police," said Leah as she grabbed her phone out of her bag.

"Right now, we just need to get to a safe place. We don't know if they are going to follow us. With Marco injured, I doubt they will. But we can't take any risks. I'm bringing you guys to headquarters. Leah, call Tyler and make sure he follows us there," Lucinda instructed her.

Leah nodded and did as she was told.

They drove for about forty minutes, passing farms and groves before slowing down as they passed through another town. Leah noticed a few small boutiques, cafés, and restaurants.

"What a cute town…where are we exactly?" Asked Leah.

"We're in Crystal Brooks, about twenty-five miles north of Hallowed Falls," said Lucinda.

They passed over a bridge and through a heavily wooded area before finally reaching the Aster Elites headquarters. The A.E. headquarters was an enormous estate. There was a thirty-foot wall with spikes at the top, surrounding the property. As they approached a set of giant iron gates, Lucinda lowered her window and scanned her ID card under the keypad. The iron gates move inwards. They drove past two dark gray stone buildings, one on their left and the other on their right. Leah could see a set of giant iron doors straight ahead. It was the entrance to the main building. Five agents stood in front of the doors. When they were close enough, Leah was able to recognize the man standing in the middle. It was Duke. The sight of him gave her a sense of relief. She knew that they would be safe, at least for now.

As soon as they parked the cars, four of the agents rushed over to help Hazel and Victor out of the car.

"Bring them to the infirmary." Duke instructed them. They carried the two of them towards the infirmary building.

"Let's get inside. Follow me this way," Duke said to them.

He quickly gave Leah a once over, then he turned on his heel and walked into the main building. Leah felt the heat rushing up to her face from her neck. They followed Duke through the doors and up a grand staircase. Once they were at the top of the stairs, they followed him into a hallway with elevators. He pressed the button at the first elevator to his left and the door opened. There were ten floors and he pressed the button for the fifth floor. When they got off the elevator, he brought them to a large room that seemed to be in the shape of a hexagon. The wallpaper was a solid maroon color and gold moldings lined the edges of the ceiling. There were five doors throughout the common room.

"Behind each of these doors is a mini suite with private bathrooms. You guys may stay here for as long as you need. I'll have the dining hall staff bring up some meals for you. Lucinda, come with me." said Duke and they both left the room.

"Are you guys okay?" Asked Tyler.

"Yea I'm okay," said Primrose. She walked over to the fireplace and sat down on a chair in front of it.

"I'm okay. Thank you for saving my sister," said Leah to Tyler as she sat down in the chair next to Primrose and stared into it. The fire flared and grew bigger.

"Leah, are you sure you're okay?" Asked Primrose.

She looked at the fire and then back at Leah. Leah snapped out of it and realized what she was doing.

"I-I'm sorry. I was just remembering the last thing Marco said as we were running out of the tunnel. He said…they needed the blood of the Summerland heir. He must have thought Hazel knew how to find the heir. That's why they kidnapped her," said Leah with concern.

Tyler and Primrose looked at each other. He crossed his arms in front of him and leaned against the wall.

"Why would he need the *blood* of the Summerland heir?" He asked.

"I don't know…maybe he's making some kind of elixir with it. But I can't think of a single spell or potion that requires a specific fairy's blood," said Leah as she racked her brain.

Primrose's mouth opened slightly, a terrified look crossing her face and Leah caught it.

"What's wrong Primrose?" Asked Leah.

"I know what he's trying to do. I-I think he might be trying to break into the center of the Hallowed Falls arboretum," said Primrose.

"What? Wait, do you actually think...he's trying to gain access to the powers that Honora was *believed* to have hidden there? But that's just rumors. There's been no evidence of it...right?" Leah asked suspiciously.

Just then, Duke and Lucinda came back into the room.

"No evidence of what?" Asked Duke.

"Um...when we were trying to escape from the mausoleum, I overheard Marco say that they needed Hazel to get the blood of the Summerland heir and Primrose believes that he is trying to access the center of the town's arboretum. But the legend about Honora storing her powers there can't be true...can it? I mean there's been nothing in the archives," said Leah.

"No one's heard from the Summerlands ever since Lavender left Hallowed Falls. What led you to believe that is what he's after?" Asked Lucinda.

Tyler glanced at Primrose and she just shook her head.

"We'll assign a couple of agents to partner with the Hallowed Falls PD on this investigation. You guys have been through a rough night. Your meals will be up soon and then you guys should probably get some rest. We'll have to keep you here until further notice. It's for your own safety. We will have someone reach out to the hospital on behalf of Dr. Charmont and Dr. Plumeria. I'll see you guys in the morning, goodnight everyone," said Duke as he turned and left.

"Luce, did you find out anything about Victor and Hazel? Are they okay?" Asked Leah.

"Hazel is fine. They found a strong sedative in her system. She was somewhat conscious when they got her onto a bed, and she mentioned that Primrose gave her a potion to counter the effects before passing out again. She should be fine by tomorrow. They are monitoring her throughout the night. But Victor…he isn't doing well. The vamp poison is slowly spreading through his body. The A.E. haven't had much research on how to handle vamp poison. The agency hasn't been able to work with vampires ever since the Alexander killings started. Pretty much any vamp families that lived in the Falls at the time left because they didn't want to be associated with the Alexanders," said Lucinda.

"Is…is Victor going to die? Is there anything I can do? I mean, I am a hematologist after all. Maybe I can use the A.E. laboratory and do some testing?" Asked Leah.

"I'll suggest it to Duke in the morning. So far, they have been able to slow down the spread of the poison. But Duke is right, we've all had a rough night. Let's just get some rest." said Lucinda. Everyone nodded and went into their own suites.

Chapter 4

T he next morning, everyone had gone down to the dining hall for breakfast.

"Hey, how'd you sleep?" Lucinda asked Leah.

"I didn't. I couldn't help but worry all night," said Leah tiredly as she took a sip of coffee.

"I'm going to see Duke in a bit and suggest getting approval for your access to the medical lab. We can go together if you want," Lucinda said with a smile.

Leah rolled her eyes but agreed to go with her. They finished their breakfast and headed towards Duke's office. Leah followed Lucinda out of the manor and towards the North building located just past the front gates. When they got there, Lucinda knocked on Duke's office door.

"Hi Duke, you got a minute?" Asked Lucinda.

"Sure, what's going on?" Asked Duke as he leaned back on his chair.

"I wanted to see if we'd be able to get an approval for Leah to have access to our medical facilities. She might be able to help with the vamp poison," Lucinda mentioned.

Duke looked at Leah and tapped his pen on the desk.

"I'll check with the Senior Director of Medical Services. I'm sure it wouldn't be a problem." said Duke.

"Well...okay then, I'm going to do some research. Why don't you... stay and chat with Duke for a bit?" Said Lucinda as she quickly rushed out the door.

"Wait...what? Lucinda!" Leah exclaimed. But Lucinda ignored her, disappearing down the hall.

She turned back around awkwardly to face Duke.

"Uh...I'll be in the common room if you need me," said Leah as she turned to walk out.

"Wait," said Duke as he scratched his head thoughtfully.

"Would you want to grab a coffee or something? I actually haven't had breakfast yet," asked Duke.

"Sure," she replied with a smile.

Duke stood up from behind his desk and walked over to Leah. He seemed much taller than she remembered. He had on a dark gray V-neck t-shirt and black cargo pants. Leah couldn't help but notice how well he filled in that shirt, the short sleeves wrapped tightly around his muscular biceps and she could practically see his defined abdomen underneath the thin fabric.

They got onto the elevator and walked into the manor. Behind the grand staircase was a small café. She hadn't noticed it when they first got there. Duke got two cups of coffee and they walked towards a set of large sliding glass doors to the right of the lobby that led to a large garden.

"I imagined the A.E. headquarters differently. Luce didn't tell me it was this beautiful," said Leah as they walked through the garden, sipping their coffee.

"This land belonged to the Summerlands. They used to live in the main building up until the death of Honora. The estate was donated to the agency, as part of her will. The North and South buildings you guys drove past when you first arrived here, were built shortly after the agency inherited the property. The original members of the Aster Elites used to hold their meetings in the great hall back then. It's located on the third floor but we just call it the Conference Hall now. It has since been renovated to fit multiple meeting rooms," said Duke.

"Wow, there must be so much history within the walls of this place," Leah said with fascination.

Then, her expression faded into a look of concern and Duke noticed it.

"What's wrong?" He asked.

"What if Marco or Heidi finds out we're here?" Asked Leah with worry.

"They won't. Even if they do, our property lines have been enchanted with the Bulwark spell, it's a protective spell. Anyone who intends on doing harm to anyone inside will not be able to penetrate the force field. There are extremely experienced witches within the Aster Elites who work hard every day to make sure of that. Lucinda, being one of them," said Duke.

They stopped at a bench in the garden and sat down. Leah closed her eyes and listened to the water coming from the fountain at the center of the garden. Then, she took in a deep breath and opened her eyes again.

"This is my fault. She wouldn't have gotten hurt if I hadn't convinced her to move to Hallowed Falls," said Leah, looking down at the coffee cup.

"Leah, you didn't *know* this was going to happen. You wanted to advance yourself in Hallowed Falls so that you can help others. If I had thoughts like that every time I put an agent in danger, I wouldn't be able to get anything done. Don't be so hard on yourself," said Duke as he took another sip of his coffee.

Leah looked at him for a second and then smiled.

"That certainly puts it into a different perspective, I guess. Maybe you're right," she said as she looked into the distance, her eyes following a monarch butterfly as it danced from flower to flower. "How do you think Marco survived all this time?"

"Well, I'm sure you've heard of the two events in Hallowed Falls history, when the killings of magical creatures began. I suspect he stored some of the blood and used it over time. He must be running out. That's probably why he's killing again," said Duke.

"Do you think that the legend is true? That the former matriarch of the Summerland family hid powerful magic in the center of the arboretum?" asked Leah.

"It's not *impossible*, but like you said, there's nothing in the archives." said Duke.

Just then, his cellphone rang.

"This is Duke…Alright, I'll be there in a few minutes." he said as he hung up the phone. "I've got to attend a meeting. I hope you feel better." said Duke.

"Yea, I do. Thanks…again." said Leah with a smile as he stood up and walked away.

Leah finished her coffee before she made her way back to the suites. When she got back, she immediately turned on the computer to access the A.E.'s private archives with the temporary access information she was given. She typed 'Summerland arboretum' into the search bar then, looked through all the articles in the system. None of the articles had any information in regard to the magic that is allegedly stored in the arboretum. Just then, Lucinda walked into the common room.

"Hey, I heard the good news. Did Duke tell you?" Asked Lucinda with a smile.

"About what?" Asked Leah.

"They approved your access to the medical facilities in the infirmary building. You can start whenever you're ready. This is your temporary pass," said Lucinda as she handed her a laminated card attached to a bright blue lanyard.

"That's awesome news! I'll head there right away. How's Victor and Hazel doing?" asked Leah.

"Hazel's a lot better. We just brought her down to the dining hall. Victor is still in critical condition and I'm afraid we are running out of time," said Lucinda.

"I'll get to the lab right away," said Leah with a nod.

Primrose walked into the dining hall and saw Hazel sitting alone, picking at her bowl of oatmeal with a spoon. She was relieved to see that Hazel was okay.

"Hazel!" Shouted Primrose as she ran over to her.

Hazel looked up and gave her weak smile, then got up to hug her.

"I'm so glad you're okay," said Primrose softly.

Hazel couldn't help but break into tears.

"I can't believe Victor's hurt. It's my fault. I wasn't strong enough to fight off Heidi and Marco." Hazel sobbed.

"Listen, it wasn't your fault," said Primrose as she held Hazel.

Tyler walked into the dining hall and sat down across from them. He felt bad for Hazel, especially seeing her this upset right now.

"Hazel, good to see you up and running. Are you alright?" Asked Tyler.

"Yea, I'll be okay. Just trying to process everything. Thank you...for saving my life," said Hazel gratefully as she wiped her tears with the back of her hand.

"Don't worry about it. I'm just glad we were able to help," said Tyler with a polite smile.

Just then Lucinda walked in and joined them at the table.

"Hey, Luce. Any updates on Victor?" Asked Hazel.

"No... I'm sorry. But Leah's in the infirmary with him now. She's going to take some blood samples and start working on a treatment," said Lucinda as she put a hand on Hazel's shoulder. "You should eat. I'll help you back to the suites when you're done."

Hazel gave her a nod. She swirled the warm oatmeal around some more before scooping up a spoonful and began eating.

After lunch, they all went back to the common room. Primrose helped Hazel into her suite while Lucinda and Tyler sat by the fireplace.

"So, this is where you work, huh?" Asked Tyler.

"Yea, it's an amazing place and I love my job," said Lucinda contentedly.

"Speaking of which, great job with the fireballs back at the cemetery. That was quick thinking." Tyler flashed her smile and she couldn't help but notice how handsome he looked. Her eyes quickly shifted back to the fireplace, hoping that it would stop her from blushing.

"Same to you, for getting Hazel out of there," said Lucinda, glancing back at him now. Her gaze was interrupted by the sound of a door opening.

Primrose quietly stepped out of Hazel's room and closed the door gently behind her.

"I used the Restoration charm and a bit of my Sleep Elixir to help her relax. She's asleep now," said Primrose, tucking the two vials back into her purse.

"Alright, I'll let you guys rest. I've still got some work to do," said Lucinda as she slowly stood up. She gave Tyler a smile before turning on her heel and walking out of the common room.

A few days later, Hazel, Primrose, and Tyler were chatting in the common room when there was a knock on the door.

"Hey guys, Duke wants us all to meet him in the Conference Hall," said Lucinda as she stayed by the door.

They all followed her down to the third floor and when they got there, Hazel noticed that Leah was already sitting at the table. Next to her, was a woman wearing gray scrubs and a white lab coat. She looked older, perhaps in her mid-forties with curly reddish-brown hair and brown eyes. There were also a few other people sitting around the oblong table.

"Good morning, we gathered everyone here this morning because we've got some updates that you should be aware of. To my left is

Dr. Milly Saunders, the Senior Director of Medical Services. She and Dr. Leah Plumeria have been working closely together to help Victor. Doctors, do you have any updates for us?" Asked Duke.

Leah cleared her throat.

"Yes, thank you. Good morning, everyone. In the last few days, we've been working on a treatment that would help fight the vampire venom that has infected Victor LaMeur. So far, we've come up with a vaccination that seems to be slowing it down further and preventing it from reaching his heart. But this is just a temporary solution. We will continue to run more tests and keep everyone updated," said Leah with a nod as she glanced back at Duke.

"Thank you, doctor," said Duke.

"Agent Evan Bradley is one of our top agents in the Department of Protective Services and has been working with the Hallowed Falls PD on this case. What do you have for us, Agent Bradley?" Asked Duke.

A man sitting to the right of Duke, stood up from his seat. He was about six feet tall with dark blonde hair and steel-gray eyes.

"Hallowed Falls PD has found another body. They alerted us last night and the body was identified as Amarie Kelly," said Agent Bradley.

"A-Amarie Kelly?" asked Primrose nervously.

"You know who she is?" Asked Duke with furrowed brows.

"She's a fairy that works part time at my flower shop...Where was she found?" Asked Primrose as she tried to hold back her tears.

"According to the police report, her body was discovered right outside the arboretum." said Agent Bradley.

"So Primrose was right," said Leah as she put her hand over her mouth.

"Are you okay, Dr. Plumeria? Right about what?" Asked Agent Bradley.

Everyone looked at Primrose. Primrose's hands were in a knot and she knew she had to tell them.

"I...I told Leah that I suspected Marco of trying to access the center of the arboretum. The powers that Honora...my great, great grandmother has hidden there," said Primrose.

Everyone gasped.

"*You're* the heir of Summerland?" Asked Leah still in shock.

"Yes," said Primrose.

"Wait, what?" Asked Hazel, sounding just as shocked as her sister.

"My grandmother is the daughter of Lavender Summerland. The rumors are true. Honora has something powerful hidden inside the arboretum and only a true heir of Honora can access it," said Primrose.

"Then why haven't you or Tyler tried to retrieve it after all this time?" Asked Lucinda.

"I was born a witch. Therefore, I am not considered a true heir. A true heir has to be a natural born fairy with Summerland blood," Tyler explained.

"You knew that she was an heir this whole time?" Asked Leah with her brows drawn together.

"Yes, it is a secret that we must keep within the family. Otherwise, we would not be able to live our normal lives or to even help others. It was better for everyone to think that the Summerland line ended with Lavender," Tyler explained.

"Do you guys know what it is that she hid in the center of the arboretum?" Asked Hazel.

"No, my grandmother said that no one knows exactly what is inside. Honora never revealed it, not even to her daughter. Anyway, I never wanted whatever was inside. I wanted to live my life as a normal fairy. But after what I've seen, I need to get to whatever is inside before Marco does. I can't let anyone else get hurt," said Primrose.

"We can't let you go alone," said Lucinda.

"We also need a plan. Agent Bradley and Lucinda will go with Primrose to the arboretum. I'll have a team standing by as backup," Duke instructed.

"Wait, Marco could be expecting us there. If he sees our agents, he'll know something is up. It could make the situation even more dangerous and who knows how many others are helping him like Heidi is. Heidi has worked for the A.E., she might already be anticipating what you'll do," said Lucinda.

"I should go along with them. I'm well practiced in my defensive magic," said Tyler confidently.

"Fine, the four of you should head to the armory tower first. Have them set you up with communication and protective gear," said Duke.

Everyone got up to leave, but Leah stalled and waited for everyone to clear out.

"Leah, you coming?" Asked Dr. Saunders as she stood by the door.

"Uh…yea, I'll meet you back at the lab," said Leah, glancing at Duke nervously.

Dr. Saunders nodded and left. Duke was still gathering his paperwork when Leah approached him.

"Hey, Duke," said Leah with a smile. Her stomach tightened and her heart was pounding.

"Hi," Duke replied as he continued to put paperwork into folders..

"I was wondering…would you like to join me for dinner tonight?" Asked Leah.

Duke stared at her for a second, then glanced down at his watch.

"Uh…I don't think I'll be able to. I've…uh…got to go. Maybe a raincheck? Excuse me," said Duke as he hurried past her and disappeared out the door.

"Oh…okay," said Leah with disappointment.

Duke was being evasive again. It reminded her of when he left the barbecue early. Leah frowned and headed back to the infirmary building.

When Duke arrived back at his office, he threw the folders onto his desk and plopped down on his chair. He replayed what just happened in the conference hall with Leah.

"Why am I being such a coward? It's just a dinner between two adults. Maybe she just wants to thank me for helping her out." Duke thought to himself.

Deep down inside he was still hurt by Savannah and he knew that getting involved with anyone else would mean that he could potentially get hurt again.

"I should at least apologize to her and explain myself." He ran a hand over his face and took a deep breath, then continued working on his computer.

Lucinda, Tyler, Primrose, and Agent Bradley went to the equipment department as instructed. The armory tower is a building diagonally behind the manor. After they were all geared up, they headed towards the front doors and got into Tyler's car. Duke offered one of A.E.'s SUVs but Lucinda suggested that they needed to be more discreet.

"What's that?" Asked Primrose as she pointed at Lucinda's right hand.

Lucinda and Agent Bradley had black fingerless gloves on with their stylus attached to the back of it.

"It's a stylus holster. All A.E. agents have them. It allows us to be hands-free during missions," said Lucinda.

"Oh, that's pretty neat," said Primrose.

Tyler started up the car and they drove towards Hallowed Falls. It took them about forty-five minutes to reach the arboretum from headquarters. When they got there, Tyler parked a block away from the arboretum and everyone got out. They walked cautiously towards the arboretum and made sure they weren't seen by anyone on the street. They couldn't afford to have any of Marco's henchmen spot them if there were any around. When they got close to the entrance, it seemed noticeably quiet. Agent Bradley stopped across the street from the arboretum and turned to face them.

"Okay, it seems clear so far. But we don't know if Marco or Heidi are inside. The arboretum closed about a half an hour ago so there shouldn't be any civilians in there. I will head in first with Tyler. Lucinda and Primrose, you will come in after we've made sure it is all clear inside. Alright, let's go," said Agent Bradley whispered as he jogged across the street with Tyler right on his heel.

They approached the entrance with their styluses drawn, then slowly opened the door and stepped into the building. Lucinda and Primrose waited a few minutes before following them, then stood outside of the entrance to wait for their signal.

"It's clear," whispered Agent Bradley through the door.

They quickly slipped into the arboretum. Lucinda looked up at the ceiling. The sky was clear and the stars twinkled behind the glass ceiling.

"I haven't been here in ages. My grandmother brought me here once. That's when she told me about the stories of Honora Summerland and our family," said Primrose as she admired her surroundings.

"Did she ever mention where Honora might have stored her magic?" Asked Lucinda, her gaze turned to Primrose.

"No, but if I were a fairy who wanted to hide something that only another fairy can find…I would probably hide it in a fairy house," said Primrose, pointing to the center of the arboretum.

"It's right in the center of the whole building. That's gotta be it!" Said Lucinda excitedly.

As they approached the fairy house, Primrose prepared herself to turn on the Micropixie aura so that she could enter the small house. When all of a sudden, they heard the front door bust open. Heidi stood by the front door with two male vampire guards with her.

"Well, well, well. Look at what we have here. The A.E. brought the heir to us. Sure saved us a whole lot of time," said Heidi with a grin and her guards snickered.

"You're not getting anywhere near her," Agent Bradley warned her as he stepped in front of Primrose.

Within a split second, Heidi was next to Agent Bradley and she grabbed him by the neck.

"Try and stop me, witch," Heidi hissed as she tossed Agent Bradley across the floor.

Agent Bradley tumbled before catching himself on all fours. Underneath Lucinda's hands, Primrose watched as misty, light blue orbs begin to manifest. Lucinda conjured powerballs. She launched the powerballs right at Heidi but she dodged them. Heidi charged at Lucinda, knocking her to the ground and the two of them rolled across the white marble floor. Tyler and Agent Bradley were each fighting with a vampire guard.

Heidi straddled Lucinda and gave her a right-hook punch, then rushed towards Primrose. Just as Primrose reached out her hand to touch the fairy house, Heidi shoved her hard, causing her to fall to the ground. Heidi reached out and touched the fairy house. There was a bright blue electrical flash and Heidi was thrown across the room before crashing onto the floor.

She groaned, "Get her!"

Lucinda got up off the floor and threw herself on top of Heidi to hold her down.

"Now, Primrose! Do it now!" Yelled Lucinda as she continued to wrestle Heidi.

Primrose looked around the arboretum. Agent Bradley and Tyler were still engaged with the two other guards. She turned her focus back to the fairy house in front of her and closed her eyes. Her wings fluttered swiftly and a golden glow surrounded her entire body. She began to shrink down in size and within seconds, the Micropixie aura had transformed her into a small fairy that stood about four inches tall.

Carefully, she turned the doorknob and pushed the door open. The interior of the fairy house was stunning and the scent of honeysuckles lingered in the air. The walls were painted gold with a satin finish and fresh white flowers lined the walls and ceiling. She walked towards the spiral staircase in the middle of the floor and started to climb up. Suddenly the whole house shook causing her to grab onto the railing. She knew she must hurry.

When she got to the top of the stairs, she saw a pedestal at the center of the room. There was a glass case over something too bright for Primrose to make out.

"*That must be it,*" she thought to herself.

She reached out to lift the glass cover but the house shook again and she lost her balance. Then, she heard a voice echo around her.

"Primrose, hurry!" Lucinda shouted.

She jumped to her feet, grabbed the lid and tossed it onto the floor. It made a loud clunking sound as it hit the wooden floor but it didn't shatter. She reached into the glowing light and felt something fall into her hands. They were small. Small like seeds.

"*Seeds?*" she thought to herself.

She put them gently into a small vial and into her purse, then ran back down the spiral staircase. When she exited the fairy house, it was quiet. She transformed back to normal size and realized why. Lucinda, Tyler, and Agent Bradley were being held by Heidi and the other two vamps. Their fangs were ready to sink into each of Primrose's friends. Then she noticed a tall silhouette behind Heidi. It was Marco.

"Ha! How kinda of you to do all the work for us. Hand over the powers of Summerland or we'll *kill* all of your friends!" Marco said with malevolence.

"Don't do it, Primrose! Just fly out of here!" Yelled Tyler.

The vampire holding Tyler punched him in the stomach. Primrose glowered at Marco.

"You'll let them go if I hand it over to you?" Asked Primrose.

"You have my word," said Marco with a grin.

Primrose reached into her purse and pulled out a vial of glowing pink liquid.

"It's all in this vial. Now let them go!" She insisted.

Marco gave a nod to Heidi and the two guards, signaling them to let go. Tyler, Lucinda, and Agent Bradley ran to Primrose's side.

Agent Bradley gave her a slight nod and Primrose tossed the vial into the air. Agent Bradley quickly put his arms around all of them and pointed his stylus towards the front door. The next thing they knew, all four of them were outside the arboretum.

"Whoa! How'd we end up outside?" Asked Primrose, feeling a little dizzy.

"Run now! Questions later!" Said Agent Bradley as he started to run towards the car and they all followed behind him.

Inside the arboretum, the vampires were searching for the group.

"Where'd they go?!" Asked one of the guards.

"Doesn't matter now. We have the Summerland powers. The most powerful of all fairy magic!" Marco declared as he popped the cork off the bottle and drank the concoction.

Suddenly, Marco felt a sharp pain in his stomach and yelled out in pain as he dropped to his knees.

"Marco!" yelled Heidi as she ran to his side. "Go after them, quick!" she demanded the two guards.

Marco started seizing out of control and smoke was coming from his body. Before Heidi could figure out what was happening, Marco combusted and turned into a pile of dark gray ashes. Her eyes were wide with horror.

"Nooo!" cried Heidi.

Heidi stared at the ground in shock, not knowing what to do next. All of a sudden, Marco's ashes began to swirl around on the floor even though was no breeze causing it to happen. It slowly turned into a large tornado in the middle of the arboretum and surrounded Heidi. The dark gray substance inserted itself into Heidi through her nose and mouth. Heidi couldn't breathe and dropped to her knees. Her eyes turned black for a second and then back to normal. She felt stronger but did not feel like herself.

"Well, isn't this a nice surprise?" A voice said inside her head.

Heidi gasped.

"No, this can't be," she said out loud.

"Oh but it is, my dear," said the familiar voice.

Marco had partially possessed her body.

Tyler jumped into the driver's seat as quickly as he could and jammed the key into the ignition. He could see the two vampires running towards them in the rear-view mirror. As soon as they all shut the car doors, they heard a loud thud on the roof of the car. Tyler stomped on the gas pedal.

"They're on the roof!" Yelled Primrose.

Lucinda quickly conjured fireballs in both hands.

"Open the window!" She yelled.

Primrose reached over to the door and pressed the button to open the window. Lucinda tossed a fireball towards the vampire guards. One of them let go and tumbled onto the street while the other one held on. She tossed another one while Tyler tried to shake him off by driving in a snake-like motion. Lucinda tossed a third fireball and was able to get him to let go.

"I got them!" shouted Lucinda, out of breath.

She looked over at Agent Bradley and he seemed hurt.

"Evan!" Yelled Lucinda.

"I'm okay, he just grazed me with his fangs," he said weakly as he held his bloodied neck.

"That looks like more than just a graze. Here, let me help you," said Primrose.

She took a small vial of Salixantho out of her purse and poured some onto her hand before patting it all over his wound.

"It'll help with the pain and slow down the spread of the vamp venom. We need to get back to headquarters, quick!" Primrose urged.

Tyler drove right up to the front doors of the A.E. manor. Duke and a handful of medical staff were waiting there.

"To the infirmary, hurry!" Duke instructed the staff.

Lucinda had one of Agent Bradley's arms on her shoulder and helped him out of the car. Two agents ran to her and took over.

"Are you guys alright?" Asked Duke, his eyes widened and brows drawn together.

"Yes, we're okay but Marco and Heidi ambushed us. There were others but we were able to shake them," Said Lucinda.

"Let's get inside," said Duke.

Lucinda turned back and watched the two guards walk Agent Bradley to the infirmary before following Duke into the manor and into the dining hall.

"Luce!" shouted Hazel as soon as she saw her.

Hazel and Leah gave her and Primrose a hug.

"Are you guys okay? It's been hours and we didn't hear from you," said Leah with concern.

"Yea...we're okay but Agent Bradley got bit by one of Marco's guards. Primrose was able to give him something to stop the bleeding on the way back. They just brought him to the infirmary. We were held hostage by Heidi and two vampire guards. Primrose had to trade the power she retrieved from the arboretum for us to be released. Agent Bradley was able to quickly cast the teleportation spell and got us out of there," Lucinda explained.

"He doesn't have it," said Primrose.

"What do you mean?" Asked Tyler.

"The vial I gave him was Zingallium, an elixir I created that is poisonous to vampires. I don't think he could've survived it. I've been carrying it around ever since a fairy was murdered by the cemetery a few months ago," said Primrose.

"Were you able find anything inside the fairy house?" Asked Lucinda.

"There was a pedestal with a glass lid over a bright golden light. When I reached into it, seeds fell into my hands," said Primrose.

She reached into her purse and took the vial of seeds out.

"Seeds? What kind of seeds are those?" Asked Lucinda.

Primrose held the vial higher and examined it. Each were a different color, dark purple, red, black, and gold.

"Actually...I think I know what they are. I read about it in the Summerland archives a while back. Years ago when the A.E. was formed, Honora and Gregoro went on a mission in the Misty Briars Forest and they discovered the Four Seeds of Desire," said Leah.

"What's are the Four Seeds of Desire?" Asked Hazel.

"The Amaranth of Life, the Rose of Passion, the Black Orchid of Death, and the Gardenia of Wealth. Each of these magical seeds bring exactly what is in their name. Gregoro and Honora felt that it would be too dangerous for these plants to get into the wrong hands. They saved the seeds from each of these plants to bring back to headquarters. Then destroyed the areas where each of these plants were growing. But they claimed that the seeds were lost on their way back," Leah explained.

"Honora must have suspected that even the A.E. headquarters wasn't safe at the time," said Duke.

"Gregoro *must* have known what Honora did if he was with her the whole time but he didn't have any of that written in his journals in the Plumeria archives," said Leah.

"I guess some people would do anything to protect someone they loved," said Duke with a shrug.

"What?!" Leah and Hazel shouted in unison.

"You guys didn't know?" Asked Duke as he scratched his head. "Uh... Gregoro and Honora were...romantically involved back in the days."

"But that's impossible, the books in the Summerland archives claim that she never had a lover," said Leah.

"Actually, we have some of Honora's original journals. The ones that are *not* part of the researches she's done. They're more…private," said Duke.

"What? Well, where are these journals now?" Asked Leah.

"They're in one of our safes," said Duke.

"Is there any way we can look at them? Maybe there's something in it that can help Victor and Agent Bradley. I mean I'm sure they've had to deal with vampire venom back then too," said Leah.

"Yes, since I've been overseeing the Department of Assets while Senior Director Griffin is away, I can probably get an approval through. But I can allow only *one* person access to them. The original journals are very fragile and too much handling might cause damage," said Duke.

"It should be Leah, she's the one who's done the most research on this issue so far and plus, she's already familiar with the lab. Perhaps she can find a better treatment," said Lucinda.

"Okay, so it's settled. I'll let you guys get some rest," said Duke as he turned to leave.

"Wait, what should we do with the seeds?" Asked Primrose.

"We can keep them in my safe for now," said Duke.

Primrose handed the vial of seeds over to Duke.

Later that evening, Leah walked into the common room and saw Hazel sitting down by the fireplace.

"Hey, you alright?" Asked Leah.

"I don't even know anymore. Victor is still in a coma and on top of that, Gregoro and Honora Summerland? How could he do that to our great-great grandmother?" Asked Hazel.

"We don't know all the details about that. I'll see what I can find out once I get access to the journals. And Victor will be fine, I promise. There's gotta be something helpful in the journals. Let's just go to bed," Leah suggested.

Hazel nodded.

The following day, Leah was working in the medical lab when Duke walked in.

"Hey Leah, I wanted let you know that I signed off the approval for you to borrow Honora's journals. They will be dropped off at my office this afternoon. You may stop by at your convenience to pick them up," said Duke in a friendly way.

"Great. I'll stop by as soon as I'm done here," said Leah flatly as she walked over to another lab table.

"Okay, I'll see you later then," said Duke as he turned to walk away. He turned back around and opened his mouth as though to speak but decided to just leave.

Later that afternoon, Lucinda knocked on Duke's office door.

"Hey, Leah sent me to pick up the journals," said Lucinda, her body peeking halfway in the door.

"Oh…they're right on the counter," said Duke, gesturing at the desk in the corner.

"You seem disappointed. I can leave them here for Leah to pick up if you want," Lucinda teased.

"No, I'm not," said Duke firmly.

"Okay then, I'll see you later," she said with a smirk.

Duke thought about what Lucinda just said. She was right, but why *did* he feel disappointed? His thoughts that day when he and Leah sat in the garden. It was nice and he felt connected to someone again.

"*Why am I fighting the fact that I care about her?*" He thought to himself. He wasn't even sure. Probably because now is not the time to think about romance. His best friend was in a coma and his top agent still recovering from an attack. He waved the thought of Leah out of his mind.

When Lucinda got to the common room, Leah was sitting in front of the computer.

"Here are the journals," said Lucinda as she set them on the desk next to her.

"Want to grab dinner in about twenty minutes?" Lucinda asked.

"Thanks, uh yea, sure," said Leah as she continued to read something on the screen.

"He seemed disappointed, you know," said Lucinda with a smile.

"What are you talking about?" Asked Leah and looked up at Lucinda.

"He seemed disappointed that *you* weren't the one to pick up the journals. He could've had the journals sent to our suites but he kept it in his office. And he *personally* came to you to let you know," said Lucinda.

"Yea…and?" Asked Leah with a raised eyebrow.

"Wow, I've never met anyone more oblivious to romantic gestures," said Lucinda, shaking her head and crossed her arms.

"Listen, I asked him out to dinner the other day and he declined. It doesn't take a scientist to figure out what's going on. He obviously hasn't gotten over Savannah Powell," said Leah, feeling annoyed.

"Didn't you guys have a nice conversation together by the garden a week ago?" Asked Lucinda.

"Yes, but he was probably only trying to be a gentleman and wanted to comfort me. Just like the time I was attacked at the library. Nothing more," said Leah.

"Okay…but answer this for me. Do you have *feelings* for Duke?" Asked Lucinda.

Just then, someone cleared their throat. They both turned towards the door and Duke was standing there awkwardly, unsure if he should leave.

"*Oh God, how long has he been standing there? He must've heard the whole conversation,*" Leah thought to herself. She could feel her face slowly turn bright red.

"Uh…Lucinda, I wanted to come tell you that Agent Bradley has been discharged from the infirmary. They were actually able to extract the small amount of poison out of his neck," said Duke.

"Oh, that's great news! I'll go see him now. Um…Leah, I'll meet you in the dining hall in a little bit? Or…not? Ok, I'm going now! See ya!" said Lucinda as she grabbed her jacket and slid past Duke.

"Leah, can we talk?" Asked Duke.

"I'm a little busy. Perhaps a *raincheck,*" said Leah as she turned back to the computer.

Duke ran his fingers through his dark brown hair.

"Look, I'm not good at this kind of thing, but I don't want you to think that I'm leading you on here," said Duke.

"You said that already and like I told you at the Siren's Cove a couple of weeks ago, I'm fine," said Leah.

"Leah, I —." His phone rang and interrupted him. "This is Duke. She's what? Alright, I'll be right there," said Duke and hung up, then glanced back at Leah. "I guess… have a good night then, Leah." Duke said and disappeared into the hall.

Leah felt a knot in her stomach as soon as Duke left.

"Maybe I'm being unfair to Duke. Afterall, he had just experienced a harsh rejection not long ago," Leah thought to herself.

Hazel waited a couple of minutes before coming out of her suite.

"Wow, you're as stubborn as mom," said Hazel.

"Oh, geez!" said Leah, clutching her chest.

"Sorry! Didn't mean to scare you but what was that all about?" Asked Hazel.

"That…was nothing," said Leah.

"It seemed like *something*. You both clearly have feelings for each other. He just doesn't know how to deal with it and you're too stubborn to accept that he *feels* something for you," said Hazel.

"He sure has a way of showing it. I'm also not interested in being someone's rebound," said Leah.

"Like I said, he probably doesn't know how to handle the new feelings he has for you while trying to put someone else in the past. Give him some time," said Hazel.

"No, it's fine. I'm over it. Let's go meet Lucinda for dinner," said Leah as she got up from the computer desk.

"Stubborn," said Hazel as she shook her head and walked towards the door.

Hazel and Leah got off the elevator to the second floor where the dining hall was. Leah noticed Duke standing to the side by the elevators with a woman. She looked about their age and was wearing a Blue Wolf's Tavern jacket.

"Oh, looks like Duke ordered take out. I didn't realize they delivered all the way here. I'm jealous, not that the food here isn't good, though. Come on, it's shrimp scampi night," said Hazel excitedly.

Everyone was sitting in the dining hall, even Agent Bradley joined them at their table. A few minutes later, Duke walked in with the delivery girl and sat on the other side of the dining hall. She had black hair and stone-gray eyes.

"Whoa! Why is the girl from Blue Wolf's Tavern in here and sitting with Duke?" asked Hazel.

"Uh…" said Lucinda hesitantly as her eyes shifted quickly to Leah and then back down at her food. "That's Savannah."

"As in…Savannah Powell? His ex?" Asked Hazel with raised brows.

"Yea…There's a Blue Wolf's Tavern in Crystal Brooks and she manages that location," said Lucinda.

Leah glanced over at their table. Just then, Duke looked up at her and she quickly looked away.

"Um, I should probably start going through the journals. I'll see you guys back at the common room." said Leah as she got up and headed back towards the suites.

"Is she okay? She barely touched her food." asked Primrose.

"Yea, she'll be fine." said Hazel as she watched Leah walk out of the dining hall.

It had gotten pretty late by the time the group got back to the suites. Leah had fallen asleep reading the journals by the fireplace.

"Leah? Sweetie? You need to go to bed," said Hazel as she shook Leah's arm gently.

"Oh...wow, what time is it?" Asked Leah groggily.

"It's a little after midnight," said Lucinda.

Leah yawned and sat up.

"Guys...You won't believe what I found in the journals. The Amaranth of Life has the powers to cure any type of illness in the world. Honora even wrote down the ingredients for the elixir. Gregoro helped her with it because he was more skilled in alchemy. They both lied about losing the seeds so that they can protect it from the Alexanders," said Leah.

"If Primrose and I can get the amaranth to blossom, maybe we can help Victor. We've got to get the seed from Duke." said Hazel.

"There's one more thing. In one of Honora's journals...she wrote about her love for Gregoro. Back when Gregoro and Honora were only twenty years old, their parents had a business together. Not long after they opened, their parents had a disagreement and the business was dissolved. When Honora's father found out that the two of them were seeing each other, he forbade her from continuing their relationship. Honora and Gregoro chose to run away together instead. They had been gone for a week when one of her father's personal guards found them and forced her to return home. She didn't see Gregoro again until she was twenty-six. By the time they met again, Gregoro was already married to Henrietta Moonflower.

Within that time, Honora had her daughter, Lavender. Lavender was five years old," said Leah.

"That's sad…they never got to be together. But if they did, we wouldn't have been born," said Hazel.

"Oh, wow," said Primrose. She plopped down onto the sofa and had a shocked look on her face.

"What?! What's wrong?" Asked Tyler as he sat down next to her.

"Gregoro and Honora hadn't seen each other for *five* years. Lavender was *five* when they saw each other again," Primrose hinted.

"Honora didn't take the Fertility Elixir. Lavender was also Gregoro's daughter. That makes Primrose…our cousin," Leah explained with a smile.

"What?! That's wonderful!" Hazel exclaimed and she went over to give her a hug.

"See? I knew it was a good idea to move to Hallowed Falls. We're bringing our families together!" Said Leah as she joined the hug.

"I wonder if Honora ever told Gregoro?" Primrose pondered out loud.

"According to her journals, she did. But Honora made him promise not to tell anyone. She didn't want to ruin what he had with Henrietta and the reputation of her family," said Leah.

"I feel sorry for them…but I'm glad we have each other now," said Primrose.

Hazel smiled and nodded in agreement.

Early the next morning, Primrose and Hazel went to see Duke about getting the amaranth seed. When they reached his office, they knocked on his door.

"Hi, Duke. Sorry to bother you but Leah has found something in Honora's journals. One of the seeds, the Amaranth of Life, may be able to help Victor. Primrose and I can tend to the plant to make sure it blooms quickly," said Hazel.

"If it'll help Victor, I'm up for trying it. I'll get it from the safe," said Duke. He got up and left the office, then came back within ten minutes and gave them the amaranth seed in a small glass vial.

"Actually, I need one more favor. I'm going to need some supplies from my shop. Is there someone who can take us there?" Asked Primrose.

"I can have someone pick them up. Just make a list and give me your shop key," said Duke.

"Thank you, Duke…for everything you've done so far," said Primrose with a smile.

Duke gave her a polite nod and smile.

Primrose started to head back to the common room but Hazel stayed behind.

"Hey…Duke? I know it's not any of my business…but are you and Savannah back together? You guys looked like you were reconciling last night in the dining hall," said Hazel.

"Me and Savannah? Uh...no, she actually came by because..." said Duke.

Hazel furrowed her brows and waited for him to continue.

"Well, when Savannah heard the address of our takeout, she recognized that it was the A.E. headquarters. So, she decided to deliver it herself and she stayed because she wanted to talk. She realized that she made a mistake breaking up with me," said Duke.

"Oh..." said Hazel.

"But it's been over two months. I told her that even though I will always care for her, I have moved on." said Duke.

Hazel smiled.

"Leah?" She asked.

"Yea," Duke chuckled.

"Leah has always been very much like my mother. Which means she's *stubborn*. You know...she's actually in the common room alone. I'll make sure to keep everyone else busy. If you catch my drift," Hazel gave him a wink and walked away.

Duke smiled and got up from behind his desk. He headed for the common room in the main building.

He knocked on the door of the common room and found Leah sitting at the computer desk.

"Oh, hi Duke. Are you looking for Lucinda?" She asked.

She got up from the desk and walked towards him.

"No...actually, I was wondering...if you'd like to have dinner with me tonight?" Duke asked shyly. "Duke...I don't think it's a good idea," said Leah as she turned back to the desk.

"Look, I know I've been hot and cold from the start, but I was dealing with a situation and that's in the past now. When we were together at the café a month ago, I realized how much I enjoyed spending time with you. I came here hoping that you felt the same way." said Duke.

Leah narrowed her eyes at him for a second.

"Okay," said Leah.

He flashed her a smile and she melted a little. She hadn't seen his smile in weeks and his dimple made him look even hotter.

"Great, can we meet around six-thirty in front of the dining hall?" Asked Duke.

Leah nodded.

Later that evening, Leah waited for Duke at the entrance to the dining hall.

"Hey," a voice from behind her said.

She turned around and Duke was standing there in a light blue dress shirt and dark gray pants.

"You look...nice," said Leah with a grin.

"And you...look beautiful as usual, doctor," said Duke.

She began to feel her face get warm. Leah was wearing her scrubs. They had been wearing clothes provided by the A.E. since they weren't able to get any of their belongings from home. She started walking towards the dining hall.

"Wait, we're not going to the dining hall. Follow me," said Duke and extended his hand to her.

Duke led her to another part of the manor. He opened the door to a common room that was much nicer than the one the group had been staying in. This one seemed more modern. There was a small round table set in front of the fireplace with candles and two plates of what looked like chicken. A bouquet of roses wrapped in clear cellophane lay on the chair and soft music was playing from the stereo in the corner of the room.

"Is this your suite? And...you cooked?" Asked Leah.

"Yes, and don't be so surprised. I'm actually a fairly good cook," said Duke with a smile.

He slid the chair out for her and she sat down.

"I hope you like chicken francaise," said Duke.

"It's one of my favorite dishes," she said with a smile.

"So, do all A.E. agents live in the manor?" Asked Leah as she took a sip of water.

"There are a few agents that use the living quarters on the sixth floor. Floors seven and eight are for directors and senior directors. The fifth floor, where you guys are staying, is where the rest of the estate's staff live. Not all of them, just the ones who have nowhere else to go. Everyone else come from the surrounding towns," said Duke.

"How long have you worked for the A.E.?" She asked as she began to cut the chicken.

"About twelve years or so. I started when I was twenty years old. It was actually Aaron Griffin who recruited me while I was in the police academy," said Duke as he put a piece of penne pasta in his mouth.

"Lucinda's father?" Asked Leah.

Duke nodded his head.

"Wow, that's pretty awesome. Luce mentioned him to us. She said he travels often?" Leah questioned.

"Yea, he comes back every now and then but he doesn't stay for long. The A.E. relies on him heavily for high level missions regarding assets. About a year ago, the Chief of Directors asked me to help oversee the Department of Assets because Director Griffin had to be away so often," Duke explained.

"So..." Leah started to say as she kept her gaze down at her plate.

"So," said Duke with a smile.

"How's Savannah?" asked Leah, glancing up at him.

Duke put his fork down and wiped his mouth with a napkin.

"She's...doing well. I guess," Duke shrugged.

There was silence between them for a second.

"What was she doing here last night?" She asked as she picked up the glass of wine.

She was never good at beating around the bush and she wasn't going to start now.

"She delivered our take-out. Her father owns the Blue Wolf's Tavern in Crystal Brooks. When she saw our address, she decided to bring it here herself...and we ended up talking," said Duke.

"You guys...*just* talked?" Asked Leah as she continued eating.

Duke smiled and took a sip of water.

"Yes, we just talked...and I told her I don't feel the same for her anymore. In the past couple of weeks, I...started to have feelings for someone else," said Duke as he gazed at her from across the small table.

Leah smiled and her ears suddenly felt like they were on fire.

"Huh...I wonder who that person could be?" She joked.

Duke chuckled and she couldn't help but laugh a little too.

He liked hearing her laugh and he knew at that moment, the spark between them has turned into a flame.

Hazel and Primrose were in the greenhouse on the east side of the estate.

"Alright, we've been singing and talking to the flower pot all day. It hasn't bloomed even a bit!" Hazel exclaimed with frustration.

Primrose tried using her Blossom charm one more time.

"It's no use. If Honora cultured the seed the way you do with your shop's plants, it's going to take weeks," said Hazel, crossing her arms.

"There's one thing we haven't tried…we can combine our Blossom charm," Primrose suggested.

"We can do that?" Asked Hazel.

"It's worth a shot," Primrose shrugged.

"Alright, let's do it," said Hazel.

They stood across from each other and held their right hands together. Their left hands hovered over the flowerpot. They closed their eyes and a bright golden light formed under their palms. It seemed to get increasingly brighter and brighter. When the charm was complete, they were able to see a short stem about half an inch tall with a leaf on it.

"It worked! We've got to keep doing it." said Hazel excitedly.

It was close to midnight when Duke walked Leah back to the common room.

"I had a great time and…I've got to admit, I totally did not expect that from you," said Leah.

They stopped in the middle of the hallway.

"I had a great time as well," said Duke, suddenly feeling a bit nervous.

They both gazed at each other for a second. Duke slowly leaned down and kissed Leah. His lips were warm and soft. She felt her heart open, sending a tingly sensation all over her body and down to her legs. The wall that she had up for weeks began to dissipate.

Then he slowly pulled away from their kiss and Leah had a huge smile plastered across her face.

"Goodnight, I'll see you tomorrow," said Duke.

"Night!" Leah replied.

Still dizzy from their kiss, she walked towards her suite. As she stepped into the common room, she saw Lucinda plop down by the fireplace.

"I know you were watching us," Leah rolled her eyes and chuckled.

"It was too romantic not to! So, you guys are together now, huh? Oh, I'm so happy for you!" Said Lucinda.

She got up and hugged Leah. Leah laughed.

"Thanks, I was definitely surprised. There was a candle lit dinner and a bouquet of roses. He cooked and everything. It was all very sweet. I never thought I was the type of girl that would be swept away by things like that," said Leah thoughtfully.

"Wait, he cooked?! I've *never* heard of him cook for anyone before," said Lucinda.

Leah blushed and grinned.

"Yea, I was just as shocked as you. Where's Hazel?" Asked Leah.

"She and Primrose went to sleep. They were able to get the seed to bloom but they were exhausted after casting the charm a few times. They're going to try again tomorrow," said Lucinda.

"That's great news! Alright, I'm going to hit the shower and then off to bed. Goodnight!" said Leah, happily.

Chapter 5

The next morning, Primrose and Hazel got up early to work on the amaranth seed. They cast the Blossom charm a few more times before quickly getting drained and feeling exhausted again. They sat down on a nearby bench to rest.

"By the way, I meant to ask you," Hazel spoke after a few minutes. "How'd you learn to make so many elixirs? You've saved our butts quite a few times."

"There's an alchemy diary that has been passed down from my grandmother. She wrote down all the potions and elixirs that she learned from her mother, Lavender," said Primrose sadly staring out into the garden.

"Wow, I wish I had an heirloom like that," said Hazel, clearly impressed.

"Well, I wish I had a sister who cares for me as much as Leah does for you. Growing up as an only child, gets lonely sometimes," said Primrose in return.

"You've got us now, cousin," said Hazel with a smile.

She patted Primrose's hand and Primrose smiled back at her.

"Alright, you ready to go again?" Asked Primrose.

Hazel nodded as they gathered their strength to try again.

As Hazel and Primrose were working on the amaranth seed, Lucinda was in the common room reading a potions book. She looked up as Tyler swung the door open and walked out to the common room from his suite. He was wearing nothing but a white towel around his waist. His jet-black hair dripping water and his hazel eyes sparkled. Lucinda stared at his perfectly carved abdomen.

"Oh, hey! Sorry, did I disrupt your reading?" Tyler asked innocently.

"Uh...um, no," Lucinda said as she looked back down.

"I'm starting to run out of undergarments. Any idea where I can get more?" He asked with raised brows.

"Um...yea, I'll call and ask...Actually, why don't I help you find some downstairs. I'll be right back," said Lucinda as she dropped the book on the chair and left the common room swiftly.

Tyler smiled, then shook his wet hair with his hands and walked back into his suite.

Lucinda went to Duke's office in the North building and knocked on the door.

"Hey, everyone's running out of clothes over there. Any chance we can help them get some of their own belongings from home?" Asked Lucinda.

Duke scratched his head.

"I guess it would be okay. It's been a while since we've heard anything about Heidi. Send *only* two at a time. It would be too difficult to protect them if they left the estate all at once. You and Agent Bradley will accompany them," said Duke.

"Yes, sir," said Lucinda with a nod.

"In the meantime, check with the infirmary staff. They should have fresh garments there that could suffice in the meantime," said Duke.

Lucinda thanked him before leaving his office. After retrieving a few sets of fresh scrubs and undergarments, she headed back to the suites. She took one set and placed the rest on a chair, then knocked on Tyler's door. He was still in the towel when he answered the door.

"Hey, here you go," said Lucinda trying to avoid staring.

"Wow! That was quick. Thanks, Luce," said Tyler.

Lucinda nodded, then moved to walk away.

"Hey, I was about to grab something to eat. Would you want to come with me?" Asked Tyler.

Lucinda turned back to face him.

"Sure, I almost forgot I haven't eaten yet," said Lucinda.

"Great! I'll just get dressed."

After a few minutes, Tyler came back out, with clothes on this time.

"How about we try the café today instead of the dining hall. They actually have some delicious buttery croissants there," Lucinda suggested.

"You guys have been hiding the café from us this whole time?" Tyler teased.

"Oops!" Lucinda laughed.

After breakfast, Tyler and Lucinda took a walk around the estate.

"So, what's your story anyway?" Asked Lucinda as she took a sip of her iced coffee.

"How do you mean?" Asked Tyler.

"What inspired you to become a doctor?"

"Oh…well, my father was a general physician. His father was a cardiac surgeon and his father before that was a pediatrician. Helping others is in my blood, I guess."

"Ah, I see," said Lucinda with a nod.

Just then, her cellphone rang.

"This is Lucinda…You did? Great! Let's meet Leah in the lab," said Lucinda as she abruptly hung up. "We have to get to the lab right now. Hazel and Primrose were able to get the amaranth to flower."

She tossed her coffee cup into the nearest trash can.

"That's great, news!" Tyler exclaimed.

They headed towards the lab as quickly as they could calling Duke to notify him on their way. When they arrived at the lab, Duke was already there.

"Good work, ladies. Leah, how soon would you be able to make the elixir for Victor?" Asked Duke.

"I'll need at least a few hours. Some ingredients need to sit for thirty minutes before I can add the next one into it," said Leah.

"Maybe I can help as well? I've also studied alchemy during medical school," Tyler offered.

"I'll try to get you an expedited approval from Employee Services," said Duke with a nod.

Hazel handed Leah the flowers harvested from the plant before Leah started showing Tyler around the lab.

"In the meantime, Agent Bradley and I can escort Hazel and Primrose to pick up their belongings from home. I'll go update him now," said Lucinda.

"I'm glad we'll be able to pick up some stuff from home. I have some more elixirs there that could be useful to us," said Primrose.

"Like the ones you used to help me and Agent Bradley?" Asked Hazel.

"Yes, I also have more of the Zingallium that I gave to Marco. I can show the A.E. how to make more just in case," said Primrose. They got ready and headed towards the manor's front doors to wait for Lucinda.

Lucinda found Agent Bradley in his office.

"Hey, Primrose and Hazel were able to get flowers from the Amaranth of Life. Leah and Tyler are working on the cure for Victor. Duke assigned us to escort Primrose and Hazel home to pick up some belongings.

"Okay, I just need to finish this report and we can head to the armory to gear up," said Agent Bradley.

Lucinda nodded.

"Hey…can we grab dinner tonight when we get back? I think we should talk," said Agent Bradley.

She sighed.

"We've already talked about this, Evan. There is *nothing* left to discuss," said Lucinda tiredly.

"You mean, *you* talked. I listened and I never got to say what I wanted to say before *you* gave up on us," he responded.

Lucinda kept her gaze at him for a few seconds before throwing her hands up in exasperation.

"Fine, we can talk when we get back." she said, rolling her eyes.

Agent Bradley got up from his chair and they headed to the armory tower.

After gearing up, they went to meet with the others at the front of the manor. Everyone got into Lucinda's SUV, the first stop was the old Plumeria estate. When they arrived, Lucinda accompanied Hazel into the manor and grabbed some of her own belongings as well. Hazel walked into her room to find Sage was sleeping in her cage. Fortunately, Amber, the housekeeper had been taking care of Sage while Hazel was gone. She grabbed a medium sized suitcase and threw some clothes into it. Lucinda stood outside of the manor and casted the Bulwark spell on the estate. When Hazel came back out, they got into the car and drove towards Primrose's house.

When they arrived at the Evans manor, Agent Bradley escorted Primrose into the house. As they approached the front door, Agent Bradley noticed that the doorknob had been broken off. He put his arm out to stop Primrose from going any further. He raised his right hand where the stylus was holstered to the glove and with a closed fist, pointed it at the door. He pressed on his earpiece and spoke in a low tone.

"Luce, the manor has been compromised," said Agent Bradley.

"Stay right there. I'll come to you," said Lucinda through her earpiece.

Lucinda turned to Hazel.

"The house has been broken in to. I have to make sure her family is okay. Stay here. I'll cast the Obscure spell on the car so you won't be seen," said Lucinda.

Lucinda quickly got out of the car and shut the door.

"*Obscura,*" Lucinda whispered as she waved her stylus over the side of the SUV.

Hazel watched as sparkly purple mist swirled all around the car.

Then, Lucinda turned and ran towards the manor. She saw Agent Bradley and Primrose standing a few feet from the front door.

"Primrose, I need you to go back to the car," Lucinda whispered.

"Don't worry, I can defend myself. I can't let him get to my elixirs and potions. He will be even more dangerous if he gets a hold of them," Primrose whispered back.

"Fine, just stay close behind us," said Lucinda.

Agent Bradley carefully pushed the front door open. The manor seemed dark and overly quiet. Their footsteps echoed in the foyer. They checked the first floor and made sure no one was around.

"It's clear. Alright, where is your room?" Asked Lucinda.

"Towards the back, there's a set of stairs that leads up to the second floor where my room is," said Primrose.

They walked cautiously through the foyer and went up to the second floor.

Lucinda and Agent Bradley checked the first two rooms.

"Something doesn't *feel* right," said Primrose.

As they moved through the house, a shuffling noise became audible in one of the rooms down the hall from where they were.

"The noise is coming from my room," Primrose whispered.

"Stay back, Primrose," Agent Bradley instructed as he slowly walked towards the room.

Lucinda readied her stylus as she followed behind. Agent Bradley kicked the door open and ran in. There was a man tied to a chair in the middle of the room. His mouth had been stuffed with a sock. Primrose ran into the room after them.

"Dad!" She yelled.

They began cutting the ropes and Lucinda removed the sock from his mouth.

"Primrose!" He shouted as he gasped for air.

"What happened?" Primrose asked with concern.

"Vamps. A female and two other male vampires. They stormed in through the front door and demanded that we tell them where you were and when we said we didn't know, they tied me up. Primrose, they *took* your mother," he cried.

"What?!" Asked Primrose. Her eyes widened with fear.

"Primrose, we *need* to get back to headquarters. Grab your belongings and anything that you will be needing. Mr. Evans, we'll find your wife. In the meantime, we'll cast the Bulwark spell over your property to protect you," said Lucinda.

"Just call me Michael. And…thank you," said Mr. Evans, still shaken up.

Lucinda and Agent Bradley casted the Bulwark spell together. Blue and purple mist surrounded the manor inside and out.

Primrose grabbed a duffle and a suitcase out of her closet. She took the suitcase, ran out to the hall, and stopped in front of another bedroom door. She punched a code into the keypad of the doorknob and it made a whirring sound before opening. It was her alchemy room. She filled the suitcase with her elixirs, then ran back into her bedroom and started shoving clothes into her duffle bag.

"Where will you guys go?" Asked Mr. Evans.

"Somewhere safe. I promise we will take care of your daughter, Michael," said Lucinda.

Primrose finished packing and walked over to her father.

"Dad, I'll bring mom back. Just stay here until I do," said Primrose as she gave him a hug and kiss.

She noticed a piece of paper sticking out from the back of the chair. She pulled it off and began to read it out loud.

"Bring the powers of Honora Summerland to the mausoleum tonight at dusk. Come alone or you will never see Violet Evans ever again," Primrose read. "Mom!" She cried.

Lucinda placed her hand gently on Primrose's arm.

"I understand how you feel right now but we are running out of time. We *must* return to headquarters as quickly as possible. Come on!" Said Lucinda as she turned towards the door and walked out.

Primrose gave her father another hug and all three of them ran out towards the SUV. Lucinda waved her stylus in front of her and her SUV reappeared. They all jumped into the car and drove off towards Crystal Brooks.

"What happened in there? Primrose, are you alright?" Asked Hazel.

"Heidi took my mother. They threatened to kill her if we don't hand over what we took from the arboretum. They want me to bring it to the mausoleum tonight…alone," said Primrose as tears began to run down her cheeks.

"We can't let you do that! Luce, what are we going to do?" Asked Hazel.

"I'm not sure but we will definitely need Duke's help to come up with a plan," said Lucinda.

Lucinda drove as fast as she could back to headquarters, even running a couple of red lights. She didn't care. More than one life was in danger now and they were running out of time. Lucinda parked right in front of the North building and they all jumped out of the car, then ran up to Duke's office.

Duke stood up from his desk as he saw the four of them running towards him.

"Whoa! What's going on?" Asked Duke with concern.

"Heidi Hendrix broke into the Evans manor and took Primrose's mother as hostage," said Lucinda, out of breath.

"She left a note, threatening to kill Violet Evans if she does not get the powers of Summerland *tonight*," Agent Bradley explained.

"She wants me to deliver it to the mausoleum at dusk, alone," added Primrose.

Duke sat back down and rubbed his forehead, then glanced down at his watch.

"Okay. We have two hours until dusk. Primrose will have to enter the mausoleum alone," said Duke.

"What?! She can't! Heidi will have her killed!" said Hazel angrily.

Duke raised his hand to calm Hazel down.

"Primrose, you will enter *alone* and you will tell Heidi about the seeds but we will use regular seeds to distract her. Lucinda, Agent Bradley, and I will walk in behind her under the Obscure spell so they can't see us. Once she is distracted, we may have to reveal ourselves and fight. When that happens, Primrose, I need you to get your mother out of there as fast as your wings can take you," said Duke firmly.

"I'll go find Leah and Tyler to let them know what happened," said Hazel.

"Alright everyone, we need to move quickly. I'm going to gear up and I'll meet you guys up front in fifteen minutes," said Duke. Everyone nodded and left his office.

Lucinda, Primrose, and Agent Bradley waited for Duke at the front doors. He showed up shortly after they got there.

"Hey, wait up!" They heard a voice yell from the back of the foyer.

Duke turned around. It was Hazel, heading towards them, outfitted in A.E. gear.

"You guys *aren't* going without me. I've got some pay back to do," said Hazel confidently.

Duke opened his mouth to say something but realized it was too late when Hazel walked past him and climbed into the SUV. Lucinda smiled and nodded her head in approval, climbing into the driver's seat as everyone else got in.

"Before I forget, here are four regular rose seeds," said Duke as he handed a vial with seeds to Primrose.

"Hazel, you will stay behind us at *all* times. Prepare to get Violet Evans out of there the second we come out of the Obscure spell," Duke instructed.

"You got it," said Hazel as she gathered her hair into a ponytail.

Lucinda slowed down as they got closer to the cemetery.

"We'll park here. It's two blocks away and they won't be able to spot us," said Lucinda.

They got out of the car once she was parked.

"Alright, Hazel. Please stand in the middle," said Duke.

Hazel stood between the three of them. Agent Bradley, Lucinda, and Duke took their stylus out and began to cast the Obscure spell. Purple and blue mist surrounded all four of them.

"I guess it worked. I can't see any of you!" Primrose whispered loudly.

"You don't see us but we can see each other. Okay, start walking towards the cemetery. Don't be afraid. We are right behind you," said Duke.

Primrose took a breath, then started walking towards the cemetery. As she approached the gate, she noticed that it was already unlocked, pushing the gate open with ease. She walked towards the back of the cemetery to find the old Alexander mausoleum.

"The last time I was here, I was the one who was kidnapped and Victor was bitten by Marco. These vamps will pay for what they did," Hazel whispered.

When they got to the mausoleum, the sarcophagus was already opened. Primrose carefully walked down the stairs. Although she couldn't see them, Agent Bradley and Duke were on either sides of her. Hazel and Lucinda were right behind them. Lucinda had her stylus pointing straight into the darkness as they approached the room at the end of the tunnel. In the center of the room, Primrose's mother was unconscious and tied to a chair.

"Mother!" Yelled Primrose as she ran to her side.

Heidi appeared out of nowhere and ran towards Primrose in what appeared to be the speed of light. Heidi grabbed Primrose by the neck and slowly lifted her off the ground. Primrose started to choke, clawing at the hand around her neck. Then, Heidi tossed her onto the ground. Primrose yelped as she landed on the ground with a loud thud. Four guards ran into the room from the door, opposite of the main entrance. There were three male and a female guard dressed in black jumpsuits. Duke saw Hazel take a step towards the room, but he stopped her.

"WHERE IS IT?!" Heidi shouted at Primrose.

Heidi's voice was different from what Hazel remembered. It sounded deeper and raspy. Primrose reached into her purse and took the vial containing the four rose seeds.

"Do you I *look* like a farmer to you, pixie?" Asked Heidi as she began walking towards her.

"No, wait! It's the four seeds of desires! The Amaranth of Life, the Rose of Passion, the Black Orchid of death, and the Gardenia of Wealth. They are the most powerful plants in the world. It's what I found at the center of the arboretum," said Primrose, hoping Heidi believed her.

Heidi grabbed the vial from her and held it up to take a closer look.

"Now!" Yelled Duke.

The three of them ran into the room, dropping the spell and becoming visible again. Lucinda started to conjure fireballs and launched them at the guards. Two of the guards threw fireballs back at them. Heidi dashed out the back door as Agent Bradley conjured two blue orbs that were made up of electrical energy. He threw them as quickly as they were conjured and it hit one of the witch guards.

"Nice, stunnerball Bradley!" Yelled Duke.

Duke did a somersault on the ground as one of the male vampire guards jumped into the air and attempted to strike down on him with a knife. They all continued to fight as Hazel ran to cut Violet lose from the chair. Primrose crawled over to Hazel and pulled out a vial filled with light blue liquid. It was the Blue Butterfly elixir.

"Here, make her drink this!" Said Primrose as she handed the vial to Hazel.

Hazel grabbed the bottle and opened it. She squeezed Violet's mouth open and poured the elixir in. All of a sudden, there was a loud zapping sound and her head turned towards the noise. Duke was hit with a stunnerball and knocked unconscious.

"Duke!" Yelled Lucinda.

Primrose gathered all her strength and flew over to Duke. Agent Bradley and Lucinda continued to fight Heidi's other three guards as Primrose casted the Restoration aura on Duke and he slowly came to. He moaned then yelled in pain as he grabbed his left shoulder and Primrose noticed the blood seeping through his fingers.

"Hold on, Duke. This will stop the bleeding," said Primrose as she put her left hand slightly over his wound. She began to cast the Mend aura but his wound was too big for her to close up. Duke cringed and yelled out in pain again.

The female witch guard threw a stunnerball at Agent Bradley. He quickly casted a force field shield and deflected the stunnerball. It hit the wall as glowing blue sparks fell to the ground like fireworks.

He immediately conjured another stunnerball and aimed it straight at the witch guard. It hit her and threw her against the stone wall, knocking her unconscious.

Lucinda was on the ground wrestling the male vampire guard. His fangs inched closer and closer to Lucinda's neck. Out of nowhere, something shot through the guard's chest from the side and threw him off of her. She jumped to her feet and noticed an ice spear in the vampire's chest and turned to see where it had come from. Leah and Tyler stood by the entrance with their styluses drawn. They continued to conjure more ice spears at the last of the guards. The last vampire guard ran against the stone wall and dodged every one of the spears.

In the blink of an eye, the vampire guard stood right in front of Hazel. He grabbed Hazel by the throat and lifted her up until the tips of her shoes barely touched the ground. Then, Hazel remembered a defensive charm that Primrose recently taught her. She fluttered her wings and her body emitted a bright white glow. Waving her left hand over him, she casted the Hemlock charm. The vampire guard froze in place and the only things moving were his eyes. Hazel knew she only had a few minutes before the vampire would be able to move again.

"Hazel! Catch!" Yelled Primrose from across the room. She tossed a vial of bright pink liquid at Hazel and she barely caught it with her hands. She opened the bottle and squeezed the vampire's mouth open. Then, she poured the bright pink elixir into his mouth. Within seconds, the vampire guard started seizing and before she knew it, he exploded into a pile of gray ashes. Hazel dropped to the floor. She grunted as she hit the stone cold ground. Leah quickly ran over to her.

Tyler ran over to Lucinda and put one arm around her.

"Are you hurt?" Asked Tyler.

"I'm fine," Lucinda replied, looking up at him.

Agent Bradley glanced over at Tyler and Lucinda. Then, walked over to Primrose and helped Duke stand up.

"Let's get the hell out of here," said Duke, weakly.

They all rushed to the car, getting in, and pulling out fast enough to make the tires squeal. When they arrived back at headquarters, a handful of medical staff and agents stood in front of the manor. Agent Bradley had called Dr. Saunders on the way back. Once the car was parked, the medical staff and agents rushed over to help them. The medical staff put Hazel, Primrose, and Duke each in a wheelchair. The rest of the group went back to their suites to rest and decompress from everything that just occurred.

The next morning, Hazel woke up in the infirmary. As she adjusted her eyes to the light, she noticed someone sitting next to her on the bed.

"Hey, stranger," said the voice. She rubbed her eyes to see clearer.

"Victor!" She yelled as she sat up and threw her arms around him.

"You're okay?!" Hazel asked.

"Yea, I feel much better. Right before Leah and Tyler left for the mausoleum, they were able to finish the Amaranth of Life elixir. Dr.

Saunders administered it to me right away. I woke up last night, not long after you guys got back. Leah and Tyler told me what happened."

Hazel hugged him again. She held him tighter and longer this time.

"Get a room would ya? Some people are trying to recover here!" Yelled Duke from across the room. Duke was sitting up on the bed and Hazel noticed the sling on his left arm.

"Are you okay, Duke?" Asked Hazel.

"I'll be fine," he replied with a smile.

Primrose was in the bed next to Duke.

"Primrose, how are you feeling?" Asked Hazel.

"My whole body is sore but nothing my elixirs can't fix," she replied.

Just then, Leah, Lucinda, and Tyler walked into the room.

"Hazel!" Leah shouted as she ran to her sister.

Leah and Lucinda hugged her.

"I'm glad you're okay," said Leah softly.

"Thanks for coming when you did. You guys saved me from that vamp," said Lucinda gratefully.

Leah and Tyler looked at each other and smiled. Then, Leah walked over to Duke and Tyler walked over to Primrose.

"Hey, your mom's going to be fine. She is recovering in the next room," Tyler told her.

"Thanks, I'll check on her in a bit," said Primrose with a smile.

"I'm glad everyone is okay. I'll come and check on you guys later. I've got a report to write," said Lucinda as she waved them goodbye and left the infirmary.

"But Heidi escaped and now she knows about the seeds," said Primrose with concern.

"Don't worry Primrose, we'll find her and hold her accountable for what she's done. I'm just glad no one got seriously injured," said Duke.

Lucinda went to look for Agent Bradley to make sure he was okay. She found him in his office and he was typing away on his keyboard. She knocked on the door.

"Hey Evan, got a minute?" Asked Lucinda.

"Yea, of course," he said.

"I wanted to make sure you were alright…and I wondered if you still wanted to talk," said Lucinda.

"Yea, I'm okay. You?" He asked as he continued to type on his keyboard.

"Just some cuts and scrapes but I think I'll live," she joked.

"Listen I…" she began to say.

"I'm just glad everyone got back safely," He cut her off and there was silence for a second.

"I thought you wanted to talk," said Lucinda, offended that he's being so abrupt.

Agent Bradley let out a breath of air.

"Look, I'm sorry. I did..." said Agent Bradley.

"But not anymore?"

"Well, yesterday when I asked you to have dinner together, I wanted to see if...maybe you still felt something for me. But I see that you've moved on."

"What are you talking about?" She asked with a confused look on her face.

"I saw the look on your faces, between you and Tyler at the mausoleum."

"Oh…" said Lucinda.

"Luce, I'm happy if you are. I wouldn't want to be the one holding you back anymore," said Agent Bradley in a friendly tone.

She stared at him for a second and tears started to build up in her eyes.

"Thank you, Evan…for understanding….and always having my back," said Lucinda fondly.

"Of course, no problem," he replied with a smile.

Lucinda nodded at him and walked out of his office. On the way back to the suites, Leah saw Lucinda walking down the hall.

"Lucinda! Wait up!" She called, jogging towards her.

She could tell Lucinda had been crying. "Hey…what's wrong?"

"It's…nothing." Lucinda said as she sniffled.

"Luce…you can trust me. What's wrong?" Asked Leah.

"After I left the infirmary, I went to check on Evan," said Lucinda.

"Agent Bradley? Why? He seemed fine when I saw him last night. What happened?" Asked Leah.

"Yea, no he's fine…It's just that, yesterday before we accompanied the girls to grab their belongings, he suggested that we have a conversation when we got back. Obviously, that didn't happen due to the events that followed. So, I went to talk to him just now," said Lucinda as she started to get emotional again.

"Let's get inside first," said Leah.

They both went into the common room and into Leah's suite.

"Okay…what did you guys talk about?" Asked Leah.

"We were supposed to talk about the break-up. He said there were things left unsaid," said Lucinda.

"Wait, what? You and Agent Bradley dated?" Asked Leah.

"Yes, I ended it a week before you guys arrived at Hallowed Falls. I felt like I couldn't do my job while having to work so closely with my boyfriend at the same time. It became too difficult. So, I broke it off," said Lucinda.

"Oh wow…okay…well, from the sound of it, he probably still has feelings for you. Right? I mean, isn't that why he wanted to speak to you yesterday? What did he say to you just now?" Asked Leah.

"He said that he wants me to be happy and that he thought I moved on…with Tyler," said Lucinda.

"Tyler? Why would he…? Oh…the mausoleum?" Asked Leah.

Lucinda nodded.

"Do you have feelings for Tyler?" Asked Leah curiously.

"I don't know. I guess…there *is* a small spark between us. We had lunch together the other day and I really enjoyed his company," Lucinda shrugged.

"Okay…do you still have feelings for Agent Bradley?" Asked Leah.

"That's the thing, I thought I had moved on. But what he just said to me, reminded me of what a good guy he is and he *always* has my back. On the other hand, there's Tyler. He's genuine, caring, and I feel so comfortable around him. He…calms me," said Lucinda.

"That's true, you are pretty high strung most of the time," Leah joked.

Lucinda slapped Leah's arm playfully.

"Ouch! Joking!" Said Leah, rubbing her arm. "In all seriousness, maybe you should spend some time with Tyler and give Agent Bradley some space before trying to talk it out again. You'll get a better clarification of what you really want."

Lucinda sighed and wiped her cheeks with the back of her hand.

"I don't know," said Lucinda. "I'm going to finish my report first, I'll meet you guys later for dinner."

"I hope you feel better by then," said Leah with a sympathetic smile.

The next day, Agent Bradley was having lunch in the dining hall when he noticed Primrose walking over to another table and sat down. He picked up his lunch tray and walked over to her.

"Hi, mind if I join you?" Asked Agent Bradley.

Primrose looked up at him.

"No, of course not," said Primrose with a smile.

Agent Bradley sat down across from her.

"I didn't get a chance to thank you," said Agent Bradley.

"For what?" Asked Primrose.

"For saving my life."

"Oh…it's no problem at all. I mean, you were put in danger because of me. I should be the one thanking you."

There was silence for a moment.

"Um…I was going to check on Duke in the infirmary after lunch, would you like to accompany me?" He asked.

"Sure, I was going to check on my mother as well," said Primrose.

When Agent Bradley and Primrose were done eating. They walked to the infirmary together. The infirmary building was right next to the manor, opposite of the garden, behind the South Building. The recovery rooms were on the third floor and they visited Primrose's mother first. Violet Evans was sitting up on the infirmary bed and reading a magazine. Her wavy dark blonde hair looked perfect, almost as if she had just come out of the salon and her vibrant blue eyes lit up when they walked in.

"Oh, hey sweetie!" Said Violet.

"Hi, mom. How are you feeling?" Asked Primrose.

"I'm doing much better. Your father will be picking me up later this afternoon. And…this is?" Asked Violet as she peered past Primrose.

Agent Bradley stepped out from behind Primrose.

"Hello, Mrs. Evans. I'm Evan Bradley. I'm glad to see that you are doing better," said Agent Bradley politely.

Violet grinned and couldn't stop staring at him.

"Thank you for accompanying my daughter to see me. He's a handsome one, Primrose," said Violet.

"Mom! This is *Agent* Bradley. He is one of the agents that helped rescue you," said Primrose. She could feel the heat rise up from her neck to her cheeks from the embarrassment.

"Oh, wow. I certainly owe you a thank you, then. How about you come by the manor for dinner one of these nights, hmm?" Asked Violet.

"I would like that very much, Mrs. Evans," said Agent Bradley with a smile.

"I'll let you guys talk. I'm going to check on Duke." said Agent Bradley.

"Okay, I'll catch you later!" Said Primrose with awkward chuckle.

Agent Bradley smiled and walked out of the room.

"Sooo? What a cute boy! Are you guys dating?" Asked Violet, grinning from ear to ear.

Primrose sat down on the bed next to her mother.

"No, mom. He was just being friendly," said Primrose, rolling her eyes.

"Well, he definitely isn't married. I didn't spot a ring," said Violet.

"Oh, geez. What time did you say dad was coming?" Asked Primrose.

"Alright, alright! I'll stop."

"Hey, did you know that we are related to the Plumerias?" Asked Primrose.

"We're what?" Asked Violet with a confused look.

"According to Honora's private journals, Gregoro was Lavender Summerland's father," said Primrose.

"Oh my…so…Honora didn't *actually* use the Fertility elixir and spell?" Asked Violet.

"No, it turns out that Honora and Gregoro were in love at twenty years old and they were forced to separate when her father found out," Primrose explained.

"Wait, so Leah and Hazel…?" Asked Violet.

"They're my cousins," said Primrose.

"Oh, that's wonderful honey. I was worried that you'd be all alone when we moved to Hallowed Falls and you having to leave all your friends behind," said Violet, feeling relieved.

"Yea, they're really good people. I'm glad to have found them."

Just then, a nurse walked over to them.

"Mrs. Evans? Your husband's downstairs waiting for you," said the nurse.

"Thank you," said Violet politely.

Primrose helped her mother off the bed and after she got changed, they went down to the registration desk on the ground floor of the infirmary. Michael Evans was sitting in the waiting area. Primrose ran over to Michael and gave him a hug.

"Hey dad," said Primrose.

"Hey, sweetie," said Michael.

Michael hugged and kissed Violet.

"I've already filled out all the paperwork. Ready when you guys are," said Michael.

"Um, actually guys…I'm going to stay here for a while. I really think I can help the A.E. with this" said Primrose.

Her parents glanced at each other and were silent for a minute.

"Alright, sweetheart. Just make sure you call us and be careful," said Violet.

"I know. I will," said Primrose.

Leah was dropping off a file at the registration desk when she saw Primrose and her parents standing in the waiting area.

"Hi, Mr. and Mrs. Evans. I'm glad to see you've fully recovered," Leah smiled.

"Oh, Leah. Sweetie!" Said Violet as she approached Leah to hug her.

"Michael, darling. Did you know that we're related to the Plumerias?" Asked Violet.

"We're what?" Asked Michael, looking confused.

"Oh, I'll catch you up at home. We really should get going," Violet said as she walked out of the automatic doors. "It's going to be an hour drive back and who knows what traffic will be like. Primrose, we love you honey. Tell me more about you and Agent Bradley when you can!" Violet shouted over her shoulder and waved at them.

Violet and Michael got into their car. Primrose and Leah watched them drive towards the gates and disappear into the road.

"Want to grab coffee?" Asked Leah.

"Sure, I'd prefer wine but coffee will do," said Primrose with a smile.

Leah chuckled. They walked into the main building and towards the café.

"Your mom met Agent Bradley?" Asked Leah curiously.

"Uh…yea, we happened to be having lunch around the same time and we ended up going to the infirmary together," said Primrose nonchalantly.

"What did she mean by you *and* Agent Bradley?" Asked Leah with a raised brow.

"Oh, she was being silly. She thought we were dating, but I explained to her that he was one of the agents that rescued her," Primrose chuckled. "Actually…do you happen to know if Agent Bradley is seeing anyone?"

"Um, I'm not really sure, but I do know that he and Lucinda broke up only recently," said Leah.

"Oh…" said Primrose.

Leah couldn't help but notice that Primrose looked a bit disappointed.

"Hey, I'm pretty much done with my temporary position at the infirmary. Do you want to check out the indoor pool today?" Asked Leah.

"Sure. That sounds like fun," said Primrose.

They stopped at the café and headed back to the common room.

When they got there, Hazel and Victor were sitting in front of the fireplace.

"Hey guys," said Leah.

"Hey!" Victor responded.

"We're heading to the pool, do you guys want to come with us?" Asked Primrose.

"Um, yea. We'll meet you there," said Hazel.

Primrose and Leah went into their own suites to change.

Hazel turned her head back to Victor.

"You sure missed a lot, but I'm *so* glad you're back," said Hazel.

She looked up at him as she smiled broadly. Victor turned his head to look at her at the same time, their noses were only a few inches apart but she didn't move away. He slowly reached for her waist and pulled her in for a kiss. His lips melted into hers and he teased her with his tongue. She reached up towards the back of his neck and pulled him in deeper. Then, they slowly pulled away.

"That was...nice," said Hazel with a smile.

"Just *nice*?" Victor teased.

She laughed and Victor felt something flutter in his stomach. Something he hadn't felt in a long time. Just then, Leah and Primrose came back out of their suites.

"Alright, you guys still coming?" Asked Leah.

"Yea, we're gonna get changed right now," said Hazel as she gave him wink.

Leah left the room with Primrose and got onto the elevator. They got off on the top floor of the main building and noticed only a couple of other agents around as they tried to find some chairs. The ceiling was made of glass panels and they were able to see the clear sky with the sun beaming down on the pool. The water sparkled as it reflect the light and Leah couldn't wait to get in. Hazel and Victor joined them shortly after. They decided to get into the hot tub first.

"Hey, so did your dad come pick up your mom yet?" Asked Hazel as she sat down next to Primrose.

"Yea, they left about half an hour ago," said Primrose.

"I'm ready to do a lap. I'll be right back," said Victor as he got up from the steaming water.

"Me too!" Leah exclaimed..

They both jumped into the pool, making two large splashes. Hazel giggled and then turned back to Primrose, who appeared to be lost in thought.

"Hey, what's on your mind?" Asked Hazel as she nudged Primrose with her elbow.

"Just thinking about how Heidi is still out there." said Primrose shaking her head slowly.

"Yea, I know. Maybe we can go find Duke later and see if there's anything else we can do to help," Hazel suggested.

Primrose nodded in agreement.

After spending about an hour at the pool, Hazel and Primrose went to see Duke in the recovery room.

"Hi, Duke. How's your shoulder?" Asked Primrose.

"Oh, hey. It's gotten a lot better. Dr. Saunders said that I'll only have to wear the sling for another week. What brings you two here?" Asked Duke.

"We wanted to check on you and also…we were wondering if there's anything we can do to help find Heidi," said Hazel.

"As of right now, we have a team of agents tracking her. Also, you guys aren't official A.E. agents and don't really have any field training," said Duke.

"You're right, but we really want to help," said Hazel.

"Okay, I'm sure there's something I can do. We don't currently have any fairies working in the agency. Primrose, your skill in elixir making would be very helpful to the Department of Magical Resources. Hazel, you can hone your charms and auras that could be helpful during certain missions. Why don't you guys head to Employee Services in the South building. I'll call ahead and let them know that I sent you there," said Duke.

"Really? You'd do that?" Asked Primrose.

"Thank you, Duke. You know, Leah's pretty lucky to have you," said Hazel.

Duke chuckled.

"Thanks, Hazel. Based on what I've seen, I feel that you guys have the skills to become official agents but you'll need training first," said Duke.

Hazel gave Duke a grateful smile and headed towards the South building.

When they walked in, they were greeted by the sight of a large grey desk, behind it was a woman with short, straight black hair and brown eyes, on the phone. The desk sat in the middle of a large room with bright white walls and large photographs with scenic views throughout the room. They could see two hallways behind the desk on either sides. She hung up the phone when she saw them walk in.

"Excuse me, hi," said Primrose politely.

The young woman looked up and smiled.

"Hello, welcome. You're Hazel and Primrose, correct?" The woman asked.

"Uh, yes. Duke sent us here," said Hazel.

"Yes, I actually just got off the phone with him. Senior Director Lyza Beth Emelio will be with you in a moment. Please have a seat in the waiting area," said Rosetta professionally.

"Thank you," said Primrose.

A few minutes later, a woman walked out, she appeared to be in her forties. Her blonde hair bouncing as she walked. Her crisp navy-blue suit brought out her brown eyes, pulling the effect of a professional, but flattering look. She smiled as she walked towards Hazel and Primrose, extending her hand as she introduced herself.

"Hi, I'm Lyza Beth. Please follow me this way."

Hazel and Primrose followed her down the hall and into an office at the end.

"Please have a seat. It is rare for a senior director to recommend civilians for the kind of work we do. You two must have really proven yourselves," said Lyza Beth, seemingly impressed.

"Yes, we have," said Hazel.

She walked around her desk and pulled out a drawer. She handed each of them a folder.

"I need you to fill out all the paperwork inside those folders. Then, I will have Department Director Rosetta take your photo up front. I'll be right back," said Lyza Beth as she stepped out of the office.

Lyza Beth walked back into the office shortly after they were done filling out paperwork. Hazel and Primrose handed the folders back to her.

"Alright, perfect. Let's get your photos taken and you guys can get started training," said Lyza Beth.

The girls followed her out of her office and back to the front desk where Rosetta was. Rosetta took them into a smaller office and took a photo of each of them. Ten minutes later, she handed them their official Aster Elites photo identification cards. Rosetta sat back down behind the front desk and typed something onto her computer.

"The barcodes on your ID cards will allow you to enter the estate and it must be on you at all times. You will now meet with Senior Director Logan Thompson in the Department of Magical Resources located on the second floor. He will be giving you further instructions on your training. The elevators are down the hall and to the left. And...good luck, ladies," said Rosetta.

"Thank you, Rosetta." said Hazel.

Rosetta smiled and nodded at them.

Hazel and Primrose walked towards the elevator and went up to the second floor. When the doors opened, they stepped out to a large office with about twenty desks all around. There were a couple of agents working on their computers and an agent who looked to be around their age approached them.

"Hi, are you ladies lost?" He asked.

"No, but where can we find the office of Senior Director Logan Thompson?" Asked Primrose.

"It's right this way. I'm Wyatt Kensington. Are you guys new around here?" He asked.

"Yes, Director Bryant recommended us," said Hazel.

"You guys must have really impressed him for him to refer you guys," said Agent Kensington.

They walked down the hall to the left of the elevators and passed about two doors before they stopped.

"Here's Director Thompson's office. Great to meet you ladies!" Said Agent Kensington.

"Thank you," said Hazel.

The door was already wide open but Hazel knocked anyway.

"Come in," said Director Thompson. He appeared to be in his mid-fifties with short brown hair and gray eyes behind a pair of reading glasses.

"Hi, I'm Hazel and this is Primrose. Rosetta sent us up here for further instructions," said Hazel.

"Oh, yes. I received the emails from Duke and Rosetta. We're happy to hear that two fairies have decided to join the agency. No offense, but since fairies are not usually social beings, we don't have too many who have interest in joining the A.E. Especially since the first Alexander killings began," he said.

"None taken. We decided to join because Marco's descendant is still out there. We know how dangerous she is and we believe that we can help," said Hazel firmly.

"Ah, yes. I had heard about that. Well, first let me tell you about our department. The Department of Magical Resources is made up of two sub-departments. One is spells and enchantments and the other is potions and elixirs. Let's see here," said Director Thompson. He looked at his computer screen.

"Hazel, I'm going to have you go two doors down to the office of Department Director Eliana Marchand. She will set you up on an aptitude test and Primrose, I'm going to have Agent Kensington take you to the potions lab," he instructed.

Hazel knocked on Director Eliana Marchand's office.

"Come on in," said Director Marchand.

"Hi, I'm Hazel Plumeria. I was sent over here for an aptitude test?" said Hazel.

"Yes, of course. I'm Eliana Marchand, pleased to meet you," she introduced herself as she extended her hand.

Hazel shook her hand. Eliana seemed to be in her thirties and had straight blonde hair that went just past her shoulders.

"Let me set you up on the computer right here. The test will help us understand where you are as far as your knowledge on magic and its history. When that is completed, I will bring you up to the spells lab and test your magical skills. These tests will help us understand where to continue your growth and help hone your magical abilities," said Director Marchand.

Right outside of Eliana's office was a cubicle with a computer desk and chair. She opened a program on the computer and got Hazel started on it.

Back in Director Thompson's office, Primrose waited for her escort. Director Thompson picked up the phone on his desk and dialed.

"Hey, Agent Kensington. Can you come by my office? Thanks," said Director Thompson and hung up the phone.

Agent Kensington popped his head into the office.

"Hi, director. What can I do for you?"

"Can you take Primrose to the potions lab and show her around?"

"Of course. This way, Miss Primrose."

"Thank you, director." said Primrose as she gave Director Thompson a nod and a smile, then followed Agent Kensington towards the elevators.

"So, what made you decide to become an agent?" Asked Agent Kensington as they waited for the elevator.

"I've watched enough friends get hurt because of me. I want to be able to do something about it," said Primrose.

The elevator doors opened and they stepped in.

"If you don't mind me asking, what happened?" Asked Agent Kensington.

"An explosive was thrown into my flower shop back in Hallowed Falls and…my cousin, Hazel burned her arm trying to put the fire out. I took her to the hospital and a day later, she was abducted by Marco Alexander. We found her at the local cemetery, tied to a chair and sedated. I tricked Marco into drinking Zingallium and it should have killed him. We saved Hazel but Heidi, Marco's great-great niece was his accomplice and she is still out there. She broke into my home, attacked my father, and kidnapped my mother. I need to stop her before anyone else gets hurt," said Primrose. As she recalled all the events that had occurred, she began to feel angry and sad at the same time.

"That's awful. I'm sorry that happened to your loved ones," said Agent Kensington.

"Thanks," said Primrose with a half-smile. The elevator doors opened and they took it to the third floor.

Chapter 6

Leah had just stepped out of the shower when her cellphone rang.

"Oh, hi Dr. Saunders," said Leah.

"Hi, Leah. I forgot to ask you something before you left for the day. Can you please come see me at my office when you get a moment?" Asked Dr. Saunders over the phone.

"Oh, of course. I'll be right over," said Leah.

Leah got dressed and headed towards the infirmary building. She arrived at Dr. Saunders' office fifteen minutes later.

"Hi, Dr. Saunders. Was there something wrong with my paperwork?" Asked Leah.

"No, no. Please, have a seat," said Dr. Saunders with a friendly smile.

Leah sat down across from her.

"You've done an excellent job here the A.E. infirmary. From what I've seen so far, your skills would be a huge contribution to our agency. I've been searching for a strong candidate like you to take on the Department Director position and I would like to offer it to you. If you accept, you would be in charge of the medical staff and report to me."

Leah's eyes widened and she smiled from ear to ear.

"That's wonderful! Yes, I accept. I will send my official resignation letter to Hallowed Falls today," said Leah excitedly.

"Great, in the meantime. You can fill out the necessary paperwork at Employee Services located in the South building," said Dr. Saunders.

"Perfect, I'll head over there right now. Thank you so much, Dr. Saunders," said Leah as she shook her hand.

Just as Leah walked out of the office, Tyler was walking in.

"Oh, hey!" Said Leah as she walked past him.

"Hey!" Said Tyler after her.

Tyler knocked on the office door.

"Hi, you wanted to see me?" He asked.

"Yes, please have a seat," Dr. Saunders offered.

"I've discussed your work with Senior Director Duke and the Chief of Directors. We would love for you to join our medical team. Would you be interested?" Asked Dr. Saunders.

"That sounds like a great opportunity. I'd love to be a part of your team," said Tyler gratefully.

"Fantastic! You can head on over to Employee Services to fill out some paperwork. I'll give the Director Rosetta, a heads up," said Dr. Saunders as she picked up her phone and began dialing.

Tyler thanked her and headed towards the South building waiting area where Leah was already sitting.

"Did you Dr. Saunders offer you a position as well?" Asked Tyler as he sat down next to Leah.

She nodded.

"Yea, she offered me the Department Director position," said Leah happily.

"That's great! Congrats!" Said Tyler.

"Thanks, I'm glad we get to work together again," said Leah.

Rosetta got up from her desk and walked over to them.

"Tyler? Leah? You may follow me," said Rosetta.

They both got up and followed her down the hallway. When they got to the office, Lyza Beth stood up from behind her desk.

"Hi, I'm Senior Director Lyza Beth. Please have a seat," she said.

Tyler and Leah both took a seat. When Leah and Tyler finished filling out the paperwork, Lyza Beth walked them back to the front to get their photos taken.

They looked over when they heard footsteps coming down the hall, noticing Primrose and Hazel walking towards them.

"Hey guys, what are you doing here?" Asked Leah.

"We wanted to continue to help the A.E. and help track down Heidi. So, Duke sent us over here. We're official A.E. agents now. Our training begins tomorrow," said Hazel happily.

"Oh, how exciting! Tyler and I were offered positions, too," said Leah with a huge smile.

They all took a moment to congratulate each other.

"Will you guys meet us in the dining hall when you're done?" Asked Primrose.

"Yea, of course!" Leah exclaimed.

Hazel and Primrose walked out the door. Rosetta took Tyler and Leah into a small office to take their photos. A few moments later, she handed them their official identification cards. Then, they headed back to the main building to meet with Hazel and Primrose.

Tyler and Leah walked into the dining hall together and joined the others at a table. Shortly after, Agent Bradley walked in with two other agents and sat at a nearby table. He waved to them and smiled at Primrose. She smiled back and tucked a piece of hair behind her ear. Lucinda noticed and was surprised by their exchange.

When they were finished eating, Tyler got up and walked over to Lucinda.

"Hey, want to take a walk with me?" Asked Tyler.

"Sure," said Lucinda.

She got up and turned to glance over at Agent Bradley. He was still chatting with the other two agents. Tyler and Lucinda left the dining hall. They went down to the ground floor and out into the garden. As soon as they stepped out to the garden, the warm evening breeze rushed towards them. There were cirrostratus clouds in the sky standing out from the background of orange, purple, and blue hues. Lucinda took in a deep breath. The air smelled like pine trees and rain. They walked towards the fountain at the center of the garden and sat down.

"I figured, we could continue our conversation from the other day," said Tyler.

Lucinda gave him a smile. She was actually excited to have some alone time with him.

"So, you asked me what my story was last time. What's yours? Did you grow up in Hallowed Falls?" He asked.

"Yes, I actually lived in Hallowed Falls with my father until I was twenty years old. That's around the time I joined the Aster Elites. We moved to Crystal Brooks after that," said Lucinda.

"That's interesting," said Tyler.

"Do you have any siblings?" Asked Lucinda.

"No, I wish I did. That would've been something. My parents actually had a hard time conceiving. They had me in their late-thirties. What about you?" Asked Tyler.

"I'm the only child as well… my mother died during a mission when I was fifteen years old," said Lucinda.

"I'm sorry to hear that, Luce." said Tyler sincerely.

Lucinda started to feel tears fill her eyes, but she didn't want Tyler to see and blinked them back.

"Um…thanks. I should head back now. I promised Hazel I'd prep her for training tomorrow," said Lucinda.

"Okay, I'll walk with you," said Tyler as they got up and walked towards the manor.

Victor looked down at his watch and he made his way to Duke's office. He hadn't really seen much of Duke ever since he recovered from his coma. Duke was sitting behind his desk when Victor knocked on his door and walked in.

"Hey Vick, I'm almost done with this report and then we can go grab dinner," said Duke as he typed away on his computer.

"That's fine. I'm in no rush," said Victor as he took the seat across from him.

"So, how's it feel to be back at headquarters after being away the last couple of years?" Asked Duke.

"It certainly feels…strange. There's so many memories inside these walls," said Victor as he cracked his knuckles.

"Are you ready to come back?" Asked Duke as he started to type again.

"I don't think so, I'm pretty content with where I am. Actually, I'm heading back soon," said Victor.

"Really? What about Hazel? Her training begins tomorrow," asked Duke with raised eyebrows.

"I'm not sure. I haven't told her yet," Victor replied. He rubbed his forehead as he thought about it.

"You know the chief will always welcome you back with open arms. I hope you do change your mind," said Duke.

"I'll think about it some more but I just need to go back and at least check on my family," said Victor.

"Alright buddy, I'm ready to eat. You comin'?" Asked Duke as he pushed himself away from the desk and stood up slowly.

"Yea," Victor answered as he stood up from the chair.

Duke and Victor walked into the dining hall. They joined Leah, Hazel, and Primrose at their table. Primrose began to feel like a third wheel as soon as Duke and Victor sat down.

"I think I'm going to get some hot tea at the café. I'll see you guys back at the suites," said Primrose as she got up and started to leave.

"We'll see you back at the suites, then," said Hazel.

Agent Bradley looked up right when Primrose started walking out of the dining hall.

"I'll catch you guys later," he said as he got up and tried to catch up to her.

Primrose pressed the button for the elevator and the doors opened.

"Hey, Primrose. Wait up!" Yelled Agent Bradley as he broke into a jog towards her.

Primrose put her arm out to hold the elevator doors.

"Where are you headed?" He asked.

"To the café for some tea…and you?" Asked Primrose.

"I'd like to accompany you if that's okay," said Agent Bradley.

"Um…sure," said Primrose.

When the elevator doors opened on the ground floor, Lucinda and Tyler were standing there.

"Oh, hey Primrose…Agent Bradley," said Lucinda.

"Hey, Luce. We're headed to the café, would you guys like to join?" Asked Primrose.

Lucinda glanced at Agent Bradley.

"Um…no thanks, you guys go ahead. I'm actually pretty exhausted. I'll see you guys tomorrow," said Lucinda as she walked past them and into the elevator.

"Goodnight, guys," said Tyler as he followed her.

"Goodnight," said Primrose.

Primrose and Agent Bradley stood there for a second, then stared at each other as the elevator doors closed. She broke their gaze by looking down at her hands, realizing she was gripping them so tightly, it was as if they were a knot. All of a sudden, she felt Agent Bradley's warm hands gently touch the top of hers.

"Hey…are you okay? Is something wrong?" Asked Agent Bradley.

He bent his knees slightly and tilted his head to look at her face. She stayed silent for a moment and pulled her hands out from under his.

"Um, yea…I think I'm going to skip the café tonight. I'm actually feeling pretty exhausted, too. I have a long day tomorrow at training," said Primrose as she kept her eyes on the ground.

"Oh…okay. Let me walk you back to your suite," said Agent Bradley as he pushed the button for the elevator.

"No!" Exclaimed Primrose. "I-I mean...I'll be okay. Goodnight... Agent Bradley."

When the elevator doors opened, she quickly stepped in and pushed the button for the fifth floor. She leaned against the wall next to the buttons and stood very still as the doors closed.

"Goodnight...Primrose," said Agent Bradley.

She felt her stomach tighten, her heart beating fast. For the first time in her life, she felt an emotion that she didn't quite understand. It was a mixture of sadness, dread, and shame. She felt dreadful because she knew deep inside, there was still something between Agent Bradley and Lucinda. She had witnessed the way Lucinda looked at Agent Bradley in the dining hall and the way she looked at him again, at the elevators. Sadness because she really didn't want to walk away from the warmth of his hands but she would never do anything to hurt Lucinda. Shame because she had feelings for someone she felt she shouldn't.

The next morning, Primrose and Hazel woke up at the break of dawn. They both had to meet Director Marchand in her office at six-thirty. When they got to her office, Hazel knocked on the door and she was typing away behind her desk.

"Come in," said Director Marchand.

"Good morning, agents," said Director Marchand as she continued to type on her computer. Finishing up, she rose from her chair. They quickly noticed, rather than a professional business suit, she was wearing a light gray track suit with two red stripes that ran along the sides.

"Alright, follow me," she said as she walked around her desk and out of the office.

Primrose and Hazel followed behind her. They stopped in front of the elevator.

"I'm taking you to the training room upstairs. We're going to start off with basic self-defense lessons," said Director Marchand.

The elevator doors opened, and they all got in. When the doors opened again, there was a large room about the same size as the entire office floor downstairs. The wooden floor reminded Hazel of her high school gym and the walls had about five inches of light gray leather padding. It looked like a large room made for asylum patients. Director Marchand walked to the center of the floor.

"Let's start with some stretches," said Director Marchand.

They spent about fifteen minutes stretching. Afterwards, she taught them some basic self-defense moves. They continued to practice for another hour and Director Marchand looked at her watch.

"He should be here soon," said Director Marchand.

"Is someone else joining us?" Asked Hazel.

Just then, the elevator doors opened and Agent Bradley stepped out.

"Agent Bradley?" Asked Hazel in a surprised tone.

He was wearing a fitted black V-neck t-shirt and black basketball shorts. Primrose felt her heart beat a little faster. She was excited to see him but at the same time, still feeling awkward from last night.

"Yes, Agent Bradley is one of the best agents in the Department of Protective Services and since their missions usually involve more combat than any other department, I figured that he would be the best to train you and provide more insight on what it is like to be out on the field," said Director Marchand.

Agent Bradley was standing up straight with his hands behind his back as Director Marchand walked past him. He gave her a nod as she got onto the elevator.

"Alright, I want to start with a particular exercise. Being fairies, you guys have the advantage of flight. It is imperative for you to have agility on the ground as well as in the air. You will begin with ten laps of flight around the room. You may begin," said Agent Bradley as he pushed the button on his stopwatch.

It took Hazel and Primrose almost twenty minutes to do ten laps of flight.

"And…time!" Yelled Agent Bradley.

Hazel and Primrose were out of breath. They floated down slowly and sat down on the ground. Hazel's wings were starting to feel strained.

"That was nineteen minutes and twenty-six seconds. You guys only began training but if you can get the time down to fifteen minutes, you should be in good shape as far as endurance goes. Now, in a combat situation, there will be times when things will be thrown at you. Whether it be fireballs or other hard objects, you will have to be able dodge anything that is thrown at you while you're up in the air. Otherwise, you lose your advantage and could get seriously injured.

"I'm going to use a low-level powerball and launch it at you. I need you to try your best to shift quickly from side to side. We'll start with Hazel," said Agent Bradley.

He raised his hands up to his sides and kept them parallel to the ground. Misty light blue orbs began to form underneath his palms. Hazel watched as the orbs grew to the size of baseballs. Primrose recognized the orbs. They were the same ones Lucinda had conjured when they were at the arboretum. Primrose observed while Agent Bradley tossed the powerballs, one after another, at Hazel. Hazel glided left and then swiftly to the right, successfully dodging both orbs. Then, as quickly as he conjured the powerball, he launched one more at Hazel. It was flying straight towards her. Hazel reacted quickly and did a somersault in the air.

"Wow!" Said Primrose as she clapped for her.

"That was awesome, Hazel. Great job!" Said Agent Bradley.

Hazel floated back down.

"Thanks!" She said as she breathed heavily, wiping a bead of sweat from her brow.

"Alright, Primrose you're up!" Said Agent Bradley.

Primrose felt her heart begin to race again. Agent Bradley began conjuring the powerballs in both hands. He launched the first one at her and she flew to the left. He launched another and she quickly glided downwards. She didn't see him launch the third powerball. All of a sudden, she felt a powerful gust of energy ram into her like an angry bull and grunted. The powerball struck her right in the abdomen and threw her across the room. She dropped and tumbled.

"Primrose!" Yelled Agent Bradley.

He ran over to her as quick as he could and dropped to one knee. He lifted her head up slightly with his left hand and his right hand supported her back.

"Primrose, are you alright?" Asked Agent Bradley.

"Yea...yea...I think I'm okay," said Primrose as she tried to catch her breath and sat up.

She supported herself with her right hand and leaned on her hip as she tried to stand up. She stood up halfway before her right knee gave out and grabbed onto his arms for balance. Agent Bradley caught her before she hit the ground again. Primrose suddenly became extremely aware of her hands on his arms. His skin felt smooth and his muscles were hard as rocks. Something about his warmth soothed her and for a second, she forgot she was just thrown across the room. She looked up at him and noticed the look of deep concern on his face.

"Hey...are you really okay?" He asked.

When she realized that he was still holding her, she quickly stood straight up and stepped out of his arms.

"I'm fine. Let's go again," said Primrose as she walked with a limp.

He shook his head slowly.

"No, that's all for today. We'll train again tomorrow," said Agent Bradley firmly as he turned and headed towards the elevator.

Hazel ran over to Primrose as she watched him get on the elevator.

"You alright? You're hurt aren't you," said Hazel softly.

"I'm fine. Really," said Primrose as she bent over and rubbed her right knee.

"Let's get cleaned up and find Leah," Hazel suggested.

Primrose nodded and put an arm over Hazel's shoulder. They made their way back slowly towards the manor and into their suites. Leah was on the computer desk when they walked in and turned to look at them.

"Oh my God, what happened to you guys?!" Leah exclaimed as she rushed over to them.

"Training. Evan was training us on flight agility and Primrose was struck by a powerball," said Hazel as she set Primrose down on the sofa.

"What?!" Asked Leah.

"Don't worry it was just a low-level powerball," said Primrose.

Leah crouched down to examine her leg.

"Your knee is swollen, it's probably just a sprain. I'll grab my kit," said Leah.

She went into her suite and came back out with a small first aid box. Leah punched into an icepack and laid it gently on Primrose's knee.

The coldness of the icepack made Primrose want to scream but she bit her lip and let out a low groan.

"Are you sure you guys want to continue to do this?" Asked Leah as she began to wrap Primrose's knee.

"Yes. I need to make sure Heidi doesn't hurt anyone else because of me," said Primrose sternly.

"I can't rest knowing that she's still out there and who knows what she'll do next," said Hazel.

"Okay, just... be more careful. I've got to head over to the infirmary in a few. I'll see you guys in a bit," said Leah as she finished wrapping Primrose's knee, then stood up and left the room.

Agent Bradley walked into his suite and lifted his shirt from the bottom, then pulled it over his head.

"I should've been more cautious. Now, she's hurt. That was a stupid move. But...I can't be overprotective of her. This is how all agents are trained. Making it easy isn't going to help her," he thought to himself as he took his shorts off.

He went into his bathroom and got into the shower. He turned the water on and let the warm water wash over his head. His thoughts drifted back to last night.

"What the hell happened? Am I scaring her off? All I intended to do was to get to know her better. Maybe I should back off. Maybe she already has her mind set on someone else," he thought as he dunked his head under the shower head and hoped that the water would just erase his memory of what happened last night. When he was done, he got dressed and headed for his office in the North building.

Meanwhile, Hazel and Primrose were resting in the common room.

"I'm starting to feel extremely sore and I'm too tired to cast the Restoration aura," said Hazel dragging her feet as she walked out from her suite.

Primrose was back on the chair by the fireplace staring into the fire. Hazel noticed Primrose fidgeting with her hands and they were in a knot. She sat down on the chair across from Primrose.

"I noticed something earlier... between you and Agent Bradley. The way he held you... it seemed like more than just a concerned friend. Is there anything you want to share?" Asked Hazel curiously.

Primrose looked up at Hazel and stared at her for a second before taking a deep breath.

"I think...no, I *know* I'm starting to have feelings for him. I've tried really hard to push it away but I just can't seem to," said Primrose, sounding disappointed at herself.

"Agent Bradley seems like a great guy. Why are you trying to push your feelings away?" Asked Hazel.

"Leah told me that he and Lucinda broke up only recently," said Primrose.

"Oh…I see…You don't think you can talk to Luce about it?"

"I've seen the way Lucinda looks at him. I know for a fact that she still *feels* something for him and I don't want to get in their way."

Just then, Victor knocked on the door. "Hey, Hazel. You got a minute? I really need to speak with you."

"Yea, sure," she replied. "I'll be right back," she told Primrose.

Hazel and Victor walked out onto the hallway.

"You should've seen me during training! Agent Bradley launched powerballs and…" Hazel began to say.

"That's awesome," said Victor flatly as he looked down at his shoes.

Hazel frowned.

"Is everything okay?" She asked.

"Yea…I'm fine. It's just…now that I'm fully recovered. I should head back to Hallowed Falls," said Victor.

"What? Why?" Asked Hazel.

"I need to make sure my family is okay. They've been left unprotected and Heidi is still out there somewhere," Victor explained.

"Oh…" said Hazel.

"Look, I hate that we won't be able to see each other as much, but I'll come see you as often as I can. I promise," said Victor. She could tell he really did feel bad about it, but she knows family always comes first and if she had been in his position, she'd do the same.

"Okay, well when are you heading back?" Asked Hazel.

"Now," said Victor.

"Promise to visit us every week?"

"I promise."

Hazel smiled and leaned in to kiss him. She made sure it was a long and deep kiss. She felt his arms slowly wrap around her. When he pulled away, he kept his hands at her waist and looked into her eyes.

"I love you," said Victor softly.

Hazel's eyes widened and then her lips broke into a huge smile.

"I love you, too," she whispered and gave him another kiss.

Hazel walked back into the common room, smiling from ear to ear.

"Is he okay?" Asked Primrose.

Hazel was beaming.

"Victor just told me he loved me," said Hazel, plopping down on the chair with a huge smile plastered on her face.

"That is so sweet!" said Primrose.

"Yea…but he's heading back to Hallowed Falls," Hazel shrugged.

"Already? Why?" Asked Primrose.

"He needs to make sure his family is okay," Hazel explained.

"Oh," said Primrose.

Hazel leaned forward on the chair.

"But back to your situation. I *really* think you need to talk to Lucinda about how you feel. You could be wrong," she shrugged. "Luce and Agent Bradley might just be friends now."

"Yea, I'll think about it," said Primrose, shaking her head and rubbing her forehead. "Let's grab lunch, I'm so hungry that I'm getting a headache."

Primrose and Hazel got up from the chairs and headed towards the elevators.

Down in the dining hall, Lucinda was heading towards the entrance as Agent Bradley was walking out and they crashed right into each other.

"Oh! Sorry!" Lucinda exclaimed as she quickly glanced up to see who she bumped into. Agent Bradley caught her in his arms and Lucinda grabbed onto him for balance. Just then, the elevator doors opened. Hazel and Primrose stepped out. The first thing they noticed was Agent Bradley and Lucinda standing there holding each other.

"Uh…You know what, I just realized I'm not hungry. I think I should go practice my defensive charms a bit more. I'll catch you later," said Primrose as she bolted towards the door and down the stairs.

"Primrose! Wait!" Agent Bradley yelled as he ran after Primrose.

Hazel walked over to Lucinda.

"What were you guys doing?" Asked Hazel.

"Nothing, I walked right into him and he just happened to catch me before I fell. Is…Primrose upset?" Asked Lucinda.

"She knows that you and Agent Bradley had a past. She admitted she has feelings for him but she doesn't want to step on your toes."

"My toes? Evan and I aren't together."

"It was apparent to her that there was still something between the two of you."

"I'll go talk to her."

"She's had quite a morning. I would give her some time. C'mon," said Hazel, tugging on her Lucinda's arm.

Lucinda glanced at the door to the stairway and then followed Hazel into the dining hall.

As soon as Primrose got to the first floor, she immediately casted the Micropixie aura and shrunk down to a tiny fairy. She looked like a two-inch glowing orb, just like she did when she was in the arboretum because she didn't want anyone seeing her upset. She flew across the foyer and out into the garden towards the fountain. She returned to normal size and sat down on the side facing away from the manor. Agent Bradley tried to catch up to Primrose but when he got to the ground floor, she had disappeared. He looked all around the foyer and she was nowhere in sight. He decided to go up to her suite just in case she went back. When he walked in, her suite was empty. He decided he would look for her again later.

"*Maybe I'll have a better chance during dinner time,*" he thought to himself. He left the common room and headed back to his office.

Primrose sat by the fountain and thought about what she had just seen in front of the dining hall entrance.

"*Why am I even upset that they were holding each other? They were a couple before. Lucinda had every right to be with Agent Bradley,*" she thought to herself. Then, she thought about the way she felt when they were together the other night after dinner and the way he held her earlier when she got injured during training. She shook her head to try and get rid of what she was feeling.

"There you are," a voice said from behind the fountain.

It startled her and she quickly turned around to look. It was Lucinda.

"We've been looking for you everywhere," said Lucinda softly.

"Oh…hey," said Primrose.

Lucinda sat down next to Primrose.

"What a gorgeous evening, huh?" Asked Lucinda, looking up at the sky.

Primrose looked up and realized it was starting to get dark. She hadn't realized how long she'd been sitting in the garden. Fireflies danced above the grass just a couple of feet in front of her.

"Are you alright? You ran away pretty quickly this afternoon at the dining hall," said Lucinda.

"Yea. I'm fine." said Primrose.

"Can I ask you something?"

"Sure..."

"What's Tyler's favorite food?" asked Lucinda. Primrose looked at her with a confused expression on her face.

"Tyler? I'm not really sure, to be honest. Why do you ask?" Asked Primrose.

"Because I'd like to cook it for him when I ask him out on a date," said Lucinda.

Primrose opened her mouth to say something but realized she was confused. Lucinda smiled.

"Hazel told me everything," said Lucinda.

She got up and stood in front of Primrose.

"I wanted to find you, to tell you that Evan and I…we're just friends. And if you feel something for him, you should let him know," said Lucinda as she put her hand gently on Primrose's arm.

Lucinda started to walk back into the manor.

"Hey, Luce?" Asked Primrose. She turned around.

"Yea?" She answered.

"Thank you…for that," said Primrose with a smile.

Lucinda smiled and nodded at her, then continued walking into the manor.

Primrose watched the fireflies for a little longer before she decided to head back to the suites.

She felt somewhat relieved after Lucinda clarified her relationship with Agent Bradley, and certainly it helped knowing she was accepting of Primrose's feelings for him. When she walked into the common room, she saw Agent Bradley asleep on a chair in front of the fireplace. She walked over to the sofa slowly and grabbed a blanket. Just as she was about to lay the blanket on him, he started to wake up.

"Primrose?" He asked.

"Yea, It's me. What are you doing here so late?" She whispered.

"You disappeared and we couldn't find you. Then, Luce came and told me everything. I wanted to make sure you were alright and was hoping to catch you when you got back."

Primrose sat down on the chair across from Agent Bradley and stared into the fire.

"I'm sorry I hurt you during training today. I felt sick to my stomach afterwards," he admitted.   "You don't have to apologize. I know what I signed up for. You were only doing your job," she said as she turned to face him.

Agent Bradley stood up slowly and stretched his arms above his head. His shirt lifted up slightly, revealing a toned abdomen with a love trail leading downwards.

Primrose quickly looked away.

"I'm glad to see that you're okay. I was getting pretty worried," said Agent Bradley as he walked towards the door.

"Hey, Evan?" Asked Primrose.

"Yea?" He answered as he looked back at her.

She stared at him for a second and suddenly lost all confidence in telling him what she felt.

"Um…never mind. Good night," she said with a smile.

Agent Bradley smiled back at her and walked out. Primrose suddenly realized how exhausted she had been and decided to call it a night.

The next two weeks were uneventful. Everyone had been busy with their new roles. Primrose and Hazel were quickly absorbing the new skills they've learned in training. Primrose showed the potions team how to create Zingallium and the Blue Butterfly elixir. Hazel learned the Mend aura which helps heal minor cuts and scrapes. Primrose also taught her the Micropixie aura.

It was a hot Saturday afternoon when Primrose and Hazel were in the gym located in the basement of the main building.

"Victor's coming to visit today for the weekend," said Hazel excitedly as she got on the exercise bike. Primrose was on the treadmill.

"I bet you can't wait to see him," said Primrose.

Hazel smiled and nodded.

"What are you guys planning to do?" Asked Primrose as she wiggled her eyebrows.

Hazel blushed as she picked up on what Primrose was suggesting.

"We'll probably just hang out on the couch and watch scary movies all day," she replied with a smirk.

"Sure, *watch* movies," said Primrose as she used her hands to make quotations.

Hazel laughed and they continued to work out for another half an hour before heading back to the suites.

Lucinda was in the common room reading a book by the fireplace when Tyler came out of his suite. She looked up as he walked out. He was shirtless and she couldn't help but stare at him. His skin looked smooth and soft. His torso was incredibly toned and his biceps were defined.

"Morning," said Tyler with a smile.

"Morning…did you run out of clean clothes again?" Asked Lucinda.

Tyler laughed and ran his fingers through his wet hair.

"Well, since you're asking…I am starting to. I think I'm going to take a trip into town and do some shopping…if that's okay," said Tyler.

"We can check with Duke. I'm sure it wouldn't be a problem," said Lucinda.

"Okay. I'm gonna go throw on scrubs. Do you want to grab breakfast with me before we go see Duke?" Asked Tyler.

Lucinda smiled and nodded.

After Tyler got dressed, he and Lucinda went down to the dining hall.

Leah had just finished an overnight shift at the infirmary and was walking back to the main building when Duke jogged up to her in a sleeveless tank top and black basketball shorts.

"Hey!" Said Duke, out of breath.

"Hey, out for a jog?" Asked Leah.

"Yea, I just finished and was coming to see if you wanted to get breakfast together," said Duke.

"Perfect timing, I just finished my shift. I'll meet you in the dining hall after I get clean up," said Leah.

"Sounds good," said Duke as he gave her a kiss on the cheek.

Leah blushed as Duke jogged into the main building in front of her. She smiled and continued walking into the manor as well.

Hazel, Primrose, Lucinda, and Tyler were all sitting together in the dining hall when Victor walked in.

"Victor!" Hazel shouted when she spotted him walking in.

She ran over to him and jumped into his arms.

"Hey!" said Victor as he caught her in his arms. They kissed and stared at each other for a minute.

"Earth to cupid!" shouted Lucinda.

Victor and Hazel laughed, then walked back to the table. A few minutes later, Duke and Leah walked in holding hands. They sat down with everyone at the table.

"This is nice, everyone together and all," said Leah happily.

"Well...not everyone, exactly," said Hazel.

"Huh?" Asked Leah.

"Agent Bradley isn't here." said Hazel as she gave Primrose a quick glance. Primrose just realized she hadn't seen much of Agent Bradley in the past two weeks.

"He's been pretty busy lately. We've both been taking turns overseeing the team that is tracking Heidi," said Lucinda.

"Wait, what? How come you haven't mentioned it earlier?" asked Leah.

"Everyone's been pretty occupied the last couple of weeks. Plus, there hasn't really been any activity. Ever since the incident at the arboretum, we've been working with Hallowed Falls PD on tracking her down," Lucinda explained.

"There hasn't been any other attacks since Violet Evans was taken, but last week when one of our officers were patrolling on the east side of town, he swore that he saw Heidi on the corner of Calm Winds Road and Pixie's Way. She was wearing a black trench coat and seemed to be headed northwest. He tried to get a closer look but a pedestrian approached him for directions. By the time he looked back, she was gone," said Victor.

"You mean...she was spotted near Hallowed Falls hospital?" Asked Leah.

"Yes, but like I said. We don't have solid evidence that it was her and we haven't heard any other potential sightings since then," said Victor.

"What about her parents? I thought they were being cooperative during the recent murders?" Asked Hazel.

"They haven't been answering any calls. They've stopped all communication with us ever since they found out about Heidi and Marco," said Victor.

"Um, since it *does* seem to be safe for now. Tyler and I were actually planning to go into town today since he hasn't been able to get any of his belongings from home," said Lucinda.

"A man can only wear scrubs for so long." Tyler joked.

Hazel and Primrose laughed.

"Can I come along? I haven't been able to get my things either," asked Leah.

Everyone looked at Duke.

"That's fine. I'll come along as well," said Duke.

"What about Hazel and Primrose? Can they come, too?" Asked Leah.

"Actually, Victor and I were going to stay in and just relax," said Hazel as she squeezed his bicep.

"I planned on doing some research in the library," said Primrose.

"Alright, let's meet in the foyer in half an hour," said Lucinda.

Everyone finished their breakfast and went their separate ways.

Primrose headed to the library as soon as she was done eating. It was located on the fourth floor of the main building. When she got off the elevator, she noticed that the library took up the entire level. On the opposite side of the elevators, there were huge floor to ceiling windows with navy-blue curtains that were pulled back. The floor was made of white marble with dark gray and gold veins running through it.

At the center of the library was a seating area with a few wooden tables and chairs. Primrose began browsing from one end of the floor and found a section on Summerland history. She grabbed a few books and walked over to the seating area, then began reading.

Lucinda, Leah, and Tyler headed down to the foyer after they got changed. Duke was standing by the doors when they came down from the grand staircase, holding a couple of iced coffees.

"Everyone ready?" Asked Duke as he handed out the drinks.

"I'm so excited! I remember passing the town on our way here. It looked like such a cute community!" Leah exclaimed.

They walked out to the front yard and got into Lucinda's SUV. It took them fifteen minutes to get to town. She parked in front of Mirabella's Boutique and went inside the store. Lucinda and Leah tried on some dresses while Duke and Tyler waited outside. When they came back out, they had shopping bags in their hands.

"Find anything good?" Asked Duke.

"Yea, I found a couple of cute outfits in there. It'll be nice not having to wear scrubs all the time," said Leah.

They continued to walk through more shops in town. It was already late in the afternoon by the time they got everything they needed.

"What's there to eat around here?" Asked Leah.

"There's Pete's Barbecue, Mermaid Café, Antonia's Trattoria, Crystal Brooks diner, and…Blue Wolf's Tavern," said Lucinda.

"Oh, I love Blue Wolf's Tavern! They have the best buffalo wings back in Hallowed Falls," said Tyler.

"Blue Wolf's Tavern it is!" Leah exclaimed.

"Are you sure?" Asked Duke.

"Yea, why do you ask?" Asked Leah.

"Because Savannah manages this one," said Lucinda.

"Oh…right. I forgot about that. We don't have to go if you're not comfortable, Duke," said Leah.

"I'm okay with it," said Duke with a shrug.

They dropped off their shopping bags at the car and walked over to Blue Wolf's Tavern. When they entered the restaurant, a young woman came out from behind the front desk with menus in her arms. A navy-blue apron wrapped around her waist with the words 'Blue Wolf's Tavern' printed in light gray on it.

"Hi, guys! Welcome to Blue Wolf's Tavern. Would you like to sit inside or the deck?" Asked the hostess politely.

"The deck, please," said Lucinda.

"Right this way," said the hostess with a nod.

She led them to the back of the restaurant and out to the deck that overlooked a lake. When they were seated, Leah looked over the wooden railing. She could see docks below where small boats could pull up to the restaurant.

"Wow, I would never have guessed that there was a lake back here. The water looks crystal clear. Ha! I guess that's why they call it Crystal Brooks. What a wondrous view," said Leah.

"I think I have the best view," said Duke as he smiled at Leah.

"Yuck," said Lucinda, rolling her eyes.

Duke nudged her with his elbow, making Leah and Lucinda laugh.

"I'll be right back. Gotta use the men's room," said Duke as he stood up from his chair.

"I'd like to wash my hands as well," said Tyler.

Leah made sure the guys were out of earshot.

"So…how are things going with you and Tyler?" Asked Leah.

"I don't know. Ever since everything happened, I haven't really had time to talk to him," said Lucinda.

"Lucinda Griffin?" a female voice came from behind them.

They turned to look and noticed a woman about their age standing there with a huge smile. Her straight black hair shined under the sun and even though she was squinting, Leah could see her light gray eyes staring back at them. The breeze gently tossed her hair around like she was a model in a shampoo commercial. She was tall and slender, she actually did seem like a model to Leah.

"Savannah…H-how are you?" Asked Lucinda hesitantly.

"I'm doing great, actually! Have you moved back to Crystal Brooks? Last I heard, you were living in Hallowed Falls," said Savannah.

"I'm back, for now. This is my cousin, Leah," said Lucinda.

"Hi, Leah. I'm Savannah Powell, pleased to meet you," she said and extended her hand.

"Leah Plumeria," Leah replied as she shook it.

"Well, I have to get back in there. It was good seeing you, Luce. Let me know if you guys need anything," said Savannah as she walked away.

"*That's* Savannah?! She looks so different from when I first saw her in the dining hall back at headquarters a couple of weeks ago. What is she? A model or something?" Leah whispered loudly. Lucinda shrugged.

"Or something…" Lucinda mumbled.

Leah caught that and tilted her head.

"What do you mean?" Asked Leah.

"She's a Powell," Lucinda hinted.

Leah looked more confused than ever. Lucinda took a deep breath.

"The Powell clan are lycanthropes," Lucinda whispered.

Leah gasped.

"You're kidding," Leah whispered back with a shocked expression on her face.

Lucinda shook her head.

Duke walked out of the restroom and just as he stepped out onto the deck, he bumped into Savannah.

"Oh, Duke! I didn't expect to see you here. What a wonderful surprise!" Said Savannah as she threw her arms around him and gave him a hug.

"H-hi, Savannah," said Duke as he put her arms back down.

Duke looked past Savannah and over to where Leah was sitting. Savannah frowned and turned to see what Duke was looking at.

"Are you here with Lucinda and her cousin?" Asked Savannah.

"Yes, actually…Leah is…my girlfriend," said Duke.

"Oh…" said Savannah, her smile fading slowly.

Just then, Tyler walked past them and back to their table.

"I'll let you get back to them, then. It was really nice seeing you again, Duke," said Savannah politely.

"Yea, you as well," said Duke as he walked back to the table.

Leah turned her head back to face Lucinda as soon as Duke looked over. She saw Savannah walk into him on his way out to the deck. She watched as Savannah threw her arms around Duke before he started walking back to the table. She couldn't help but wonder what they said to each other.

"Hey, you ladies ready to order?" Asked Tyler as he sat down and propped up the menu in front of him.

"Yep," said Lucinda.

Leah nodded with a half-smile.

Duke sat down next to Leah and smiled at her. Leah smiled back for a second, then turned her head back to where Savannah had been standing. Savannah was watching them from the patio entrance and then quickly went back inside when she saw Leah glance over.

"I can't believe he's moved on already...but can I really blame him after what I've done." Savannah thought to herself and shook her head. She walked over to the bar and grabbed her laptop.

"Everything alright boss?" asked the bartender.

"Uh...yea, can I get a glass of Jameson on the rocks please?" She asked him.

The bartender raised an eyebrow at her.

"What? Just one shot, that's all," she said.

"You got it, boss," said the bartender with a smile.

The sun was setting by the time the group got back to headquarters. Lucinda and Tyler were walking ahead of Leah and Duke.

"You've been quiet since lunch. Are you feeling alright?" Asked Duke.

"Yea…I'm okay, just tired," said Leah as she picked at a hangnail.

Duke stopped walking and grabbed her hand.

"Follow me," said Duke.

He led her towards the back of the foyer and through the sliding glass doors into the garden. All the way to the back was a wooden bench and behind it was a small waterfall built into the wall. The temperature felt cooler than it did earlier. The breeze rushed through the trees making the sound of waves within the branches. They sat down and Duke kept Leah's hand in his. His hands were warm and it kept her goosebumps at bay. The air smelled like fresh cut grass and tiny glowing neon lights floated in front of her.

"Fireflies," she whispered.

"They're cool, aren't they?" Asked Duke.

Leah smiled and nodded. She turned her head to face Duke and he looked at her. In the corner of her eyes, the tiny fireflies became glowing blurs. His eyes slowly moved down to her lips. His face inched closer and closer to Leah's. His warm lips brushed hers gently. Then, their lips collided like magnets. Her hands cradled the sides of his face. His eyes were still closed when she pulled away and when he opened them, Leah had a really big smile on her face.

"You're a *really* good kisser," said Leah in a surprised tone.

"You are constantly underestimating me, Dr. Plumeria," Duke joked.

Leah recalled the first date they had a couple of weeks ago. He had prepared an amazing candlelit dinner and she remembered being surprised that he even cooked at all.

Duke and Leah hung out in the garden until it was completely dark and he walked her back to her suite. Just as they approached the common room, Leah stopped and looked up at him.

"Hey…um, what did you and Savannah talk about at the restaurant when she bumped into you?" Asked Leah.

"Not much, really. I told her we were there together," said Duke.

"Oh," said Leah.

"Is something wrong?" Asked Duke.

"Uh…no. I was just…curious," said Leah as she continued walking.

Duke stopped and pulled her back to him. He rested both hands were on her waist and looked deep into her green eyes as if he were searching for something. Suddenly, he felt nervous and excited as her body leaned up against his. Goosebumps began to form on his biceps and Duke realized just then that no one's ever had that effect on him before, not even when he was with Savannah.

"You have *nothing* to worry about," he assured her.

He brushed a piece of hair away from her face and she stared back into his eyes.

"Okay," said Leah as she gave him a quick kiss on the lips. Duke continued to walk her all the way to her suite.

"Goodnight, beautiful," said Duke with a wink.

Leah chuckled.

"Goodnight, handsome," Leah teased.

Duke left and headed back to his suite.

Chapter 7

Primrose was halfway through the second book from the Summerland archives when she looked up at the window. It was already dark out and she realized she'd spent the whole day reading up on her family's history. When her stomach suddenly growled, she shut the book, gathering the stack of books in her arms. She walked over to the librarian's desk and signed them out. Then, she headed for the elevators.

The elevators stopped on the third floor, the doors opened revealing Agent Bradley standing there.

"Oh, hey…Primrose," Agent Bradley greeted her as he stepped onto the elevator. "I see you're heading to the dining hall as well. How have you been?"

"I'm doing well, and you?" Asked Primrose.

"Good," said Agent Bradley with a nod.

There was an awkward silence between them.

"Um…" they both said at the same time.

They looked at each other and chuckled. It felt like forever before the elevator doors finally opened again. Primrose walked out first and Agent Bradley stepped out after her. She sat down at an empty table while Agent Bradley joined a a couple of agents at another table. Shortly after, Hazel and Victor walked in. Primrose smiled and waved at them.

"Hey, I'm surprised you're here so late but I'm glad. I haven't seen you all day!" Hazel exclaimed.

"Yea, I spent the whole day reading about the Summerlands in the library and lost track of time," said Primrose.

"We lost track of time as well. We spent some time at the pool and then watched movies the rest of the day. Somehow we both fell asleep and woke up just before we came down here," said Victor.

"We were going to start a new movie if you'd like to join afterwards?" Asked Hazel.

Hazel happened to glance past Primrose and noticed Agent Bradley sitting at another table. She got up and walked over to him. Primrose watched as Hazel spoke to Agent Bradley and then walked back with a huge smile.

"I just asked Agent Bradley if he was free later. He's going to join us for movie night!" Said Hazel excitedly.

Although Primrose felt excited, she managed to avoid letting on. She glanced over her shoulder to look at Agent Bradley and he glanced at her at the same time. They both smiled and returned their attention to their company. After dinner, they went back up to the common room. Hazel's phone rang as soon as they sat down on the sofa.

"Hey, Agent Bradley. Oh…okay. No worries. Sure, goodnight," said Hazel.

As soon as she hung up, Hazel pouted.

"He won't be able to make it. He just got called back to work," said Hazel, disappointedly.

Primrose was disheartened, she was looking forward to seeing him. Just then, Lucinda rushed out of her suite.

"Hey, Luce! We're about to start a movie, want to join?" Asked Victor.

"Sorry, I'd love to but I just got called in. I'll catch you guys later," said Lucinda as she hurried out of the room.

Lucinda jogged over to the elevators and got on as soon as the doors opened. As soon as the elevator stopped on the third floor, she ran to the first conference room on the right. Duke had just called her to say there had been a confirmed sighting of Heidi in Hallowed Falls. When Lucinda walked into the conference room, Duke and Agent Bradley were sitting at the end of the table. Agents Wyatt Kensington, Skylar Everard, Zoe Salvatore and Mark Lyle walked in a few minutes after her.

"Alright, everybody take a seat," said Duke as he opened a folder in front of him.

"We just got intel that Heidi had been spotted an hour ago in Hallowed Falls. This time, she was spotted *inside* the hospital. It was later discovered that she'd stolen some of the hospital's blood supply," said Duke.

He laid a couple of print outs on the table. They were screen shots of Heidi from the security cameras. She was wearing all black and her face had been captured on one of the photos. It was a blurry photo of her but Lucinda could tell it was Heidi.

"Do they have any idea where she is now?" Asked Lucinda with concern.

"No, but my guess is that she's either hiding at the Alexander's manor or the mausoleum at Bloodstone Cemetery. Hallowed Falls PD is working on getting warrants for the two locations. Agent Bradley and Agent Griffin, you will lead the team and head over to the Hallowed Falls precinct. Once the warrant is issued, you will assist them in tracking down Heidi Hendrix at the two locations. Any questions?" Asked Duke.

Everyone stayed silent.

"Alright, let's head to the armory tower," said Agent Bradley.

Everyone got up from the table and went to get prepped. When all five agents were geared up, they got into an A.E. SUV and headed towards Hallowed Falls.

When they arrived at the Hallowed Falls precinct for a briefing on the action plan. It was a little after two in the morning by the time they headed towards the Alexander estate. The streets were incredibly quiet and a low-lying fog had rolled in from the woods at the west end of Dragon's Breath Trail. The French-style manor sat on a small hill and a four-foot stone wall lined the entire property. Two of the Hallowed Falls officers accompanied them. They walked in single file and slowly approached the manor's front gates. One of the officers tried to push the gate open only to find it was locked. Lucinda walked up to the gate and waved her stylus over it. They heard a click and the sound of rusted iron creaking before the gate slowly swung open. The two officers walked in first with their pistols drawn and the rest followed behind them.

They climbed a set of cement steps that led up to the manor's front door. Lucinda, Agent Bradley, and the two officers slowly approached the manor. The others took cover behind a couple of nearby trees and waited for further instructions.

"Hallowed Falls Police Department!" Yelled one of the officers as he banged on the door. They waited about a minute before knocking on the door again.

"Hallowed Falls PD! Open up!" He yelled again.

They waited a few minutes longer this time and still, no one answered.

"I guess they want to do this the hard way," said Agent Bradley sarcastically as he walked up to the door. He pointed at the lock with his stylus.

"*Fulminate!*" He shouted.

There was a small explosion and the front door swung inwards. Agent Bradley walked in and the team followed. The foyer was dimly lit by the moonlight coming in through the large windows. The officers swept the entire first floor while Agent Bradley and Agent Everard swept the second floor. Agent Lyle and Lucinda cleared the third floor. Everyone gathered again at the center of the foyer once the manor had been cleared.

"The manor is empty," said Agent Lyle.

Lucinda walked back down the hall and looked to the left where she noticed a door slightly ajar. She pushed the door open wider and saw a set of stairs leading down to the basement. Agent Bradley walked up behind her. She kept her stylus in the glove holster and raised her arm up, pointing straight into the darkness.

"I've got your six," said Agent Bradley.

He pointed his stylus downwards as he followed behind her. As she descended the stairs, it began to smell musty, getting colder with each step. The stairs creaked and echoed around them. When they got to the bottom, they noticed some kind of dim blue light that seemed to be coming from behind the stairs. Lucinda conjured a glowball and Agent Bradley did the same. As soon as Agent Bradley's glowball was conjured, they were able to see the rest of the basement. Ten glass pods spread about the basement and were about seven feet long with small blue lights on the sides. Each one contained a body.

"What the *hell* are these?" Asked Lucinda. The look of confusion and shock spread across her face.

"I believe these are preservation pods. A vamp's body lasts only as long as a human's, assuming that they only feed on animal blood.

These pods extends the shelf life of their bodies longer, for a lack of a better term, while they rest and is also used to preserve those who are long gone. It's got state-of-the-art technology and are *extremely* expensive," explained Agent Bradley.

"So, the rumors were true. They *do* keep their elders down here," said Lucinda as her eyes wandered over to two empty pods. She walked over to them to get a closer look.

"I wonder who these belong to," she said thoughtfully.

"Who knows, they probably belongs to Heidi's parents. But it seems like the whole place is clear. Let's get out of here," said Agent Bradley.

As they went up the stairs, Lucinda gave the pods another glance. Something felt off about them, but she quickly brushed that thought aside to focus on their next task.

Everyone got back into the SUV and headed for Bloodstone Cemetery. When they arrived, Lucinda led the team towards the back where the old Alexander mausoleum was located. They were only a few feet into the cemetery when they spotted the silhouette of someone laying on the ground ahead. Agent Lyle ran up to the body and checked for a pulse. He looked up at them and shook his head. Lucinda walked over to examine the body. She turned the body over and clenched her jaw, then stood up again.

"Damn it. It's the caretaker, he works here at the cemetery. There's bite marks on the left side of his neck," said Lucinda.

"Heidi's got to be around here somewhere. C'mon," Agent Bradley said urgently.

Lucinda continued to lead the team into the old Alexander's mausoleum. The sarcophagus was already opened when they walked through the door. They slowly walked down the dark tunnel and as they approached the room at the end, Lucinda held her fist up signaling the team to stop. She leaned against the wall and slowly peeked into the room. She made sure the room was empty before she carefully stepped in. There was a table and a chair at the center of the floor. The table had knives and needles laying on a square piece of gray suede fabric. Next to the chair was an IV stand. The room looked the same as the last two times she'd been there except there were no vampires and no hostages.

Agent Bradley looked around and his eyes landed on the black metal door on the other end of the room.

"Agent Everard and Agent Kensington, stand guard here. Everyone else follow me," Agent Bradley directed.

The door was locked and there was a keypad on the doorknob. Agent Bradley cast the Fulminate spell again and the doorknob blew right off, causing the door to swing open. Once they were through the door, the lights automatically turned on and they were able to see their surroundings.

"It looks like a medical laboratory," said Agent Bradley as he looked around the room.

On the other side of the laboratory, he noticed another black metal door and walked over. A cold blast of air hit him as soon as he opened it.

"What in the…" said Agent Bradley.

Lucinda walked over to him and stuck her head into the room. It looked like a walk-in freezer with glass shelves lining the walls. Every shelf had trays of clear bags filled with blood.

"They've been storing the blood supply here. This must be how Marco had been surviving this entire time," said Lucinda.

"I'll alert the captain and the hospital," said one of the officers.

Within fifteen minutes, the Hallowed Falls PD had the cemetery surrounded.

"What do we do now?" Asked Agent Kensington.

"We let these guys do their jobs and we'll return to headquarters to report our findings," said Agent Bradley.

"But we haven't found Heidi," said Agent Kensington.

"No, we didn't. But she's gotta turn up again soon since we've taken away their blood supply," said Lucinda sternly.

They got into the SUV and drove back to headquarters. The sun had already come up by the time they got back to Crystal Brooks. Agent Bradley and Lucinda went to see Duke. He looked up when he heard footsteps coming down the hallway.

"What'd you guys find?" Asked Duke as they entered his office.

"We swept the entire manor, but it was empty. It seems that Heidi and her parents have abandoned the place. We also found about ten preservation pods down in the basement and two of them were empty," said Agent Bradley.

"So they've been using preservation pods. That's probably how Marco has been kept preserved all this time," said Duke thoughtfully.

"At the mausoleum, we found another body. It was the caretaker of the cemetery…his blood had been drained. We went back down to the mausoleum where Hazel and Primrose's mother were held hostage and we discovered a lab in the back where they hid the stolen blood supply. We've searched the *entire* property but there was no sign of Heidi," Lucinda added.

"Alright, keep me updated on this. I'm sure she'll turn up again, soon. In the meantime, get some rest. Great job, team," said Duke.

Lucinda and Agent Bradley left Duke's office, then walked out of the building together.

"Don't you find it odd?" Asked Lucinda as she unstrapped her stylus holster from her right hand.

"Find what odd?" Asked Agent Bradley.

"Well, two of the pods were empty. Even if one of them belonged to Marco, who does other one belong to?" Asked Lucinda curiously.

"I wondered the same thing at first but it could've been Heidi's parents or even Heidi herself," Agent Bradley shrugged.

Lucinda agreed there was a strong possibility that it could've Heidi's pod but she was too tired to think about it any further. Agent Bradley and Lucinda went their separate ways when they got back to the main building.

Another few days had gone by and the team had not heard of another Heidi sighting. It was a humid Tuesday morning and July fourth was only a couple of days away. Hazel, Leah, and Primrose were in the dining hall having breakfast together before their shifts started.

"I wonder if they do anything special to celebrate Independence Day around here. It would be fun to have a party or something," said Hazel, pursing her lips in thought.

"I heard that Crystal Brooks usually has an Independence Day parade that runs through town," said Leah.

"Maybe we can ask Duke if we can go to the parade?" Asked Hazel, brightening at the thought.

"I'm not sure about that. Heidi's still out there," said Leah cautiously and shaking her head.

"It's been weeks since anyone's seen her," Hazel said in a slightly exasperated tone.

"Maybe we can convince Duke, somehow," said Primrose, chiming in.

Just then, Duke and Agent Bradley walked into the dining hall. Duke spotted the girls and joined them at the table. Agent Bradley smiled at Primrose. Primrose smiled back and fidgeted in her seat.

"Just the man we were looking for!" Said Hazel cheerfully.

"What's going on?" Asked Duke with his brows drawn together.

"We were wondering...since the fourth is coming up...if we could attend the parade in town?" Asked Primrose.

"I wouldn't advise it but if you go, we can't stop you. You are adults, after all," said Duke sternly.

"Also, Primrose and I have been through intense training for the past month. We can protect each other," said Hazel, hoping he would agree.

"That's fine," Duke nodded as he ate his cereal.

After breakfast, Primrose and Hazel headed to the South building to continue their training.

Over at Blue Wolf's Tavern, Savannah was sitting at the bar on the deck and was working on her laptop ordering supplies for the restaurant, staring at the photo of votive candles on her screen. For a second, her mind drifted, flashing back to when Duke was at the restaurant last time. Lately, she'd been feeling the weight of regret and each time she saw Duke, it felt heavier. Deep inside she knew that she had made an *enormous* mistake for declining his proposal three months ago.

She remembered that night vividly. Duke had made a reservation at Antonia's Trattoria for their three-year anniversary. When they got to the restaurant, he opened the door to let her walk in first. The quaint restaurant was empty and beautifully decorated. There were string lights hung throughout the ceiling. Every table had three votive candles and small vases with three red roses in each of them.

She remembered how perfect everything was, from the delicious meal and the buzz she got from the champagne.

After the waiter had cleared their plates, Duke took her hand in his and told her how much he loved her. No one has ever said those words to her before and she was happy to say it back. But just as she opened her mouth to respond, he got out of his chair and knelt down on one knee.

"Savannah, will you marry me?" She recalled Duke asking.

She remembered her entire body was frozen with shock, then a feeling of dread and fear washed over her. She was content with the way their relationship had been going but marriage had *never* crossed her mind. The thought of it, at the time, freaked her out.

"I'm…I'm sorry…I can't," her voice echoed in her mind and she cringed.

Those were the last words she said to him before she stood up and ran out of the restaurant. It was the last time she had seen him until recently when she delivered his take-out to the A.E. headquarters a couple of weeks ago.

"Hello, Savannah," a voice came from behind her quickly snapping her out of her thoughts. She turned to find Heidi standing there.

"Heidi?! What are you doing here?" Asked Savannah, surprised to see her.

"I was in the neighborhood and figured I'd come visit my old friend," said Heidi with a smile.

"Who are you calling *old*?" Savannah joked.

Savannah got out of her chair and gave Heidi a hug.

"It's nice to see a familiar face again. How are you and Duke? Married with children yet?" Asked Heidi as she sat down next to her.

"Um…actually, we broke up about three months ago," said Savannah, her smile slowly fading.

"Oh, I'm sorry to hear that…what happened?" Asked Heidi.

"He proposed and…I freaked out. I've been regretting it ever since but it's too late now," said Savannah, sadness reaching her eyes.

"It's never too late. I'm sure you can just talk to him. I remembered how much he said he loved you," said Heidi.

"He's dating someone else," said Savannah with a shrug.

"Oh? Who's the unfortunate gal?" Asked Heidi.

"Leah Plumeria, Lucinda's cousin," said Savannah.

"Oh…really." said Heidi, interest peaked.

"You know her?" asked Savannah, a little curious.

"Uh…no. Not at all. Listen, I've got to go but we should have dinner and catch up some time. I'm staying in town at my old house," said Heidi, getting up from the chair.

"Yea that sounds great, you still have my number?" Asked Savannah.

"Of course!" Heidi smiled and waved as she walked away.

"Leah Plumeria…a descendant of Gregoro Plumeria," Heidi thought to herself.

Heidi was forced to run off to Crystal Brooks and had just arrived there a day ago. Hallowed Falls was crawling with cops who were looking for her and it was too risky to stay there. Back when she was working for the A.E. she had purchased a small house at the edge of town on Airy Lane.

"Snap out of it! We've got pixies to track down!" A voice in her mind startled her.

It was Marco's voice. When he was tricked into drinking the bright pink concoction given to him by the fairy in the arboretum, his soul had partially taken over Heidi's body. She recalls Marco telling her that shortly after he returned to Hallowed Falls, he had gotten a hold of the Enchantress elixir but it had no physical effect on him. When he drank some of the fresh fairy's blood, it must have mixed with the elixir in his system and strengthened his immortality, enabling him to become something else after his physical body had been destroyed.

"They must be under the protection of the Aster Elites. You need to find a way to get into their headquarters no matter what it takes!" Marco's voice echoed eerily in her mind.

"That's not possible. The A.E. headquarters is under the Bulwark spell, I would be detected within a quarter mile of the estate." Heidi thought back.

"Then, you need to lure them out. Don't forget if you fail you can say goodbye to your parents...forever." said Marco ominously.

Heidi's parents disappeared shortly after Victor rescued Hazel at the mausoleum. Heidi refused to help him any longer, so Marco waited until Heidi fell asleep one night and took complete control over her body. He had his vampire guards sedate her parents and took them to a secret location. When Heidi woke up and realized her parents were missing, Marco confessed to what he did. He'd taken her parents and would not reveal the location to her until she helped him with what he needed, which was to capture the heir of Summerland and to retrieve the Four Seeds of Desire. Heidi winced and slowly headed back to her house to brainstorm on an action plan.

Back at headquarters, Lucinda and Agent Bradley were called to the conference hall. When they arrived, they noticed that the Chief of Directors, Conrad Everard sitting at the front of the table. Next to him were all the department directors and their senior directors.

"Chief Everard," said Lucinda with a nod as they walked past him.

"Good afternoon Agent Griffin and Agent Bradley. Please have a seat," said Chief Everard in a friendly tone.

They took their seats next to Duke.

"I've summoned all of you here today because I've got some exciting news. The agency's commissioner has decided to open an A.E. headquarters overseas, in Belle Montagnes. I've been charged with overseeing that office," said Chief Everard proudly.

Everyone clapped.

"Thank you. In addition, I'd like to announce a couple of other promotions. Under careful observation and thorough decision making, I've selected a successor to continue leadership here at Crystal Brooks headquarters. Duke Bryant, please come up here," said Chief Everard with a smile.

Duke stood up from his chair and walked over to Chief Everard. Everyone cheered and clapped. Chief Everard shook Duke's hand and handed him his new badge. Then, he stood behind the chief.

"Evan Bradley," Chief Everard announced.

Evan got up and walked to the front of the room.

"*Senior* Director of Protective Services," said Chief Everard as he shook Evan's hand and handed him his new badge.

"Lucinda Griffin, *Department* Director of Protective Services," announced Chief Everard.

Lucinda walked over and stood next to him.

"Your father will be so proud when he hears about this, Director Griffin," said Chief Everard as he shook her hand.

Lucinda smiled and gave him a polite nod.

"And last but not least, Skylar Everard. Department Director of Assets," said Chief Everard, proudly.

Skylar stood up from her chair. Her blonde hair was dyed light blue at the bottom half and was up in a ponytail that swung as she walked confidently towards the front of the room. The chief handed her a badge and gave her a hug.

"Congratulations, Directors! I want to thank each and *every* one of you for the blood, sweat, and tears you've put in all these years. Even though I will no longer serve Crystal Brooks, I am just a call away. So, don't be a stranger. And Skylar, your mother and I are *so* proud of you. Good work everyone!" He exclaimed as he walked out of the room.

"Oh my God!" Lucinda shouted excitedly as she hugged Skylar.

"I knew we would make it!" Said Skylar.

"Your father is one of the best. He will be missed dearly," said Lucinda.

"Thanks," said Skylar shyly with a smile.

Lucinda smiled and patted her on the back.

It was the day before Independence Day and Savannah was getting the restaurant prepped for the celebration. She was hanging streamers inside the restaurant when her phone rang.

"Savannah, it's Heidi. I was wondering if you'd be free this afternoon for lunch?" Asked Heidi.

"Uh…yea sure, why don't you stop by Blue Wolf's around noon?" Savannah suggested.

"Perfect! I'll see you then!" Said Heidi.

Some time passed, Savannah was finishing up with the preparations for tomorrow's festivities and going over the playlist with the DJ on the deck.

"Savannah!" Yelled Heidi from the entrance.

Heidi was wearing a pair of black sunglasses and a large sunhat. Savannah barely recognized her behind those oversized sunglasses.

"Hey!" Savannah greeted her.

"What are you up to?" Asked Heidi.

"We're throwing an Independence Day party here on the deck tomorrow. There's going to be games and giveaways," said Savannah.

"Oh, how fun!"

"It will be! You should join us tomorrow. C'mon let's sit inside."

Heidi followed Savannah to the bar inside the restaurant. When they sat down, the bartender set two champagne glasses on the counter and poured mimosas into them.

"Order whatever you'd like. My treat," said Savannah as she sipped on the mimosa.

Heidi looked around the restaurant.

"It's been such a long time since I've been here," said Heidi.

"You're right! I think the last time you were here, was when..." Savannah began to say but stopped herself.

"Victor and I celebrated his twenty-eighth birthday," Heidi finished for her.

"I'm sorry," said Savannah as she bit her lip.

"It's okay," said Heidi with a shrug.

Heidi gave her a half-smile but deep down inside, she really *wasn't* okay. Victor had been the one person she'd actually fell *hard* for. No one understood her the way he did. She remembered the first day they met and it was right here at Blue Wolf's Tavern. She had just completed her general surgery residency program at Crystal Brooks Medical Center and a group of colleagues had invited her out one night to celebrate. Savannah tossed back one too many tequila shots and Heidi had to take her outside for fresh air. Heidi herself started to feel the effects of the vodka sodas and figured that the fresh air would do her some good as well.

Once they were outside, Savannah walked to the curb, threw her head forward and started to puke. Heidi held her friend's hair and looked away. When Savannah was done, she swayed a little and leaned on Heidi. Before she knew it, Savannah dropped like a bag of potatoes onto the ground.

"Oh my God, Savannah!" Heidi shouted.

Two men rushed over to help them.

"What happened?" The man asked as he crouched besides Savannah. His dark gray eyes pierced Heidi's as he hovered over Savannah.

"Uh…uh…she had one too many shots," Heidi managed to say.

The other man, who seemed to be a little taller and bigger than the other one, kneeled down by Savannah's head. He bent down and listened for her breathing. Then, he took his black leather jacket off and laid it gently under Savannah's head. Savannah moaned as she started come to.

"What's her name?" Asked the man by her head.

"S-Savannah," said Heidi as she swayed.

"Hey…Savannah. Are you okay?" He asked.

"Hmmm?" asked Savannah.

"You just passed out on the street," said the man.

Savannah's eyes closed again as she fell back asleep.

"Let's get her inside," said the man with the gray eyes.

"Thanks for helping us out. I didn't catch your name," said Heidi.

"My name's Victor. That's Duke. And you are?" Asked Victor.

"Heidi," she answered with a smile.

Duke slid his arms under Savannah and carried her back inside. Heidi led them to the office in the back of the restaurant and waited for the girls to sober up. It was already close to four o'clock in the morning when Savannah woke up again.

"Oh God…" said Savannah as she held her forehead and tried to sit up on the sofa.

"Savannah!" Shouted Heidi as she rushed over to her.

"What the hell happened?" Asked Savannah, groggily.

"You passed out in front of the restaurant. These two guys were nice enough to help carry you in here," Heidi explained.

Savannah looked up and noticed the two men standing behind Heidi.

"Oh…I'm sorry to have troubled you," said Savannah, running her hands through her hair in hopes that it didn't look too disarray.

"It was no problem at all. We just wanted to make sure you were okay," said Victor with a polite smile.

"We should probably go now," said Duke, seemingly exhausted as he headed for the door.

"Wait, maybe you guys can come back this weekend? I'd like to treat you guys to a meal for helping me," said Savannah.

Duke and Victor looked at each other.

"That sounds great. We'll see you then," said Victor as they exited the office.

"Remember back in high school when we used to hide behind the bar on the deck and sneak shots of tequila?" Asked Savannah as she began laughing.

Her voice brought Heidi back from her thoughts.

"Yes, of course!" Heidi replied.

"Till this day, my father still doesn't know the truth about why he'd always find empty bottles. He still thinks someone had been breaking into the deck at night," said Savannah.

They both laughed.

"So, this party…will you be inviting Lucinda?" Asked Heidi.

"No, actually the thought hadn't crossed my mind," said Savannah as she continued to sip on the mimosa.

Heidi waited for Savannah to look back at her. Her eyes flashed black, instantly hypnotizing Savannah with her gaze.

"Send Lucinda a message and get her to come to your party tomorrow," Heidi instructed.

Savannah took her phone out and began texting.

"*Good* girl," Heidi smirked.

Back at headquarters, Hazel and Primrose were sparring in the training room. Hazel did a spinning roundhouse kick at Primrose. Primrose ducked down and while supporting herself with her right arm, she used her left leg to kick Hazel from underneath. Hazel landed on her side. When she looked up, Primrose was in the air ready to strike her. Hazel rolled over quickly before Primrose landed on top of her. Then, Hazel flew up and kicked towards Primrose. Primrose used her hands to block two of the kicks before falling backwards She grunted as she landed on her buttocks. Hazel floated down and helped her up. They walked over to a bench against the wall to get a drink of water.

"I think we should have a girls day out tomorrow and go see the parade," Hazel suggested as she tried to catch her breath.

"Yea, I think we definitely deserve a girls' day out," Primrose agreed as she wiped sweat off her forehead.

After they got cleaned up for lunch, they met Lucinda and Leah in the dining hall.

"I've got some *exciting* news to share!" Said Lucinda with a huge grin and her hands clasped in front of her.

"Agent Bradley got promoted to Senior Director and I got promoted to Department Director!" Lucinda exclaimed excitedly.

"And Duke got promoted to Chief!" Leah added.

"Congrats, Lucinda!" Said Hazel as she got up and gave her a hug.

"That's fantastic news about Agent Bradley and Duke!" Said Primrose with a smile.

"This is perfect timing. We were actually going to suggest for us to go into town for a girls' day trip tomorrow. We can do some shopping and watch the parade afterwards," said Hazel.

"That's a great idea. We should make an appointment at Calytrix's Spa. They have the best pixie dust body scrub there," Lucinda suggested.

"That sounds like a great plan!" Said Primrose cheerfully.

"Can't wait!" Leah responded.

The next morning, the girls got up early to head into town for their nine o'clock reservation at the Calytrix's Spa. Lucinda was waiting in the common room when Tyler walked out of his suite.

"Hey, Luce," said Tyler.

"Hi," said Lucinda with a smile.

"Are you free today?" Asked Tyler.

"Um…actually the girls and I were going to head into town for a girls' day out," Lucinda replied.

"Oh…that sounds like a good time. Enjoy your day at the spa then," said Tyler. He gave her a smile as he started towards the door.

"Tyler, wait," said Lucinda as she bit her lip.

Tyler turned around.

"Would you…like to catch a movie with me tomorrow night?" Asked Lucinda.

"Lucinda Griffin, are you finally asking me out on a date?" Asked Tyler with a smirk.

"Uh…I guess?" Lucinda responded as her face started to turn bright red.

"I'd love to," he said as he gave her a wink.

After he walked out of the room, Lucinda let out a mouthful of air and fanned herself with her hand. She never had to ask anyone out before and she was prepared to hide under a rock for the rest of her life, had he declined.

When everyone was ready, the girls got into Lucinda's SUV and headed into town. Calytrix's spa was at the center of town. The interior of the spa was bright, modern, and clean. The scent of lavender welcomed them as they stepped through the door. There were two women behind the counter near the entrance, having a conversation. They turned to face them when as they approached the counter.

"Good morning, ladies. Lucinda Griffin's party?" Asked one of the women.

"Yes," Lucinda answered.

"Great! My name is Aurora. Follow me this way ladies," said Aurora.

She led them to a small room with lockers.

"You may leave your personal items in these lockers. There are three changing rooms in the back. Please change into these robes and I will be back shortly," said Aurora politely.

She stepped out of the locker room and the girls started to change into their robes. Aurora knocked on the door after a few minutes.

"Is everybody decent?" She asked.

"Yep!" Said Lucinda, opening the door.

"Alrighty, please follow me this way," she replied

She led them down the hallway and into a larger room with four beds.

"You may remove your robes and lay under the sheets. Your masseuse will be in shortly," said Aurora as she closed the door behind her.

The girls removed their robes and laid on the beds. A few minutes later, four masseuses entered the room and introduced themselves. They dimmed the lights and lit a couple of candles. The room started to smell like lavender and peppermint. Then, the women began to massage them.

"This is definitely a well-deserved treat for all of us. Especially since Lucinda got a promotion and all of us joined the Aster Elites. Everything seems to have fallen into place," said Hazel.

"It sure has," said Leah, sounding very relaxed.

Her eyes were closed as she enjoyed every moment of it. Primrose closed her eyes and the image of Agent Bradley immediately popped into her head. Her thoughts flashed back to the night he had fallen asleep in the common room waiting for her to return. He looked so peaceful and she had noticed that he let his facial hair grow out a bit and it made him look so damn sexy. Then she recalled the moment when he rushed over to her after he had thrown a powerball at her and knocked her to the ground. She remembered the terror that was plastered across his face when he dropped to his knees next to her.

He had been so busy the last couple of weeks that she had barely even caught a glimpse of him. Every morning as she got ready for training, she had some hope that they'd run into each other.

"Why am I so afraid to tell him that I care about him?" She thought to herself.

Whenever she did see him, she wanted to run. To run away due to fear and to run into his arms because she *wanted* him at the same time. She couldn't understand why she so conflicted.

"Maybe I'm afraid of being let down…again."

She'd gotten her heart broken before and it wasn't something she wanted to go through *ever* again.

"Chad Wesley, my first love. The boy who broke my heart," she recalled in her mind.

Primrose met Chad Wesley back in college. He was in her chemistry class during her junior year and he had chosen her to be his lab partner. They dated for two more years after they graduated. One day, when he failed to meet her at the café, she decided to go over to his house to make sure he was okay. She was about to cross the street when his front door swung open and Ariella Mason walked out of his house. Primrose watched in slow motion as Ariella gave Chad a kiss on the lips before walking to her car. When Chad looked up, he noticed Primrose standing there across the road. Primrose turned and ran up the street. He tried to run after her but she had quickly turned a corner and casted the Micropixie aura to hide in a rose bush. As soon as he was out of sight, she returned to normal size and went straight home.

"*Primrose*. Primrose!" Yelled Hazel as she shook her on the shoulder.

Primrose snapped out of her thoughts.

"We're going to rinse off, come on," said Hazel.

The girls showered and went back to the locker room to change.

"I'm starving. Where should we eat?" Asked Hazel.

"Huh," said Lucinda, looking down at her phone.

"What's wrong?" Asked Leah.

"I just noticed a text from Savannah. She invited us to the party at Blue Wolf's Tavern she's having today," Lucinda replied.

"A party? That sounds like fun!" Said Primrose.

"We don't have to go if you're not okay with it, Leah," said Lucinda.

"No…it's fine. I mean that's what we came out for right?" Leah said with a shrug.

"Yes!" Hazel celebrated.

They quickly finished changing and walked over to Blue Wolf's Tavern which was only a couple of blocks away. The streets were packed with people and the girls struggled to get to the front door of Blue Wolf's Tavern. When they got inside, they walked right up to the bar.

"Hey, Lucinda!" Savannah yelled and waved from the other side of the bar.

Savannah made her way towards them as she slid between the crowd.

"I'm glad you guys made it! C'mon, I have a table for you," said Savannah with a smile.

She led them up the wooden stairs and out to a large balcony. She sat them down at a table where they were able to see the party on the deck below. There was a DJ set up at the front of the deck with the lake glistening behind him as he blasted upbeat party music. Savannah looked at Primrose and Hazel.

"Oh wow, and who are these fairies?!" Asked Savannah in amazement.

"This is Hazel and Primrose, they're my cousins," said Lucinda.

"You sure have a big family! I'll send over a waitress for you guys. Have fun, girls!" Said Savannah as she headed back downstairs.

Heidi was sitting on the far end of the restaurant when Lucinda, Leah, Hazel, and Primrose walked in. She kept her eyes on them as they made their way to the bar and kept watch as Savannah led them up to the second floor of the restaurant.

"*They're here. Now get the fairies away from the witches,*" Marco ordered her.

Heidi rolled her eyes. Just then, Savannah came back down the stairs. Heidi got up and walked over to her.

"Great party! You did such an incredible job! C'mon, let's have a toast!" Heidi yelled over the music.

Savannah nodded and they walked back to the table on the far end of the restaurant.

"I see that Lucinda made it…and she brought her friends?" Asked Heidi as she plopped down on the leather seat.

"Yea, two of her cousins are actually *fairies*," said Savannah with fascination.

"Fairies, huh? That's…interesting," said Heidi as she poured vodka and orange juice into Savannah's glass.

Meanwhile, the waitress approached the girls' table with a tray of drinks and set them on their table.

"This is so much fun! We haven't been out in such a long time!" Hazel shouted over the music.

"Look at all those people down there. I want to go dance!" Leah exclaimed.

"You guys go, I think I'm just going to relax," said Lucinda as she poured herself a cocktail.

"Me too," said Primrose.

Hazel and Leah got up and went downstairs to the lower deck. They held hands while trying to squeeze through the crowd. It seemed like more people had come in since they got there. They walked past the indoor bar and through the sliding doors that led outside. There were tables that lined the perimeter of the deck. Hazel and Leah started dancing as soon as they got to the middle of the dance floor.

Heidi continued to fill Savannah's glass with vodka and orange juice as Savannah continued talking. Heidi nodded along and pretended to listen.

"And after he proposed I just…r-ran! Ran out of there like a bat outta hell!" Savannah slurred. "But I…I still love him. Ya' know?" She said as she swayed a bit.

"So, why don't you do something about it?" Asked Heidi as she set the bottle of vodka back into the ice bucket.

"H-Huh?" said Savannah.

"You should get the love of your life *back*," said Heidi with narrowed eyes as she sipped on her cocktail.

"B-but he's with Leah now," said Savannah.

Heidi leaned towards Savannah.

"Well then…maybe we need to get *rid* of her," Heidi suggested with a sinister tone.

Savannah stared at Heidi for a second, then broke into laughter.

"You're joking!" Said Savannah as she laughed hysterically.

"I'm not," said Heidi with a straight face.

"W-what?" Asked Savannah, seemingly confused and beginning to feel a bit afraid.

"It's simple. We'll pull her aside and tell her to leave. Tell her that she doesn't *deserve* Duke," said Heidi with a smirk as she chomped down on a piece of ice.

"W-will that really work?" Asked Savannah.

"*The lycan is vulnerable. Do it now,*" said Marco.

Heidi's eyes flashed black for a second.

"Go over to the deck and spill a drink on Leah. Then, get the fairy alone and bring her to the restroom," Heidi instructed.

Savannah stood straight up with her drink in hand and walked towards the deck. She spotted Leah and Hazel in the middle of the dance floor and sped towards them with her drink. The drink splashed all over Leah's top.

"Oh!" Shouted Leah with her mouth gaping.

Hazel gasped.

"Oh my gosh! Leah, I am so sorry!" Said Savannah.

"It's okay...I'll just rinse this off," said Leah as she patted her top with her hand.

"I'll come with you," said Hazel.

"No. Why don't you stay and dance? I'll take good care of her," said Savannah.

"Yeah, stay and have fun. I'll be right back," said Leah as she walked back inside.

Savannah followed Leah back into the restaurant and Heidi made her way towards the restroom as soon as she caught sight of them.

"*She was supposed to get the fairy!*" Yelled Marco, making her wince.

"Don't worry. I've got a backup plan," Heidi said out loud.

"*You better,*" Marco warned.

Leah walked straight to the sink and started to clean herself off. When all of a sudden, she heard the door lock behind her and she quickly turned around. Leah gasped.

"Heidi," Leah scowled.

"Long time no see, Leah," said Heidi as she walked around Savannah.

Savannah stared straight ahead and swayed a bit. Leah noticed that she wasn't even blinking.

"What have you done to her?" Asked Leah as she slowly reached into her purse.

"Ah, ah! I wouldn't do that if I were you," said Heidi as she grabbed Savannah's wrist and raised it to her mouth. Then, slowly licked it.

"Savannah!" Yelled Leah.

Savannah stood still and had no facial reaction.

"She will *only* listen to me. The girl always had trouble holding her liquor. Everyone knows a vamp can hypnotize a snupe when they are vulnerable," said Heidi with a smirk.

"Let her go!" Leah shouted angrily.

"I will. But first, you will drink this," said Heidi as she tossed a small vial filled with clear liquid at her.

Leah caught it and stared at her.

"How do I know you'll let her go after I drink this?"

"Vampires *always* keep their word."

Leah slowly pulled the cork off the vial.

"Bring her back *first*."

"Fine," said Heidi, rolling her eyes.

She turned Savannah to face her. Her eyes flashed black.

"*Disenchant*," said Heidi.

Savannah blinked a few times and then gasped.

"Leah…?" Savannah said as she came to.

She looked at Leah and then Heidi, whose fangs seemed ready to sink into her neck. Heidi hissed at her.

"Run!" Leah yelled.

Savannah hesitated for a second and then turned towards the door. She struggled to unlock it for a second then swung the door open and bolted out. Heidi locked the door after her.

"Drink!" Heidi demanded.

Leah slowly raised the vial up to her lips and then drank the concoction. A few seconds later, she became dizzy and Heidi became a blur. Suddenly, Leah passed out and dropped onto the cold tiled floor. Savannah darted up the stairs and found Lucinda.

"Luce! Luce!" Yelled Savannah.

She ran towards Lucinda and almost knocked her over. Primrose shot up from her chair.

"It's Leah! Heidi..." said Savannah as she started to cry.

Lucinda grabbed her by the shoulders.

"What?! Where's Leah?!" Yelled Lucinda.

Savannah shook her head and sobbed.

"Savannah, get it together! Where's Leah?!" Asked Lucinda as she grabbed her shoulders.

Hazel ran over to them as she got to the top of the stairs.

"What's going on?" She asked.

"Heidi...s-she not the same anymore. I think something's wrong and she's still with Leah in the restroom..." said Savannah.

Lucinda let go of her and ran towards the stairs. Hazel and Primrose ran after her. She busted through the restroom door. It was empty and there was no sign of Leah or Heidi.

"Look!" Said Primrose pointing towards the floor.

She crouched under the sink and picked something up.

"That's Leah's stylus!" Said Hazel as she covered her mouth and her eyes filled with tears.

"Heidi must have taken her. You two stick together. We'll meet back at the car!" Lucinda instructed them as she dashed out of the restroom.

Hazel and Primrose stayed close to each other and searched the entire first floor of the restaurant. Then, they began to search the streets. About thirty minutes later, they headed back to the car and saw Lucinda jogging towards them.

"Anything?" Asked Hazel.

Lucinda shook her head and tried to catch her breath.

"I called Duke. He and Agent Bradley are on their way," said Lucinda.

Hazel started to tear up again.

"Oh, Leah," said Hazel as she put her face in her hands. Primrose put her arms around her.   "We'll find her," said Primrose.

Duke and Agent Bradley got there within twenty minutes and the sun had begun to set. They parked behind Lucinda's SUV. Duke jumped out of the driver's seat and ran over to Lucinda.

"What happened?!" He asked with bulging eyes.

"Heidi took Leah…she left her stylus behind," said Hazel sadly as she held it up.

Duke took the stylus and held it tight.

"Damn it!" Duke shouted angrily as he paced around.

"Where's Savannah now?" Asked Agent Bradley.

"She's probably still at the restaurant," Lucinda responded.

Duke sprinted towards Blue Wolf's Tavern and everyone ran after him. There were still a lot of people back at the restaurant. They searched the entire first floor and couldn't find Savannah. Lucinda ran upstairs to the second floor and found her sitting at a table alone with a bottle of vodka in her hand. Her hand was shaking as she took another sip. Duke and the rest of the group ran up the stairs.

"Savannah…" said Duke softly.

Savannah looked over. Her eyes were bloodshot from crying.

"Duke!" Cried Savannah as she sat up straight.

Duke sat down next to her and set the bottle of vodka on the table. He took his black leather jacket off and put it around her.

"Are you okay?" He asked.

"Y-yea…I'm okay. Duke, I'm so sorry. Leah…she saved me," said Savannah as she began to cry again.

"Savannah…I need you to try and remember *anything* that Heidi might've said to you when she took Leah," said Duke.

Savannah shook her head and closed her eyes. Tears trickled down her cheeks.

"Did she say where she was taking her?" Asked Lucinda.

"No," said Savannah as she put her face in her hands.

"What do we do now?!" Asked Hazel as panic began to set in.

"Wait…I remember something," said Savannah as she lifted her head up. "Heidi mentioned that she was staying at her old house on Airy Lane. It's on the south side of town."

Lucinda and Duke looked at each other.

"I know where it is," he said as he got up and ran down the stairs.

The group followed him back to their cars. It took them ten minutes to get to 906 Airy Lane. Heidi's house was the last one on a dead-end street. Duke parked a block away from the house and Lucinda parked right behind him. Everyone got out of the cars and gathered on the side of the street.

"Alright, we don't know who else she has in there. Everyone needs to be extremely aware of your surroundings and be prepared to defend yourselves. Hazel and Primrose, as soon as we have eyes on Leah, get her out of there. We'll take care of Heidi. Are you guys ready?" Asked Duke sternly.

"Yes," everyone replied in unison.

"Wait, why can't we go under the Obscure spell like we did back at the cemetery?" Asked Hazel.

"Witches can't use magic when we're under the Obscure spell. That's why we became visible again when we had to fight last time," Lucinda explained.

"Oh," said Hazel.

"Alright, stay behind me," Duke instructed.

He led them towards Heidi's house. It was a two-story building with white paneling and black shutters. None of the lights seemed be on inside. They slowed down as they got closer to the front door. Duke signaled for Agent Bradley to approach the door first. Agent Bradley waved his stylus over the doorknob. They heard a click and the door slowly creaked opened. Agent Bradley and Lucinda walked in first with their styluses drawn. They conjured glowballs once they were inside. Duke walked in as Hazel and Primrose followed behind him.

Agent Bradley and Lucinda went upstairs to search the second floor. Duke started walking down the hall to the left of the front door as Hazel and Primrose stayed right behind him. They looked inside the first two rooms which seemed to be empty. Then, they walked into the third room. It was slightly larger than the other two. They noticed an enormous wardrobe against the wall and the doors were slightly ajar. Duke walked towards the wardrobe and slowly opened the doors. Behind it, was a set of stairs but it was too dark for them to see what was at the bottom. Duke conjured a glowball and began to descend the stairs. The temperature seemed to drop as they walked down. When they got to the bottom, they noticed four rooms throughout the hallway. Duke checked the first room on the left and then the next one on the right.

When Duke reached the last room on the left, he noticed someone laying on the ground.

"Leah!" He shouted.

Hazel and Primrose ran in after him. Leah was laying on her side against the floor with her right arm stretched out. Duke lifted her up and noticed a small pool of blood underneath her. She'd been bitten on the right side of her neck. Primrose quickly took a vial of Salixantho elixir out of her purse and patted some of the substance on Leah's wound. Then, she took out a vial of Blue Butterfly and poured it into Leah's mouth. Hazel cast the Mend aura but it didn't have any effect on the wound. Duke lifted Leah off the ground with both of his arms and headed for the door. All of a sudden, a small explosion blew the door wide open. Hazel and Primrose were knocked down to the ground. Duke was tossed and slammed against the wall causing him to drop Leah onto the floor.

Duke grunted as he hit the wall. Hazel looked up and saw Heidi with three guards behind her, one was holding a stylus. She quickly jumped to her feet and threw a right hook at Heidi. Heidi dodged it by ducking down and when she stood up again, she backhanded Hazel. Hazel grunted from the strike and landed on her side.

Primrose quickly did a spinning roundhouse kick at Heidi, sending Heidi crashing into the wall. Two of the guards grabbed Primrose and the other one grabbed Hazel.

"Let them go!" Shouted Duke as he pointed his stylus as Heidi.

"Do you really think *that's* a smart move?" Asked Heidi as she turned her head towards the girls.

The vampire guards opened their mouths, ready to sink their teeth into Hazel and Primrose's necks.

Duke lowered his stylus.

"Take them to the car," Heidi ordered the guards.

The guards held Hazel and Primrose with their arms against their backs and forced them out of the room. Heidi locked the door behind them. They went up the stairs and through the wardrobe. Heidi led them out of the house and into the backyard. They turned left onto the driveway and headed towards the two black sedans. Out of nowhere, there was a whooshing sound and they were thrown by an unseen force.

Primrose yelped as she was tossed against the side of the house. Hazel was thrown to the ground and landed on all fours. When

Primrose looked up, she saw Lucinda and Agent Bradley standing there in the yard. They quickly conjured powerballs and launched them at the three guards. Then, they conjured stunnerballs and sent them flying at them again.

Hazel and Primrose quickly jumped to their feet. Then, stood on either sides of Agent Bradley and Lucinda. One of the guards began to conjure fireballs and launched them towards the four of them. Agent Bradley and Lucinda casted force fields. The fireballs sizzled as it crashed into their invisible shields.

Hazel jumped up five feet into the air with her hands on her sides, parallel to the ground and began to cast the Tempest charm. A small tornado began to form right below her and grew to about seven feet tall as it moved towards one of the vampire guards and engulfed him. The guard tried to escape the tornado but Hazel successfully trapped him inside.

The other two guards charged at Lucinda and Agent Bradley. Primrose glanced past the guards and saw Heidi running towards the black sedans. She flew towards Heidi and kicked her in the back. Heidi grunted as she dropped down on one knee and caught herself with both hands. She slowly stood up with her back to Primrose. Primrose landed on the grass and watched Heidi suspiciously. Heidi turned and smirked, then charged at Primrose. Primrose readied herself as Heidi ran towards her and lunged at her. She jumped up and lifted herself off the ground with her wings. Heidi quickly grabbed Primrose's left ankle and threw her onto the grass.

Down in the basement, Duke slowly got up as he groaned with pain and walked over to the door. He pointed his stylus at the doorknob.

"*Fulminate!*" Duke yelled weakly.

The doorknob blew off the door in a loud explosion. Duke walked back over to Leah and picked her up with both arms. He carried her out the door, up the stairs, and through the wardrobe. Then, ran through the front doors and towards his SUV. When he got to the car, he gently laid Leah across the backseat and shut the door. Then, he casted the Obscure spell over it and ran back towards Heidi's driveway.

Hazel was getting drained from holding the Tempest charm. All of a sudden, the tornado started to dissipate, as Hazel dropped to the ground, exhausted. When the vampire guard was released from the tornado, he charged at Hazel. She quickly fluttered her wings again to lift herself back up into the air. The guard reached up and grabbed Hazel's ankle, then yanked as hard as he could. Hazel fought to stay up in the air. She quickly cast the Hemlock charm, paralyzing him. As soon as he froze, she tried to loosen her ankles from his grip.

As Duke walked up the driveway past the two black sedans, he noticed one of the guards grabbing Hazel's ankle at the end of the dirt path. He ran towards the guard and launched himself at him, causing both of them to tumble onto the grass. The vampire guard quickly jumped back up and punched Duke in the face.

Duke grunted. While still up in the air, Hazel kicked her feet towards the guard and forced him to walk backwards. He tried to block her kicks with his hands but fell backwards onto the grass. Hazel landed on top of him and punched the side of his head several times in quick succession, knocking him unconscious.

On other side of the yard, Lucinda conjured fireballs and threw them towards the guard she was fighting. He did a somersault on the ground, dodging her fireball. He jumped to his feet and ran towards her with his fist in the air, ready to throw a punch. Lucinda conjured a stunnerball and kept it in her right hand as she dodged his punches. He threw a right-hook at Lucinda and she dodged it by ducking down. Then, she threw the stunnerball right at his throat. The guard started to shake as smoke plumed from his neck. The guard passed out and dropped to the ground. Lucinda watched him for a second to make sure he didn't move again just as Agent Bradley landed on his back in front of her.

The witch guard he was fighting had kicked him in the abdomen. She saw a fireball begin to form in the witch guard's palms and she charged at the guard. The guard saw her running towards him and jumped to the left causing him to lose the fireball in his hand. Just as she ran past him, he grabbed her hair and kicked her in the back of her knees. She dropped to the ground and caught herself with both hands. Agent Bradley jumped to his feet and grabbed the guard by his vest. But the guard slipped out of his grip and ran towards Heidi. Agent Bradley quickly tackled him to the ground. They landed right next to Primrose and Heidi in the middle of the driveway. Lucinda quickly assisted Agent Bradley by placing handcuffs on the guard.

Hazel flew over to Primrose who was still fighting Heidi. Heidi kicked Primrose in the abdomen, causing her to tumble backwards onto the ground. Heidi jumped on top of her and opened her mouth exposing her fangs. Her fangs were only a couple of inches away from Primrose's neck when Hazel grabbed Heidi's hair and pulled her back. With her right hand, she punched Heidi in the side of her face. Heidi groaned.

Primrose reached into her purse and pulled out a vial of Zingallium. Hazel saw what Primrose was doing so she grabbed

Heidi's hair again. Then, she grabbed Heidi's right arm and held it behind her back, forcing her to sit up. Primrose took the cork off the vial and walked towards Heidi. She straddled Heidi's legs and squeezed her mouth open to pour the bright pink elixir in. Heidi fell on her side, against the ground, and began to gasp for air. They got off of her and stepped back. Heidi wrapped both of her hands around her throat and started coughing uncontrollably. They watched as black ashes floated out of Heidi's mouth and into the nostrils of the witch guard that was being held down by Agent Bradley.

"No! Stop!" A voice yelled from behind Hazel.

Everyone looked up and Hazel turned around. Victor was standing there at the front of the driveway. Behind him, was Agent Zoe Salvatore and Agent Mark Lyle.

"Vic-tor," Heidi managed to whisper before passing out.

Victor ran over to Heidi and crouched down. He reached into his pocket and pulled out a vial filled with purple liquid, then poured it into her mouth.

"Why are you wasting the Amaranth of Life elixir on her?!" Asked Hazel.

"We need to know what happened to Marco. He could still be out there," said Victor.

Agent Salvatore and Agent Lyle ran over to help Victor. They put Heidi in handcuffs and carried her off. Victor turned to face Hazel and then wrapped his arms around her. Primrose walked over to them and joined the hug. Agent Bradley and Lucinda forced the witch guard to stand up. They kept him restrained while walking him out of the driveway. Duke grabbed the other unconscious guard and threw handcuffs on him. Victor jogged over to help Duke, together they dragged the witch guard up the driveway. Hazel and Primrose followed behind them back to the cars. When they were close to the SUVs, Duke let the other agents handle the unconscious guard and ran over to his SUV. He waved his stylus over his car and as it reappeared, he quickly opened the passenger door.

"Victor! I need you!" He yelled.

Victor ran over and noticed Leah laying across the backseat. He reached into his pocket and grabbed another vial of the Amaranth of Life elixir. He popped the cork off and squeezed Leah's mouth open, then poured the elixir into her mouth.

"We've got to get to the infirmary! Quickly!" Victor shouted.

Everyone got back into their cars and sped towards headquarters. Duke drove up to the manor's front doors and stopped with a screeching halt. Dr. Saunders and a handful of infirmary staff were waiting there for them with gurneys. Agent Bradley helped Duke carry Leah onto a gurney and they wheeled her into the infirmary.

"We administered the Amaranth of Life elixir about fifteen minutes ago," said Duke as he ran besides the gurney.

"We've got to get an IV started," Dr. Saunders instructed one of the nurses. "Duke, I need you to stay back while we work on her."

Duke let go of the gurney as they wheeled her into the emergency room. He walked over to the waiting area and sat down. His knuckles and left brow bone had minor cuts. Lucinda, Hazel, and Primrose ran in a few seconds later.

"Duke! Where is she?" Asked Hazel.

"They took her into the emergency room," said Duke.

Just then, Agent Bradley walked in. Primrose noticed that he was clutching his left ribcage. She walked over to him.

"Hey, are you alright?" She asked him.

"Yea...I'm fine. Probably just a bruised rib," said Agent Bradley as he managed a half-smile.

Tyler ran over to them.

"Luce! What happened? Are you alright?" Asked Tyler as he crouched down and examined her.

"I'm fine. Don't worry," said Lucinda.

"You've got cuts on the side of your face and knuckles. Come with me," said Tyler as he helped Lucinda up.

Tyler and Lucinda disappeared behind the double doors. A minute later, a few more doctors came out to check on the rest of them.

The following morning Hazel, Primrose, and Lucinda went back to the infirmary. Duke was sitting in the waiting area.

"Duke…have you gone back to your suite at all?" Asked Hazel with concern as she sat down next to him.

"No," he replied, shaking his head as he ran his hand down his face.

Hazel saw Dr. Saunders come out of the double doors and ran over to her. Duke shot up from his chair.

"Dr. Saunders! How's Leah? Is she okay?" Cried Hazel.

"Yes, she's okay for now but she's still unconscious. Thank goodness for the Amaranth elixir. We've got her hooked up to an IV and I'll call you as soon as she wakes," said Dr. Saunders as she walked over to the front desk.

"That's good news. Duke, you should get some rest. We'll let you know as soon as we hear anything," Lucinda suggested.

"Yea…I guess I should. Just make sure you call me as soon as she's awake," said Duke.

Lucinda nodded and patted him on the back as he turned to walk out.

"We should get something to eat and then we can check back here afterwards," said Lucinda.

The girls nodded in agreement. As they were walking towards the main building, they saw Agent Bradley walking towards them. Hazel and Lucinda looked at each other.

"We'll wait for you in the dining hall," Hazel told Primrose with a smile and a wink.

Agent Bradley waved at Lucinda and Hazel. The girls waved back and continued to walk towards the main building.

"Hey," said Agent Bradley.

"How's your rib?"

"Still bruised. How about you?"

"Hazel, Lucinda and I used some of the Salixantho on our cuts and scrapes. I'm pretty much all healed up."

They stood there awkwardly and avoided eye contact.

"Uh…Do you have time to grab a cup of coffee with me?" Asked Agent Bradley, scratching his head.

"Sure," she replied with a smile.

His face lit up. They slowly walked towards the main building.

"I saw that right-hook you threw at Heidi. Great job taking her down," said Agent Bradley.

"I had a good trainer and good thing she can't throw powerballs," said Primrose with a grin.

Agent Bradley chuckled.

"Ow! Damn it!" Agent Bradley clutched his left rib and curled his torso.

"Are you okay?!" Asked Primrose as she jumped in front of him and put her hand over his.

He stared down at her and she gazed into his eyes. As he slowly leaned closer towards her face, she held her breath and watched as he closed his eyes. She suddenly felt panicked and took a step back. Agent Bradley's eyes opened again.

"Here, this should help," said Primrose.

Her wings began to flutter and increased in speed as she waved her left hand over the left side of his torso. A bright glow surrounded her entire body. When she stopped glowing, she put her hand back down.

"How's it feel now?" She asked with furrowed brows.

Agent Bradley pushed around his rib with his fingers.

"It doesn't hurt anymore," said Agent Bradley with relief.

Primrose smiled contentedly.

"You're my hero," Agent Bradley joked.

They both laughed and continued to walk towards the café.

In the dining hall, Lucinda and Hazel grabbed bowls of cereal and sat down at an empty table.

"I hope she wakes up soon," said Hazel as she stirred the bowl of cereal.

"She will," Lucinda assured her.

Just then, Victor walked in and Hazel's face lit up.

"Hey," said Victor with a sympathetic look on his face.

Hazel stood up and stared at him for a second before throwing her arms around his neck. He held her tight for a moment and gave her a kiss on her forehead.

"I wasn't sure if you were still mad at me," he said, feeling relieved.

"Why would I be mad at you?" She asked.

"Because I gave Heidi the elixir."

"You did what you had to do and you were right, we need to know what happened to Marco."

"How are you feeling Luce?" Asked Victor.

"I'm still bruised and a little sore but I'll be okay. Thanks for asking," said Lucinda with a smile.

"How'd you know where to find us last night?" Asked Hazel as she sat back down.

"I drove over here when I got off work and got here in the early evening last night. I was hoping to catch the fireworks with you. When I walked in, I bumped into Agent Salvatore and Agent Lyle on their way out. They told me that Lucinda called Duke and that Heidi had taken Leah. I insisted that I go with them and that we grab some elixirs just in case," said Victor.

"And good thing you did. If you hadn't, Leah probably wouldn't have made it," said Lucinda. The terrifying thought made her shift in her seat.

Hazel nodded and gave Victor a kiss on the cheek.

"What's going to happen to Heidi and her two guards now?" Asked Hazel.

"They're in the holding tower behind this building. We will try to get more information out of Heidi before we decide what to do with her." said Lucinda.

"But what about the witch guard that was helping her? Won't he be able to cast a spell and break out?" Asked Hazel.

"He's been put under special handcuffs that blocks his magic and the tower is *heavily* guarded," said Lucinda.

"I've got to head back to Hallowed Falls now, but I'll be back to see you in a few days," said Victor as he gave Hazel a kiss.

"Okay, love you," said Hazel.

"Love you, too," said Victor with a wink.

He got up and left the dining hall.

"You two are so cute," Lucinda teased.

Hazel laughed.

"Thanks. What about you and Tyler? He seemed really concerned about you at the infirmary last night," said Hazel.

"Yea...he was really sweet. Before we left for the spa yesterday, I actually asked if he'd like to catch a movie with me. But I don't think it's going to happen," said Lucinda.

"Why not?" Asked Hazel with a frown.

"Because...we don't know when Leah will wake up and there's just... too much going on," said Lucinda.

"I hope you guys get together soon. I can tell he really likes you," said Hazel with a conspiratorial tone.

Lucinda rolled her eyes and smiled.

Chapter 8

It was the following Monday after Independence Day. Duke, Director Marchand, and Lucinda were all heading for the holding tower together. They walked into the west building behind the manor and got on the elevators to get to the third floor. An enclosed bridge connected the west building to the holding towers and armory tower on either sides. The three of them got off on the third floor and walked over the bridge to the holding tower.

Heidi had been brought into an interrogation room prior to their arrival for questioning. There were two armed agents standing guard outside of the room. Heidi was wearing a cobalt-blue short sleeved jumpsuit with 'A.E. Inmate' printed in silver on the back and thick iron handcuffs wrapped around both wrists and chained to the ground. The room was dull, with walls painted a dark gray and was dimly lit by a few flood lights.

"Heidi Hendrix, sixth generation of the Alexander clan. Half-vampire and former A.E. agent. Are you aware of all the charges held against you?" Asked Lucinda.

Heidi lifted her head to look Lucinda dead in the eyes and smiled but did not speak.

"You can hold your tongue all you want, Heidi. But you know better than anyone that we are well equipped, and we *will* get you to answer. We can do this the hard way…if that's the way you want to go about it," said Lucinda firmly.

Heidi's smile faded away and she tried to get up. The chains crashed loudly against the metal chair and Lucinda smirked, she knew she had gotten to Heidi.

Lucinda nodded at Director Marchand, who was holding a rolled-up pouch under her arms. She walked over to the table that was a foot away from where Heidi was sitting. As she unrolled the pouch, there were clinking sounds and Heidi could see small vials inside. Heidi's eyes flashed black as she stared into Director Marchand's eyes.

"Oh, silly girl. You know your powers don't work here," said Director Marchand.

"Uuggh!" Heidi groaned as she shook the chains again.

Director Marchand picked up a small vial filled with bright green liquid. She walked over to Heidi and popped the cork off. Lucinda went behind Heidi and put her in a choke hold. Heidi squirmed to get loose but Lucinda held her tightly. Director Marchand squeezed Heidi's mouth to get it open and poured the concoction in. Lucinda let go of Heidi and walked around to face her again.

Director Marchand pointed her stylus at Heidi.

"*Candor sincera*" Director Marchand chanted.

A glowing white mist floated out of her stylus and surrounded Heidi.

Heidi pursed her lips to prevent herself from talking.

"Is Marco still alive?" Asked Duke.

Heidi fidgeted in the chair and tried to keep her mouth closed.

"I-I...d-don't kn-ow," said Heidi as the Candor spell forced her to speak.

Duke took a step forward.

"What do you mean?" Asked Duke in a serious tone.

Heidi looked up at him and tilted her head.

"Hm, Duke Bryant. That fiancée of yours was so easy to hypnotize. Her low tolerance for alcohol and broken heart made her so weak. She still loves you, you know. You should've seen her *pathetic* little heart pouring out the details of the night she rejected you. Oh, but wait...you've got yourself a *witch* now, right? Leah Plumeria? She didn't put up much of a fight either. Seems like your taste in women goes down with age," said Heidi with a grin.

Duke slowly conjured a stunnerball in his right hand then, squashed it and took a breath. He walked up to her then, put both of his hands on the arms of the chair and shook it.

"Cut the bullshit, Heidi! Where is Marco?!" Duke shouted angrily in her face.

Heidi opened her mouth and licked her fangs. Lucinda pulled Duke back.

"I don't *know*," said Heidi nonchalantly.

"Is he still alive?" Asked Lucinda.

"I. don't. know," said Heidi.

Lucinda raised her arm and pointed her stylus at Heidi.

"He is no longer in his *physical* form," said Heidi as she sat up straighter.

"What? How is that possible?" Asked Director Marchand.

Heidi squeezed her eyes shut then took a deep breath.

"When Marco returned to the Alexander manor a few months ago, he told us that he would make the Alexander name reputable again. He promised us powers, the *Summerland* powers. He eventually got his henchmen to retrieve a small vial of Enchantress elixir but it didn't work on him. I guess magical transformation doesn't work on someone who's pretty much already *dead* but drinking the blood of Serena Bennett and the fairy at the flower shop must have activated the elixir. Then, when the Summerland heir tricked him into drinking the elixir at the arboretum, he exploded and turned into a pile of ashes. I thought that was the end of him, but somehow, he partially possessed my body afterwards. His physical body was destroyed but his vamp soul lived on...*inside* of me. After I was forced to ingest the same elixir, he was released from my body," said Heidi with a hint of regret in her voice.

"Partially possessed your body? So, that means you still had some control over yourself and yet you *continued* to help him? Did you know Victor could have died?!" Lucinda spat as she took a step towards her.

Duke held Lucinda back and Heidi frowned as she shook her head.

"After you saved Hazel, I told him I no longer wanted to serve him, but he got angry and waited until I fell asleep one night to fully take over my body. He sedated my parents and took them to a secret location. The following day, he threatened me and said If I didn't help him capture the heir of Summerland, he was going to kill them. I didn't mean for Victor to get hurt, I would never..." said Heidi as she stared down at the ground.

Duke looked at Director Marchand and Lucinda, then signaled for them to walk out of the room. Director Marchand grabbed her pouch off the table and walked towards the door. All three of them walked out of the interrogation room and closed the door behind them. Duke walked down the hall and they followed.

"We need to find out where Marco's *soul* is," said Duke.

"Wait, when Agent Bradley and I were holding down the witch guard, I saw something that looked like black mist come out of Heidi and into his nostrils. I didn't think much of it at the time because of what was going on, but that's probably where Marco is," said Lucinda.

Duke turned back around and started to walk back down the hall. He walked past the interrogation room where Heidi was. The room right next to it was where the witch guard was being held. There were another two armed agents standing in front of the door. Duke opened it and walked in with his stylus drawn. Lucinda and Director Marchand followed behind him. The witch guard was sitting on the chair in the center of the room and he was wearing an inmate jumpsuit. His head was facing downwards.

"Wake up!" Duke shouted as he walked up to the chair.

The man began to laugh wickedly as he lifted his head up.

Director Marchand set her pouch on the table and picked up the vial containing the Candor elixir. Duke grabbed the man from behind to keep him from moving then Director Marchand squeezed his mouth open and poured the elixir in. When Duke let go of him, he spit the elixir out and laughed again. Lucinda walked up to him and punched him in the side of his face.

He grunted and spat on the floor.

"Bring Hazel here," Duke ordered.

Lucinda nodded and hurried out of the room.

"So it seems that you Alexanders like to do things the hard way," said Director Marchand as she pointed her stylus at him.

"We know you're in there...*Marco*," said Duke sternly.

The witch guard's expression changed to anger. He growled and tried to get up but the chains held him down. They waited until Hazel arrived.

"What's going on?" Asked Hazel as she stepped into the room and looked at the man sitting in the center of the room.

"Marco's soul has taken over this witch's body. I need you to cast the Hemlock charm," said Duke.

Hazel nodded and walked towards the chair. She began to flutter her wings and as her entire body began to glow, she waved her left hand over him. He suddenly froze. When she was done, Hazel left the room. Duke and Director Marchand forced the elixir into this mouth again. This time, they made sure it went down his throat. Lucinda kept her stylus pointed at their prisoner.

"Where is Marco?!" Lucinda asked.

"Come and get me, Lucinda Griffin," Marco growled and licked his lips.

"Where are Heidi's parents?" Asked Duke.

"Hidden in a cave down b-by R-rose Gold Beach," said Marco, twisting his neck.

His shook his head as he tried to stop himself from saying more.

"Are they alive?" Asked Lucinda.

"Yesss..." he hissed.

"Where exactly is the cave?" Asked Duke.

"Down...on the east end...of the beach...by the boulders...nooo!" Shouted Marco as he fidgeted in the chair causing the chains to make loud clunking sounds.

Duke walked out of the room. Lucinda and Director Marchand followed him.

"Send a team to Rose Gold Beach. We need to rescue Heidi's parents," Duke instructeas he continued down the hallway. Lucinda and Director Marchand nodded as they followed him out of the holding tower.

Lucinda assembled a team which included Hazel, Agent Kensington, Agent Lyle, and Agent Salvatore. She called the team, including Director Bradley into the conference hall for a briefing. When everyone got seated, she began.

"As you guys may know, we have both Heidi Hendrix and Marco Alexander in custody at the holding tower. Marco has taken control over the body of one of his henchmen and has admitted to the kidnapping of Heidi's parents. Due to the fact that they are civilians who may be innocent, we are responsible for returning them to safety. We will need to gear up and meet in the foyer in twenty minutes and head over to Rose Gold Beach in Hallowed Falls. Hazel, I need you to grab an elixir kit. Everyone must be on high alert at all times and be prepared to defend yourselves. We anticipate that more of Marco's henchmen may be guarding the hostages. Our mission is to search and rescue Britannia and Robert Hendrix. Any questions?" Asked Lucinda.

The room was silent.

"Alright, let's go!" Lucinda shouted.

Everyone got up and headed towards the armory tower. The team met up in the foyer shortly after. Agent Lyle pulled up to the front in an A.E. SUV and they all jumped in.

"So, it's true then? Marco is still *alive?*" Asked Hazel with a worried look on her face.

"Yes, unfortunately. But we've got him secured at the holding tower, he is no longer a threat to us," said Lucinda.

The team arrived at Rose Gold Beach late in the afternoon. When they got out of the SUV, they gathered in a circle.

"There are civilians on the west end of the beach. We need to go around the back so that we don't alarm anyone. Follow me this way," instructed Lucinda.

The team followed Lucinda out of the parking lot and down a path lined with tall grass. Gradually the path turned into pink sand. They walked towards the east end of the beach and reached a wall of boulders that led out to the ocean.

"The cave must be on the other side of these boulders," said Lucinda.

The jagged wall stood about six feet tall and Lucinda was able to climb up with ease. The rest of the team followed. Once they were on the other side, they could see the opening of the cave about half a mile down the beach.

As they approached the opening of the cave, they could feel a cool breeze blowing at them. Hazel tried to look as far into the cave as she could but it was pitch black. The smell of salty ocean lingered in the air as the wind caused her hair to whip against Hazel's face. Lucinda began to conjure two glowballs.

"I'll walk in first. Stay close behind and *don't* make any unnecessary noises," said Lucinda.

Everyone nodded and Lucinda slowly walked into the cave. The crunching of sand and rocks echoed around them as they walked. It got colder and the sound of the waves became more distant as they walked further into the cave. Soon, Lucinda spotted a dim flickering light and as they approached what seemed to be a room lit by two torches that stood at the center. She waved her hand and the glowballs dissipated. Between the two torches were two glass preservation pods just like the ones Lucinda found at the Alexander manor. She looked around the room with her stylus pointing straight out in front of her. She carefully approached the pods while the rest of the team searched the remainder of the small cave. Hazel stayed close behind Lucinda, prepared to cast a defensive charm if necessary.

Hazel peeked into the pods as she approached them. She gasped loudly and covered her mouth with both hands. The team ran over to make sure they were okay and discovered that within each pod, was a body. A male in one and a female in the other. Agent Lyle examined them.

"They're completely stiff. I believe they've been petrified. We were too late," said Agent Lyle.

"Damn it!" Shouted Lucinda angrily. Suddenly, they heard running footsteps heading towards from the opening of the cave. The team huddled with their styluses facing outwards. Out of nowhere, a woman's laughter echo around them and before they knew it, there was a strong gust of wind that surrounded them like a tornado. It blew the torches out, leaving them in complete darkness.

Lucinda tried to conjure a glowball but before she was able to toss it into the air, she was punched in the abdomen. She let out a grunt and gasped for air. It felt as if her lungs closed off and the pain grew as she curled forward. She caught a glimpse of a woman with green eyes and reddish-brown hair before she disappeared.

"Luce!" Hazel shouted with panic in her voice.

She could hear the rest of the team being attacked and she knew she had to do something, so she jumped up into the air and cast the Glare charm. Her entire body emitted an incredibly bright white glow and when she looked down, everyone was shielding their eyes. Agent Lyle conjured two glowballs and tossed them into the air. When Hazel saw this, she turned off her aura, then floated back down next to Lucinda.

"Luce, are you okay?" Asked Hazel with conern.

Lucinda glanced around the room.

"Yea...I'm fine," she replied.

"Where's Agent Kensington?" Asked Agent Salvatore.

Everyone glanced around and there was no sign of Agent Kensington. Lucinda got up and ran towards the opening of the cave. The rest of the team ran after her. When they got to the opening, she found his badge in the sand but Agent Kensington was nowhere to be found. Lucinda stood there for a second, then grabbed his badge off the sand and shut her eyes.

"Powers help me find, what my eyes cannot seek, before I am out of time, help me find what is lost," Lucinda chanted.

She was silent for a minute.

"Shit! It didn't work!" Said Lucinda as she kicked the sand.

"What do we do now?" Asked Hazel.

"I have to report the bodies to the Hallowed Falls PD. Then, we head back to headquarters," said Lucinda.

The team walked back to the wall of boulders and climbed over it. When they got back to the SUV, Lucinda made the call to the Hallowed Falls PD. After she hung up, they all got into the car and drove back to headquarters. Lucinda went to look for Director Bradley as soon as she returned and found him in his office with Duke.

"Luce, what'd you find?" Asked Duke as she walked in.

"Heidi's parents...but we were too late. They've been petrified. There's one more thing, Duke…we lost Agent Kensington," said Lucinda dejectedly.

"What? How?" Asked Duke with serious concern.

"After we discovered the bodies in the cave, there was a woman in there with us. She blew out the torches and we couldn't see anything. Just as I conjured a glowball, she punched me in the stomach. I caught a glimpse of her green eyes and reddish-brown hair before she disappeared into the darkness. By the time we could see again, we realized Agent Kensington was gone. We found his badge at the entrance to the cave." Lucinda explained.

"Did you try the Locator spell?" Asked Duke.

"Yes, but I couldn't see anything. All I saw was darkness," said Lucinda.

"Then I think we need to pay Heidi another visit," said Duke grimly.

Duke, Director Bradley, and Lucinda made their way to the holding tower. They walked up to the interrogation room where Heidi was being held and Lucinda walked in first. Director Bradley and Duke walked in behind her.

"Agent Bradley, what a treat," said Heidi with a sly grin.

"Heidi…My team and I just came from Rose Gold Beach, where Marco kept your parents hostage. Heidi… they had been petrified before we got there. It was too late to save them," said Lucinda.

"W-what? No. That's not possible! He promised! Nooo!" Cried Heidi as she fought the chains holding her down.

"Heidi, I'm so sorry about your parents. In order to get them justice, we're going to *need* your cooperation," said Director Bradley.

"There was a woman in the cave with us and it seemed like she had been guarding the cave. She had green eyes and reddish-brown hair. Who else were you guys working with?" Asked Lucinda.

"There is *no one* else. I was Marco's only right hand. The rest were snupes we recruited from Hallowed Falls and Crystal Brooks," said Heidi as she continued to weep.

"When we raided your parent's manor, there were two empty pods in the basement. Who did they belong to?" Asked Agent Bradley.

"T-two…?" Asked Heidi.

She looked down on the ground and shook her head.

"That can't be. There's always been just one empty pod, Marco's. But...if there is a second empty pod like you say...then the name should be on the side of the pod," said Heidi.

Duke walked over to the door and went into the hall.

"Take her to her cell. Make sure she gets sustenance," Duke instructed the two agents next to the door and started to walk away.

Director Bradley and Lucinda followed him down the hall.

"I'll take a team with me to the Alexander manor first thing tomorrow morning," said Lucinda. Duke nodded and they all left the holding tower together.

When Lucinda got back to the suites, she saw Primrose, Hazel and Leah in the common room.

"Luce!" Shouted Leah as she got up and pulled her into a hug.

"Are you okay? Let me take a look at your abdomen," said Leah.

"I'm fine, really," said Lucinda. She was exhausted and although her abdomen was sore, she'd rather just lay in bed.

"Hazel told me what happened. Did you find out who the woman was?" Asked Leah, curiously.

"No, Heidi didn't know who it was but I recall seeing two empty preservation pods back at the Alexander manor. Whoever the woman was must be the owner of that pod and her name should be on the side of it. We will have to go back there tomorrow to check it out," Lucinda told Hazel.

Hazel nodded.

The next morning, Lucinda had the team meet her in the foyer. Agent Salvatore, Agent Lyle, and Hazel got into Lucinda's SUV and they drove towards Hallowed Falls. Once they arrived at the Alexander manor on west end of Dragon's Breath Trail, they got out of the car and walked towards the manor. Lucinda slowly approached the front door and noticed that it was slightly ajar.

"Probably left open from the last time we were here," Lucinda thought to herself.

She pushed the door open and stepped into the foyer.

"Agent Lyle and Agent Salvatore, I need you to make sure the rest of the manor is cleared. Hazel, you're with me," said Lucinda.

Agent Lyle and Agent Salvatore headed upstairs, and Hazel followed Lucinda to the back of the foyer. They stopped at a door leading down to the basement. Lucinda instinctively drew her stylus and pointed it down the stairs in front of her then, looked at Hazel. Hazel nodded at her, signaling that she was ready.

They slowly descended the stairs and Hazel could feel the air get colder the further down they got. Lucinda conjured two glowballs so that they could see when they got to the bottom. She led Hazel over to where the two empty pods were.

"Oh my God. Are these…?" Asked Hazel as she examined the pods.

"The old Alexander clan? Most likely," Lucinda replied as she made her way to the empty pods.

"This is *incredibly* creepy," said Hazel as she continued to scan the room.

Lucinda walked around one of the empty pods and bent down to where she saw a gold plaque on the side.

"This one belongs to Marco," said Lucinda as she stood up and walked around the other empty pod and read the plaque.

"Cassidy Alexander," Lucinda read out loud.

"Who's that?" Asked Hazel.

"I don't know but that's got to be who attacked us in the cave," said Lucinda.

A loud crash suddenly came from upstairs. Hazel and Lucinda ran upstairs as fast as they could. When they got to the hallway, Agent Salvatore was sitting on the ground with blood running down her forearm and Agent Lyle was kneeling next to her. Lucinda ran over and kneeled down as well.

"Zoe!" Yelled Lucinda.

"I'm alright. Just a cut on my right elbow," said Agent Salvatore reassuringly.

"What happened?" Asked Lucinda.

"We were coming back downstairs when we heard some shuffling down the hall. I went to investigate while Agent Salvatore stayed in the foyer. When I went into the first room on the left, I caught a woman with reddish-brown hair rummaging through the drawers. She saw me and ran past me but Agent Salvatore was able to grab her arm as she ran into the foyer," said Agent Lyle.

"She grabbed a nearby vase and threw it at me. I used my arm to block it," explained Agent Salvatore. She happened to look past Lucinda and noticed the photographs hanging on the wall next to the stairs. "Wait a minute...that's her! That's the woman that was just here," she said, pointing towards the stairs.

Lucinda walked over to the wall and climbed halfway up the stairs. She stopped in front of the photograph where Agent Salvatore had pointed to. The woman in the photo had reddish-brown hair and green eyes. Lucinda recognized her as the woman she saw at the cave.

"It *is* her. She's the one who was in the cave with us, Cassidy Alexander," said Lucinda, stunned at the photograph.

She took the photo off the wall and walked back down. Agent Lyle helped Agent Salvatore stand up.

"This might help," said Hazel.

She fluttered her wings and her left hand hovered over the cut on Agent Salvatore's elbow. A golden glow surrounded Hazel's entire body and once she finished casting the Mend aura, she put her hand back down. Agent Salvatore inspected her elbow and there was no longer any sign of a laceration.

"Wow! Thank you." said Agent Salvatore, in awe.

Hazel smiled and nodded at her.

"We've gotta head back. C'mon," said Lucinda as she led them back to her car.

As they drove up past the front gates of headquarters, Lucinda parked her SUV off to the side of the main building. The late afternoon sun was beaming down on them as they got out of the car. Lucinda headed for Director Bradley's office in the North building while the rest of the team went to the dining hall. She knocked on Director Bradley's office door.

"Come in," said Director Bradley.

He glanced up from his computer as Lucinda walked in.

"Oh, hey Luce. Did you get a name from the pod?" He asked.

"Yes, Cassidy Alexander," said Lucinda as she held up the photo.

"Alright, let's go see if Heidi recognizes who this is," said Director Bradley as he got up from behind the desk

Lucinda and Agent Bradley headed towards the holding tower to question Heidi. They were waiting in one of the interrogation rooms when two agents brought Heidi in. They put her in the chair in the middle of the room and attached chains to her handcuffs.

"Heidi, I took this from your house in Hallowed Falls. Who is she?" Asked Lucinda as she held up the photo.

Heidi stared at the photo.

"Cassidy Alexander…she was the wife of my great-great granduncle, Dean Alexander. He was Marco's brother. Why do you have that photo?" Asked Heidi.

"She's the one who was with your parents in the cave. She must've been working for Marco on the side without you knowing," said Director Bradley.

"That's…not possible. *How* is that possible?" Asked Heidi.

"That's what we're going to find out," said Director Bradley as he walked out of the room.

Director Bradley and Lucinda went up to the fourth floor where the holding cells were. They walked up to where Marco was being held. Two heavily armed agents were standing guard right outside. One of them unlocked the door to let Director Bradley and Lucinda in. They found Marco laying on the twin-size bed against the wall. His hands were cuffed in front of him and each of his ankles had an iron cuff around it. He watched as they stepped into his cell and closed the door behind them.

"Ah, you really are a sight for sore eyes, Lucinda. Just like your great-great grandmother, Rosa," said Marco with a smirk.

Lucinda raised her stylus at him.

"Who is Cassidy Alexander and why is she working for you?" Asked Lucinda.

Marco's smirk slowly faded and clenched his jaw.

"She was my brother's wife," said Marco.

Lucinda conjured a stunnerball her left hand.

"Why is your brother's *wife* helping you? Has she survived with you all this time?" Asked Lucinda as she began to lose patience.

"Yes. My brother was *weak*. He couldn't comfort her when they lost their first child. Cassidy turned to me for comfort. We fell in love and I helped her survive all these years," said Marco.

"Why did you order her to kill Heidi's parents?" Asked Director Bradley.

"Kill them? I have nothing to do with that. She must've done that on her own," said Marco. Director Bradley and Lucinda looked at each other, then they walked out of the cell.

"What do we do now?" Asked Lucinda.

"He's not going to give up much intel. We need to continue our efforts in finding Agent Kensington. We also need to be on high alert as Cassidy could come for Marco," Director Bradley instructed.

Lucinda nodded and they headed back to the main building.

Meanwhile in the common room, Hazel and Primrose were resting in front of the fireplace when Hazel's cellphone rang.

"Hello? Yes. She is?! We'll head over there right now," said Hazel as she hung up.

"What is it?" Asked Primrose.

"Leah's awake," Hazel said with relief in her voice.

They both got up and hurried out of the common room. When they got to the infirmary, Dr. Saunders led them to the room where Leah was recovering. Duke was sitting down next to her when they got there.

"Hazel! Primrose!" Cried Leah.

Hazel and Primrose ran over and wrapped their arms around her.

"How are you feeling?" Asked Primrose as she pulled away.

"Like I'm having the worst hangover, ever. But I'm alive thanks to you guys," said Leah with a smile.

"I was afraid that we might have lost you," said Hazel as she began to tear up again.

"But you didn't and I'm fine," said Leah as she put her hand on Hazel.

"Alright, we're going to let you rest some more. I'll see you tomorrow, okay?" Said Hazel, wiping her tears with the back of her hand.

"Okay," said Leah with a smile.

They gave Leah another hug and left.

Leah turned her head back to face Duke.

"Hey," Duke said softly.

"Hey," said Leah as she continued to smile.

Duke leaned down to give her a quick kiss.

"She's right, we almost lost you. What the hell happened at Blue Wolf's Tavern?" Asked Duke.

Leah tried to sit up and Duke adjusted the pillow for her.

"I don't really remember much. We were all having such a great time. Hazel and I were dancing on the deck when Savannah…Savannah spilled a drink on me," she said as began to recall the events of that day. "She walked me to the restroom and then…*Heidi*! Heidi, locked us in there. Savannah had been hypnotized but once Heidi released her, she made me drink something and I don't remember anything after that."

Leah reached up and touched the gauze pad over her neck. Duke reached for her hand and held it in both of his and kissed it. Leah felt his warm lips gently touch the back of her hand and it instantly warmed her entire body.

"I'll let you rest and I'll swing by first thing tomorrow when you get discharged and help you back to your suite," said Duke as he stood up and kissed her forehead.

Leah nodded and smiled. She slowly shut her eyes as Duke left the room.

Chapter 9

Agent Kensington began to stir and when he fully came to, he realized he was in some sort of warehouse. He tried to get up from the chair but his wrists were bound behind his back and his ankles were tied to the chair legs.

"Oh, good. You're finally awake," said a female voice.

He turned his head in the direction of where he heard the voice.

"Who are you?" Asked Agent Kensington, groggily.

A woman who seemed to be in her mid-forties with wavy, reddish-brown hair, and green eyes walked over to him. She wore a black tight-fitting short sleeve dress with a pair of red high heels.

"Cassidy Alexander, please to meet you," said Cassidy with an almost devilish smile.

"What am I doing here? Untie me!" Agent Kensington shouted.

"Sorry, kid. But I need you," said Cassidy as she walked over to a table and began mixing different liquids into a flask.

"For *what*?" He asked suspiciously.

She walked back over to him with a flask.

"First, you'll tell me where Heidi Hendrix is," said Cassidy.

"No," said Agent Kensington.

"No?" Asked Cassidy.

She walked over to him and squeezed his mouth open

"Wait! She's being held at the Aster Elites headquarters," said Agent Kensington.

"Ah ha," said Cassidy with a smile.

"You'll never get past the Bulwark spell," said Agent Kensington.

"Oh, but I will. The silly protection spell only detects those who wants to do harm to the people inside. All I want to do is break my love out of there," said Cassidy in a sinister tone.

"Who?" Asked Agent Kensington.

"Don't you worry your pretty little head about that," said Cassidy as she squeezed his mouth open.

She forced the clear brown liquid into his mouth and made sure it went down his throat before she let go of him. He began to choke and cough. Then, he slowly began to feel drowsy.

"What'd...you...give me?" He asked weakly.

"Just a little *something* to help you relax," said Cassidy with a sly smile.

Cassidy waited until Agent Kensington passed out, then she grabbed his face again.

"Wake up!" She shouted.

Agent Kensington moaned and his eyes were fluttering.

"Open your eyes!" Cassidy continued to shout in his face. Agent Kensington's eyes slowly opened. Cassidy bent down and stared deep into his eyes. Her green eyes flashed black for a second. She examined his face for a second before standing up straight again.

"Cute one, you are. Too bad I can't keep you. Now, be a good little boy and bring me to the Aster Elites Headquarters," said Cassidy with a smirk.

The next day, Leah was getting changed when she heard a knock on the door.

"Come in," said Leah as she threw her shirt on.

Duke opened the door and walked in.

"Hey, how are you feeling today?" Asked Duke was he walked over to her.

He put her hands on her waist and gave her a kiss on the lips.

"Much better now," Leah said with a smile.

"Are you ready to go?" Asked Duke.

"Yea, I'm ready. Let's go grab some breakfast," said Leah.

They left the infirmary and headed towards the dining hall. When they got there, Hazel and Primrose were already waiting for them at one of the tables.

"It's good to see you back on your feet, Leah," said Primrose.

"Thanks, Primrose. I'm glad to be back," said Leah, happily.

"We should have a proper celebration since we never got to celebrate your promotions. Why don't we host a cocktail party here in the dining hall?" Asked Hazel.

"That actually sounds like a great idea," said Duke.

"I'm glad you agree, Chief," Hazel teased.

Leah laughed.

Dusk had fallen as Agent Kensington drove up to the front gates of the Aster Elites Headquarters with Cassidy in the passenger seat of a black sedan. He drove up to the keypad and scanned his ID.

She watched as the giant metal gates slowly swung inwards. Agent Kensington drove the car towards the manor.

"So this is headquarters. See? I told you. The Bulwark spell wouldn't stop us," said Cassidy with a smirk.

Agent Kensington was silent, his eyes bore straight ahead. He parked the car off to the side in front of the manor under a huge oak tree. They both got out of the car and Cassidy walked over to face him. She was dressed in a black jumpsuit. Her hair was put up in a ponytail and she wore a black baseball cap over it. She looked into his eyes.

"Take me to Heidi Hendrix," Cassidy whispered into his ear.

Agent Kensington began to walk across the gravel road. Cassidy followed closely behind him and pulled her cap farther down. They walked past the main building and turned right onto another gravel road. Up ahead, Cassidy could see a stone tower ahead of them. He led her into the holding tower and walked up to the front desk where there were two other agents.

"IDs please," said one of the agents behind the desk.

Agent Kensington showed him his ID.

"Um...and yours ma'am?" Asked the agent.

"Uh...I'm so sorry! You see, I'm brand new here and I've completely forgotten my ID at my suite. Can't you just let me go this *one* time?" Asked Cassidy as she batted her lashes.

He narrowed his eyes at her for a second before looking down at Agent Kensington's ID.

"Go ahead and sign in on the clipboard," said the agent, flatly.

Agent Kensington put his ID in his back pocket and they both signed their names on the clipboard, then got on the elevators to the fourth floor where the holding cells were.

They walked down the hall towards Heidi's cell and immediately noticed the two agents guarding the door. Cassidy grabbed Agent Kensington's arm to stop him from walking any further. She stood in front of him and looked into his eyes again.

"I need to get into that cell. Get *rid* of those guards," whispered Cassidy.

Cassidy stood to the side and allowed Agent Kensington to continue walking. She watched as two stunnerballs began to form underneath his palms.

"Hey, you there! What are you-" shouted one of the guards.

Before he was able to finish his sentence, Agent Kensington launched a stunnerball at him. It hit the agent and sent him crashing against the wall. The other agent launched a stunnerball at Agent Kensington but he dodged it and quickly returned a stunnerball. The stunnerball hit the center of the agent's chest and he fell to the ground, unconscious.

"Good job, handsome," said Cassidy cheerfully as she patted him on the back.

Agent Kensington walked towards the cell door and pointed his stylus at the doorknob.

"*Fulminate!*" Shouted Agent Kensington.

Cassidy walked over to him as she stepped over the guard laying on the floor. Heidi gasped at the sight of Cassidy. She jumped out of the bed and she tried to run but the chains pulled her back.

"My love!" Said Cassidy as she walked over and wrapped her arms around her.

"C-Cassidy?" Asked Heidi.

"Yes, don't you recognize me my love?" Asked Cassidy with concern.

"*She must think that Marco is still inside of me,*" Heidi thought to herself.

"Y-yes, my love. W-what are you doing here?" Asked Heidi.

"To get you out of here, of course! Oh, what have they done to you?" Asked Cassidy as she pulled Heidi in for a hug.

Cassidy pulled away and turned to Agent Kensington.

"Why are you just standing there? Get her out of these chains!" Cassidy demanded.

Agent Kensington pointed his stylus at Heidi's handcuffs and casted the Fulminate spell, then he did the same with the chains around her ankles. Heidi finally felt free again and she knew it was only *minutes* before the other agents would be alerted. She looked at up Cassidy with hatred.

"M-Marco…what's wrong with you?" Asked Cassidy.

"I'm not Marco," said Heidi as she launched herself at Cassidy, pushing her down onto the bed. Heidi wrapped her hands around Cassidy's throat. Cassidy responded by grabbing Heidi's fingers and attempted to loosen her grip. Then, Cassidy punched Heidi right in the jaw. Heidi fell to the side and Cassidy quickly jumped to her feet. She gasped for air and stared at Heidi. Heidi got up and tried to throw a punch at Cassidy but she missed and Cassidy kicked her right in the stomach. Heidi yelped in pain as she curled her torso.

"You're *weak*. Marco was right. That's why you were just his little pawn. Now, where is Marco?!" Shouted Cassidy.

Heidi used all the energy she had left in her and rammed herself into Cassidy like an angry bull. They both fell onto the hard cement floor and Cassidy tried to slap Heidi but Heidi punched her in the face as hard as she could. Cassidy was knocked unconscious. Heidi stood up and looked at Agent Kensington. He stood very still with a blank expression on his face. She waved her hand in front of him and he didn't even blink.

"She must've hypnotized him. I've got to get out of here," she thought to herself.

Heidi searched his pockets. She found a set of car keys and his ID in his pockets. Then, she bolted out of the holding cell and down the hall. She heard the elevator doors open and looked around for somewhere to hide. There was a staircase to her right and she ran through the door to wait for the footsteps to pass.

Meanwhile, Lucinda was in her office with Agent Lyle when her cellphone rang.

"This is Lucinda...What?! We're on our way!" Said Lucinda as she jumped up from behind her desk and ran towards the door.

Agent Lyle ran out behind her.

"What is it?" Asked Agent Lyle with concern.

"That was the security team, they said that Agent Kensington used his ID at the front gates. They just reviewed the surveillance footage and he was heading for the holding towers with someone. It's got to be Cassidy. We have to hurry!" Said Lucinda urgently as she ran down the stairs.

Agent Lyle stayed close behind her. They ran across the gravel road, past the main building and towards the holding tower. As soon as they got off the elevators on the fourth floor, they ran over to where Heidi's holding cell was. Lucinda examined the two agents laying on the ground and made sure they were still breathing.

"Call the infirmary!" She instructed Agent Lyle.

Agent Lyle whipped his cellphone out and made the call. Lucinda drew her stylus out as she approached the cell. The door was already opened and she noticed Agent Kensington standing there.

"Wyatt!" Yelled Lucinda.

She stood in front of him and shook him. He didn't respond to Lucinda at all. She turned around to check out the holding cell and noticed another body on the ground.

"Cassidy Alexander?" Said Lucinda, in shock.

Still hiding in the stairway, Heidi sped down the stairs as soon as it was clear. When she got to the first floor, she peeked through the small window in the door. She was able to see the front desk in the middle of the floor where two agents sat behind the desk. One was on the phone and the other had his eyes the computer screen.

"I've got to run for it. It's the only way I'll ever get out of here," she thought to herself.

She slowly pushed the door open and darted towards the exit.

"Hey!" Shouted one of the agents.

He got up and ran after her while the other one called for backup on his radio. Heidi ran past the infirmary and across the front yard of the main building. She saw the black sedan parked under an oak tree and she quickly unlocked it with the car keys. She jumped into the car just as the agent rounded the corner of the main building.

"Stop!" He yelled.

Heidi jammed the key into the ignition and started up the car. The car screeched loudly as she stomped on the gas pedal and drove towards the front gates. She could see the agent in the rearview mirror. He conjured stunnerballs and aimed it at the car. One of them hit the trunk of the car causing her to swerve but she kept driving until she reached the gates. When she got to the keypad, she quickly scanned Agent Kensington's ID and the gates slowly opened. As soon as it was opened wide enough, she stomped on the gas and disappeared down the road, heading towards town.